BEAR
EDGES

At his isolated ranch southwest of Jackson, the middle-aged, scruffy looking pilot, wearing Pacs, loose tan trousers, a beat-up bomber-crew jacket, and an old fedora, hurried to the Bell JetRanger 206B that was parked in a field near the frame house, flipped various switches, checked various gauges, and began warming up the engine.

"Bears," he mumbled to himself. "I hate bears, Jack. Why'd it have to be bears?"

* * *

It looked like a convention of Ford and Firestone Tire executives. Almost all of the Teton County Sheriff's Department's off-road force—most of the vehicles new Ford Expeditions—were assembled at the East Broadway end of Elk Refuge Road, waiting for the word to start rolling. A cold fog filled the air....

* * *

"Harrison, I hope you don't mind my askin'," Wilson deadpanned, "but what are you plannin' to do with the bear?"

"I'm working on it, Jack," the pilot replied. In truth, he didn't have any idea what he was going to do with the grizzly that was hanging on to the helicopter. He was really hoping that it would just fall off.

* * *

All of a sudden there was not an empty lodging bed to be found, and you could not get a quick seat in a local barbeque restaurant if your name was Maria Shriver....

* * *

"What are you doing?" Ellie exclaimed, subconsciously looking around for anyone else on the trail. "Soaking your feet is one thing, going skinny-dipping in a national park is another."

* * *

It did not snow. And then it did not snow. And then it did not snow some more. It was beginning to look like this was going to be a long, cold, snowless winter in Jackson Hole.

* * *

BEAR EDGES

By Fred Whissel

Printed by Lulu.com
Morrisville, N.C.

The author would like to thank Paul Schullery and The Yellowstone Association for permission to quote from his very helpful book, "The Bears of Yellowstone."

For purchase or other printing or publication information, please contact Lulu, 3131 RDU Center, Suite 210, Morrisville, NC 27560 USA, on the web at http://www.lulu.com

ISBN: 978-0-6151-5176-2

Lulu first edition 2007

Printed in the United States of America

To My Family.

Again, Thanks for Bearing with Me.

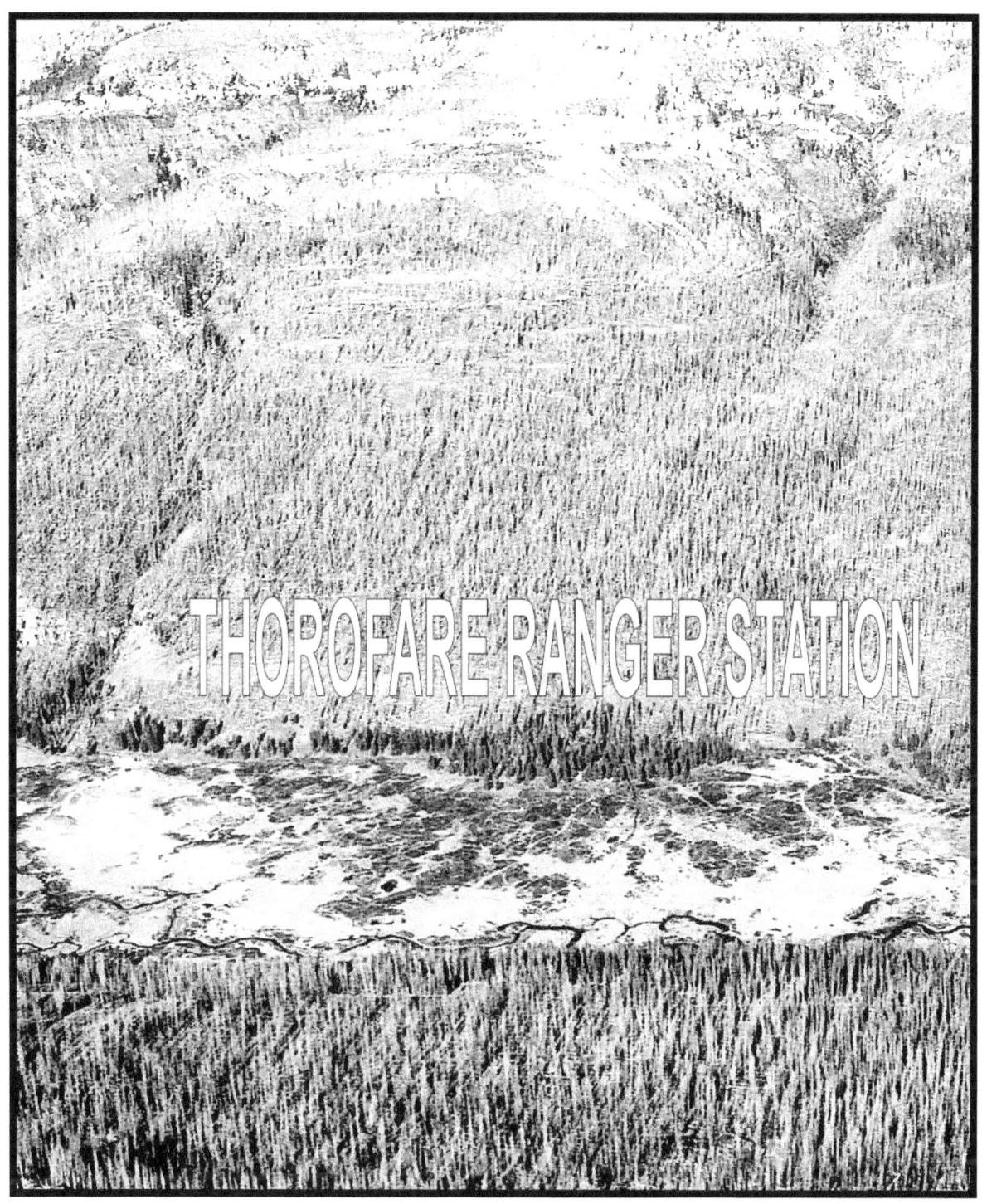

Thoroughfare Ranger Station, located at the southeastern corner of Yellowstone National Park, is the second-most remote location in the United States. In this view, the Yellowstone River flows from the right edge (south) through a marshy bottom towards Yellowstone Lake. (Photo by the author, with thanks to Patrick Smith for the aerial assist.)

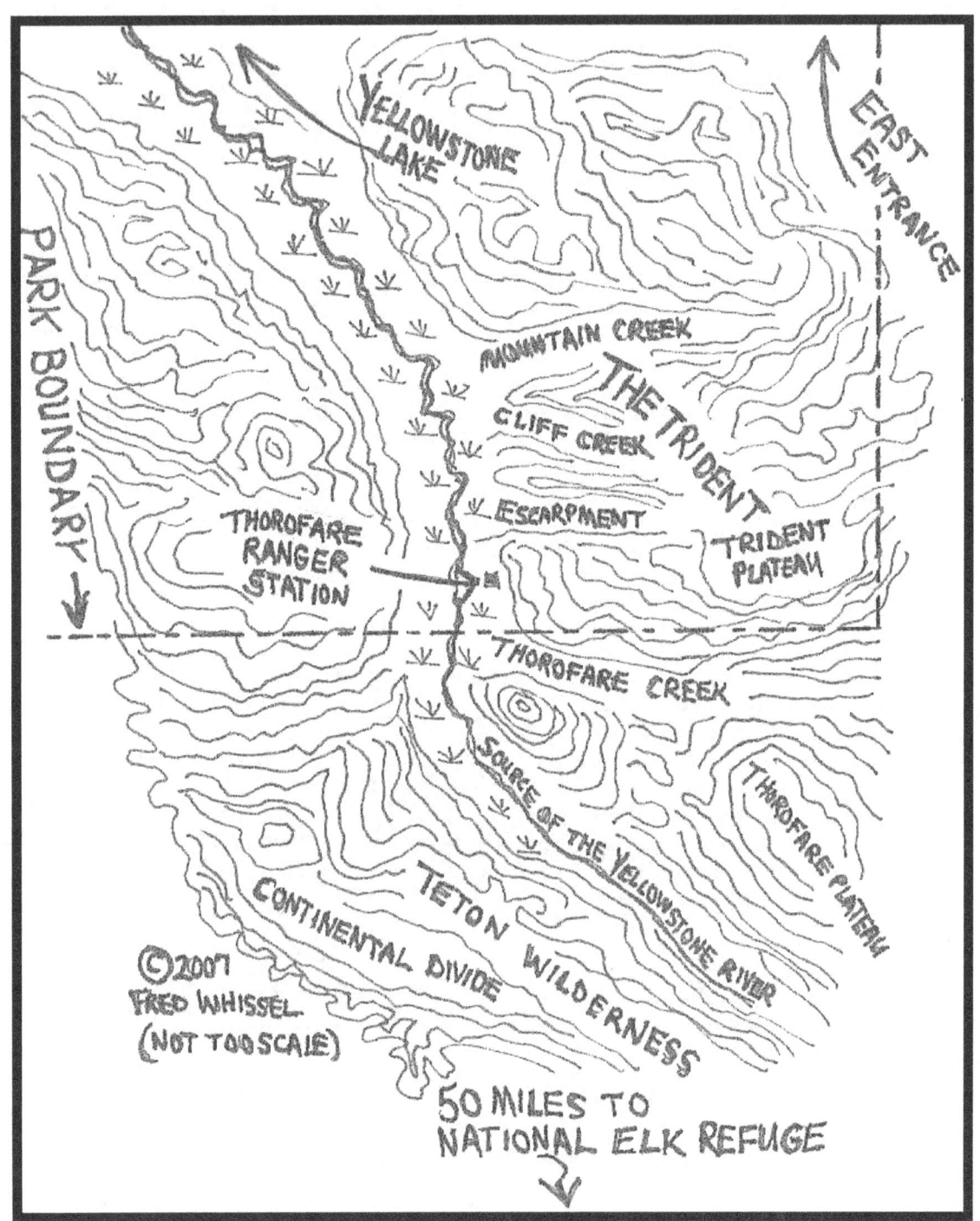

Thorofare Ranger Station is just south of the three creeks (Mountain, Cliff and Escarpment) that comprise "The Trident." The source of the Yellowstone River, which flows north, lies to the south of the station, in the Teton Wilderness. (Drawing by the author)

CONTENTS

PROLOGUE

Sixty miles north of Jackson, Wyoming, beyond the towering Tetons that rise free of foothills from the glacial valleys to the east and the west, is the world's oldest national park. Yellowstone.

Roughly rectangular in outline, some fifty-four miles east-to-west and sixty-three miles north-to-south, Yellowstone is a land of rugged, often astonishing beauty, even after foreseeable fires blackened one-third of the park's acreage in 1988. Although the healing process continues, Yellowstone remains a natural paradise and wildlife wonderland extolled by connoisseurs and mere slip-through sightseers alike.

Here, broadly blanketing Yellowstone's 2.2 million acres are dark green forests of staff-straight lodgepole pine dense enough to conceal, at a distance of only a few feet, a granite boulder emplaced by a melting glacier only a few feet away. Here arc small sub-alpine meadows never seen by most park visitors, a river-riven gorge with steep yellow-rock walls that approaches Arizona's Grand Canyon in its grandeur, mighty misty waterfalls that sparkle in the morning sunshine like founts of falling diamonds, one of the world's largest volcanic calderas and its greatest concentration of geysers, including the world's highest spouting and most faithful, simmering hot springs, noisy fumaroles, boiling mudpots—a total of some ten-thousand thermal features providing on-surface evidence of the earth's upset stomach.

Here are broad plains populated with aromatic, silver-green sagebrush, and grasslands in which bistort, biscuitroot, fireweed, foxglove, horsetail, yampa, and the more-familiar Indian Paintbrush take shallow root. Here are both mixed and singular stands of whitebark pine, Douglas fir, Engelmann spruce, and quaking aspen. Here are high craggy cliffs and distant windblown buttes—mere adolescents in the annals of geologic history. Here are badger, beaver, bison, bighorn, cougar, coyote, elk, fox, marmot, moose, mountain goat, mule deer, prairie dog, pica, pronghorn antelope, recently reintroduced packs of gray wolves, and dozens of other animal species.

Here are some eight-hundred miles of world-famous waterways like the Snake, the Madison, the Firehole, and the historic Yellowstone River, all fed from frigid waters of melting mountain snow almost all year-round. Here are more than four-hundred fishable lakes, including the ice-cold Yellowstone that accounts for more than half of the park's angling activity. Here swim a fly-fisherman's dozen of fabled freshwater fighters, including brook, brown, cutthroat, lake, and rainbow trout, mountain whitefish, and grayling.

And here, last retreating from uncivilized civilization in Yellowstone's wildest, roughest, and most remote regions, are uncountable hundreds of bears, including the black (which may also be blond or brown) and the largest predator in the lower forty-eight states, *ursus arctos horribilis*, the once-feared, still-fearsome grizzly.

Tourists migrate to Yellowstone in the millions each summer, coming by bus, bicycle, automobile, motorcycle, pickup truck (with and without camper shell), lumbering recreational vehicle, and even afoot, to spend a few hours or a few days camping, fishing, hiking, horseback riding, snapping scenic photographs, or merely watching the wildlife, in particular the bears. In almost any corner of the park, at almost any day-light hour during the summer sightseeing season, one or many vehicles at a time can be seen sitting to the side of a narrow road while the daily doings of this animal resident or that are notched neatly in memory, stored on digital media, or captured on photographic film, while the subject under scrutiny all but ignores these nosy two-legged intruders and their noisy shouts of fascination.

The highlight of any summertime visit to Yellowstone is now and has always been the infrequent sighting of a nearby bear, although many unfortunate encounters have taken place at such near distances. (Grizzlies are best viewed from afar.) There are historically significant photos of Teddy Roosevelt marching merrily along an Old Faithful area pathway accompanied by playful black bears (*ursus americanus*) as wary members of the president's bodyguard remain poised to protect the nation's interest with one simple squeeze of a trigger finger. There are three million (maybe more) home movies made in eight-millimeter black-and-white and faded Kodak color featuring Mom feeding a bear while visiting Yellowstone prior to the 1970s with a dozen or so other bruins in the background shuffling and sniffing through piles of park garbage. There are movies, books, slide strips, paintings, posters, photographs, plastic and metal moldings, rock carvings, wood chiselings, stuffed animals, and even floppy fake-fur slippers fitting all sizes of feet to celebrate and commemorate Yellowstone's world-famous bears.

There are today some four- to six-hundred grizzlies and an even larger number of black bears residing in what is known as the Greater Yellowstone Ecosystem—a sort of animal homeowner's association that encompasses around eighteen million acres of Wyoming, Idaho, and Montana. Even those bear and wildlife management specialists who study and safeguard the wide-ranging bear population of the GYE have only a general idea of where most of the bears are at any given point in time. The area they occupy is simply too vast and too wild to maintain accurate records of their whereabouts. At best, a few are captured and collared with electronic transmitters to track their movements, but the rest occupy an unknown home where the buffalo roam, where the deer and the antelope play, and the sick and the injured and both young and old prey had just better watch out if they know what's good for them.

In the hours after daybreak, and those just before dusk, Yellowstone's bears join most other animals in searching for a meal, and park visitors can be found out in force during these shoulder-hours witnessing that foraging, with hand-held binoculars, telescopes on tripods, and poorly focused cameras hastily aimed. In the dead of night as well Yellowstone's bears are ever on the prowl making their quiet food forays, although few tourists or professional film makers are fearless or stupid enough to be out recording those darkened quests.

The watch for bears goes on from Yellowstone's official opening around late May—when the roads are almost cleared of snow—through the park's closing to nearly all vehicles around late October or early November, when the first big snows and sub-zero overnight temperatures drive away fair-weather visitors and begin to make many of Yellowstone's pathways impossibly passable. As the gates swing shut for the coming winter, in the higher elevations, in Yellowstone's most-inaccessible regions reaching above 11,000 feet, the park's black and grizzly bears continue their search for those final few morsels of food that will be turned into fat and used to get them through the next five or six months of hibernation in a quiet cave, in a deep crevasse, in a hollowed-out hole, or simply tucked in under a pile of fallen limbs and branches on some secluded back country mountain. They will pursue these meals most often at the interface of meadow and forest, in what those who study such bruin lifestyles term "edges."

The normal diet of the mainly herbivorous black bear consists of ants, fish, carrion when available, berries, bushes, and other plants (no garbage now), with a little water on the side to wash it all down. Yellowstone's more-omnivorous grizzlies, much larger and thus forced to be less choosy about their food supplies, expand upon that menu by including whitebark pine seeds stolen from the stores of red squirrels, an assortment of roots, spawning cutthroat trout, and up to an amazing 40,000 army cutworm moths a day in the higher elevations towards the end of the summer. While the black bear's shorter, curved claws require it to find most of its meals above the ground the grizzly's longer, straighter claws enable it to look below the surface for some of its food. Whether found on or under ground, a grizzly's food is normally eaten immediately, but it is occasionally cached away under dirt, leaves, and branches for a later snack.

Both black bears and grizzlies in Yellowstone rely on the park's normally severe winters to provide piles of rotting carrion each spring from the unfortunate ungulates that, because of age, sickness, injury, or an unexpected step into one of Yellowstone's unforgiving thermal features fail to make it through the winter. Upon awakening from a five-month hibernation around mid-March, the hungry bears usually find enough winter-kill carcasses to satisfy their demands for food until the snow finally melts and succulent plants start growing. Craftier and harder to corner than that dead meat are spring-spawning trout, which seemingly have their own special appeal for fun-loving grizzlies. In recent years, thanks to the reintroduction of wolves and their increasing harvest of elk and bison calves, Yellowstone's carnivorous grizzlies have found it easy to confiscate those catches from their initial owners, or to take down the sick and the lame at any time of year.

As long as there is food to be found by foraging, particularly in the park's remotest reaches, Yellowstone's bears will spend the spring, summer, and fall putting on pounds, procreating, or just getting their bodies prepared for the arrival of another brutal mountain winter. Within marked territories they will follow their food supplies from season to season, adapting their dietary desires to the ever-changing sources of nutrition. But if some or all of those normal sources of food dry up, the bears will soon find alternatives, if merely to ensure their own survival. And if those alternative sources happen to be found in the back yards of humans, there will inevitably be both confrontation and conflict. And both the bears and the humans will lose. This is a story of such losses.

Chapter One

THE PEAKS

Some twelve miles south of Yellowstone's east entrance, and about the same distance east of the southern shore of Yellowstone Lake, is the highest point in the park, located in an area that is one of the least-reachable by tourists. Almost lost among the surrounding mountains of similar height is Eagle Peak, which at an elevation of 11,358 feet is certainly not one of Wyoming's highest mountains but one that has been glorified over many generations by hunters, trappers, explorers, anglers, American Indians, and mountain men alike.

Here, in what is known as the Absaroka Range, at the western edge of the Shoshone National Forest and the northern neck of the Teton Wilderness (a part of the Bridger-Teton National Forest) sit some of Wyoming's ruggedest mountains. The nearest evidence of civilization to Eagle Peak is found at either Yellowstone's east entrance, some fifteen miles north, or Thorofare Ranger Station, an equal distance south, where for only five months of the year the Park Service assigns a single ranger. From the ranger station to the nearest road in Yellowstone is, therefore, a distance of roughly thirty miles, or at least three days of hiking through a region challenging the character of many would-be woodsmen.

Eagle Peak crowns one of several large mountains in the southeast corner of Yellowstone that feed, with their melting snow, a half-dozen sparkling streams that serve as spawning sites for the park's famous cutthroat trout. Each spring the icy cold meltwaters roar down the steep slopes to replenish such crystal-clear creeks as Cliff, Cabin, Howell, Escarpment, Mountain, Trappers, and Thorofare in the immediate drainage area, all of which combine to feed the Yellowstone River. In turn, the Yellowstone carves a serpentine course northward to Yellowstone Lake, one of the country's coldest and deepest. Anglers who make the extra effort to fish these mountain streams often return to the civilized world with some of the broadest smiles they have ever worn, having landed fair-sized fish at a rate of up to three per hour.

Since at least the days of the pre-reservation Indian and the rendezvousing mountain man, and probably well before, the whole area south of Eagle Pass (near what is now the park's southeastern border) has been crisscrossed by heavily traveled game trails—producing an obvious name for the ranger station, the creek, and Thorofare Plateau. Even today, these animal highways are still stomped into submission by elk, moose, deer, bear, bighorn sheep, and other large animals. The valley also has long been one of the major north-south routes for migrating elk. Each fall, most of Yellowstone's thirty thousand elk seek warmer southern climes, with about a third of them vacationing in the more-palatable National Elk Refuge just north of Jackson. Each spring these antler-shedding ungulates make the return trip north to Yellowstone's high country—leaving behind whole industries based on shaping or pulverizing their discarded head-wear—and are accompanied on their homeward trek by hundreds or thousands of new calves. Reached mainly on horses carrying provisions supplied by numerous outfitters, the Thorofare area still abounds with resident and migrating wildlife, and is renowned for offering some of the best elk hunting in the world.

The few backpackers who visit the Thorofare Ranger Station either hike south on Thorofare Trail along the east shore of Yellowstone Lake (roughly paralleling the course of the Yellowstone River) or leave from Eagle Creek Campground on the combined U. S. Routes 14, 16, and 20 near Yellowstone's east entrance, hike through Eagle Creek Meadows and Eagle Pass, then take the Mountain Trail until it intersects Thorofare Trail about six miles north of the station.

Although the Thorofare Trail is just east of the Continental Divide, from which waters flow west into the Pacific or south and east into the Atlantic or the Gulf of Mexico, the Yellowstone River here supports some of the marshiest terrain in the park, for a distance of almost fifteen miles. The Thorofare Ranger Station is at the edge of this valley, east of the river, near The Trident Plateau.

Just northeast of the ranger station is a group of three ridges that resemble the tines of the nautical tool for which they were named. The station keeping job tends to be so tedious that, in the mid-1990s, the ranger on duty forewent his obligation to seek official permission and blazed a trail all the way up to the 10,969-foot peak of The Trident. When his remarkable efforts were discovered, rather than being rewarded, he was reprimanded by park administrators under the notion that it's not nice to redo Mother Nature without prior approval from the government.

Chapter Two

THE RANGER

John Reston was a ranger. To the National Park Service that meant that Reston was fully qualified to collect assorted user fees, to hand out park maps and unread newspapers, to wave thousands of vehicles through any of Yellowstone's five entrances on any given day, to talk summertime honeymooners through the many pitfalls of new marriage and outside-inn camping, and to escort an occasional elected official on a fact-finding junket around the hottest spots in the Park Service west of the Potomac.

To John Reston, being a ranger simply meant spending his second summer in Yellowstone assigned to the Thorofare Ranger Station. For most others it could be a lonely assignment, even with the infrequent visit of a fisherman bringing his exaggerated stories about the ones that got away. But to Reston, in these young adult years of his life, having little human company over the next five months didn't much matter. The slim but sturdily constructed young man in his early twenties actually looked forward to spending the summer in one of the most isolated corners of Yellowstone, almost always alone.

It wasn't as though Reston would be entirely out of touch with civilization. He would have a small library of books, a VCR (with movies), a multi-band radio, and a regular microwave communications check-in with park headquarters in Mammoth. He was amazed to realize that Mammoth was some sixty-five miles away, as the eagle flies, diagonally opposite his point in the park—about as far away as it could be without leaving Yellowstone's boundaries, so far in fact that Reston's routine radio reports had to be relayed by metal antennas mounted atop tall hidden towers along the way, instead of going direct line-of-sight.

Reston was comforted by his firm conviction that this area ranked as one of the most beautiful in the entire park, even with the black marks given it by the devastating fires of 1988 and all of the lesser ones since. His immediate surroundings were idyllic. He could look north up the marshy valley of the Yellowstone River and see almost all the way to the big lake. At 8,000 feet the station was still almost 3,000 feet below the forks of The Trident; that peak was only six straight-line miles away. And the animals were everywhere.

It was Reston's love for wildlife that had drawn him into this taxpayer-paid profession in the first place. He had spent many school vacation days at the National Zoo in Washington, D. C., first as a mere awe-struck visitor, then as a citizen volunteer, and finally as a paid part-time summer employee, in all of which positions he managed to migrate most days towards the exhibits that featured North American mammals. He loved the bears, especially the grizzly, with its long claws, humped back, strong frame, and upturned snout that always reminded him of Bob Hope. He sometimes daydreamed about the days when Yellowstone—established in 1872—was not even a gleam in Teddy Roosevelt's eye, when the mountains were so full of grizzlies that they had a hard time keeping their distance from the marauding humans who passed through their territories. Reston found it both incredible and discomforting that these now-reclusive creatures were not too long ago found from Manitoba to Mexico, from the middle of North America to its West Coast, and at most points in between, in total numbers thought to approach 100,000. He remembered reading one account (a *History of Colusa County,* wherever that was—he could not now remember) that reported grizzly sightings as high as forty in a single day.

Only three years after Yellowstone was established, all of the Park's bears—both black and grizzly—had been placed on a "no hunting" list but nevertheless continued dwindling in numbers. In 1974, a moratorium had been placed on grizzly hunting in the lands abutting Yellowstone. In 1975, the grizzly joined the bald eagle as an Endangered Species in the lower forty-eight states. In more recent years the bear had made enough of a comeback that some politicians (mainly Republicans) were now considering de-listing it.

Reston loved grizzlies. He loved hiking the mountains east and west of the valley to monitor their comings and goings, usually at a distance by using binoculars. On a few occasions he had hiked out of the park, to the south and west, along Falcon and Mink Creeks, where the concentration of grizzlies was even greater than in the southeast corner of Yellowstone itself, due to the better food supply—the larger normal concentration of elk in the Teton Wilderness.

That area had also been less affected by fires than Yellowstone itself, which had lost some 800,000 acres of mainly lodgepole pine in 1988 and lesser amounts since. It was not the fires, however, that took the greatest toll on the grizzlies. They had usually been able to detour around those conflagrations. The larger problem was what the hot-as-hell fires had done to the grizzly's fragile habitat. While the long-term impact of fire in thinning the forests was to encourage even greater growth of plants previously stymied by the thick canopy that had blocked their sunlight the more-immediate result was to deprive the bears of the forage that they depended on, both late that summer and the subsequent fall, to help build up layers of fat for their forthcoming hibernation. Then, too, the bears had immediately lost a second source of food—their suddenly cindered succulent underground roots—and a third, the rich whitebark pine seeds cached away at higher elevations by red squirrels, and even a fourth, the tasty and nutritious moths that made up an important part of their diet in late autumn. To make matters even worse, the needed next-spring spawn of cutthroat trout was significantly reduced by the alkaline run-off of the charred trees, or in some cases chemically choked out by poorly aimed fire drops from fly-over aircraft. One benefit of the fires, however, was that they had also barbequed several elk, bison, deer, and moose, which put more meat than usual on the tables of the grizzlies in the following spring.

Chapter Three

THE FIRES

It had been a long, hot, fish-in-the-frying pan summer. The searing sun had scorched almost every blade of grass in Yellowstone, along with the parched grasslands throughout much of the Rocky Mountains and Southwest. In the national park, and in the surrounding forests, millions of trees suddenly had become so many standing matches, just waiting to be struck and ignited by a bolt of lightning or kindled by a tourist unable to understand that the omnipresent signs saying "Campfires Prohibited" meant exactly what they said.

Clearly the park's animals were suffering. While the big ruminants roamed in search of any edible plants at all to provide their necessary sustenance, the carnivorous predators were eyeing anything that moved, regardless of size, strength, likely resistance to the idea of being some other animal's meal, top speed in a short sprint, or possible caloric content. As for Yellowstone's fish, their lakes and rivers were now rapidly drying up and were already lower than anyone could ever remember seeing them. Many smaller streams had disappeared entirely months ago.

The sere conditions portended an autumn of forest fire outbreaks in Yellowstone making those of 1988 look like a suburban backyard barbeque. Once the predictable fires flared to life, as they inevitably would, they would race rapidly from tree to tree, stand to stand, and area to area. Virtually all of the park's trees and its two thousand assorted buildings were at-risk, including the historic Old Faithful Inn.

All summer long Park Service supervisors, in preparing themselves for the expected holocaust, had been ready to issue both all-out calls for help and quick public denials that their policy of unnatural fire suppression had caused the unintentional stockpiling of understory fuels for fires even more devastating than could have been expected. Fire lookouts all around the park had been ordered to report even the first suspected signs of smoke or flames that appeared in their binoculars. Updated satellite images were scrutinized carefully and constantly for any telltale indications of potential problems. The park's many motorized firefighting vehicles—as outmatched as they certainly would be in the anticipated battle—were all fully fueled and manned on a standby basis around the clock. And all entering park visitors—up to 50,000 a day—were given handouts cautioning them about the drought conditions and asked to do everything they could to help prevent forest fires.

But all of those who monitored the desperate conditions in Yellowstone knew that the opening day of fire season was only a matter of time. It had not rained in months. The water table had fallen so low that even Old Faithful was spouting less and less often. Animals were dying of dehydration and starvation on their feet. At this point even several days of steady rain would not be enough to put an end to the tinderbox conditions, to restore the park's wildlife to health, or certainly to save the animals that had already suffered and died. Only the inevitable first few heavy snow-falls of the forthcoming winter would signal any sort of lasting relief from the fires and give Yellowstone's animals and administrators some room to breathe.

The sky-filling clouds had first formed very early in the morning all along the park's western border, in northern Idaho and southern Montana, almost as though they were so many artillery guns being massed for an all-out assault on the tree-troops of Yellowstone. Bulbous, boiling, dark, and dangerous, the thick cumulus clouds had gathered size and strength all morning long while drifting almost inconspicuously eastward, until some silent command had ordered them all to charge en masse into the park, to launch constant spears of lightning towards the ground, to snap towering trees as though they were toothpicks—blowing them all apart in explosions of superheated steam that rivaled the park's most powerful geysers—and to set countless fires, from the minerals-made terraces of Mammoth in the north to Pitchstone Plateau near the south entrance.

For the first time in its 130-year history the entire park was ordered closed immediately, and instructions were sent from the Mammoth headquarters to every possible in-park point of contact to evacuate every car, every camper, every person with or without a valid park permit, and every domestic animal that they may have brought in with them. All souvenir shop and service employees in the park were to lock their doors and leave the premises without delay. The governors of Wyoming, Idaho, and Montana were telephoned immediately and asked to respond all available assistance as soon as humanly possible, including even semi-trained firefighters in their National Guard units. All on-call U. S. Army units on nearby bases were also requested. And every local community with a spare fire truck or an extra garden hose around the perimeter of Yellowstone was invited to help. It would be the single most-massive firefighting effort in the history of the world, an attempt to contain fires that threatened to torch an area larger than the states of Delaware and Rhode Island combined.

One thing the Park Service had learned—too late—from the 1988 fires was to hit all mass-murdering fires quickly and hard, holding their size and strength to the absolute minimum. In 1988, such fires at first had been allowed to spread, and strengthen, until the soaring columns of flame and hot air created their own winds and weather conditions, and leaped across roads, meadows and rivers that would have contained any lesser fires before they became uncontrollable. The historic inn at Old Faithful, and its many surrounding buildings, had been spared destruction only by a miraculous last-minute shift in the wind that whipped the flames away from the feeble firefighting force assembled to confront the approaching fiery fingers of hell. Only a few outlying buildings around Old Faithful had burned to the ground. Across the park some 800,000 acres of trees and grasslands had been blackened, often creating puzzling patterns of smoking charcoal stubs where soft winds once whispered through stately lodgepole giants. This time there would be no waiting, no second thoughts, no administrative concerns about over-estimating the potential for disaster on the fear of spoiling some wealthy German or Japanese tourist's vacation.

All roads leading into and out of Yellowstone were packed, with all sorts of vehicles being escorted out—some almost sandwiched by burning trees—and many new ideas in firefighting equipment ushered in. Panicked animals were running everywhere, seeking safe refuge, and many were run over or run down by speeding vehicles. As expected, there were many vehicle collisions. Near Madison Junction, in a meadow found suitable for the purpose, Army and National Guard helicopters were landing troops and taking on huge loads of water and fire-retardant, to be dropped wherever needed, which was in nearly any direction that they flew. The light-brown, water-starved meadow was instantly repainted an easy-to-see yellow, as hundreds of skilled veteran firefighters and large numbers of half-trained troops en route to their first real live forest fires hustled around in flame-resistant pants and coats. Some of them, upon first seeing the fiery forests, had troubling thoughts that they might not be returning home from this war.

The evacuation of park visitors went on throughout the first day, all afternoon, and all night, always illuminated by red and orange flames and rising balloons of incandescent smoke in the same colors. First the west entrance, and then the north, had to be completely closed to leaving or entering traffic when flaming trees fell across the narrow roadways. Two families in separate cars were trapped, and all nine persons therein died by burns or injuries when large lodgepoles tumbled onto them as they inched too-slowly towards safety, the falling burning trees crushing the cars like ants under anvils, setting both the interiors of the vehicles and the occupants ablaze. Other vehicles were soon simply abandoned, their drivers and passengers eventually rescued and redirected towards safer passageways out of the park.

It was not until mid-morning of the second day that park administrators could declare Yellowstone empty of all visitors except those hiking, camping, and fishing in the deepest, wildest reaches, who had been flown over and warned of the danger by park rangers in helicopters using electronic megaphones. These backwoods people were still being evacuated, aided wherever possible by the weary firefighters.

Yellowstone's tens of thousands of animals, of course, had to fend for themselves. Whole herds of bison, whole packs of wolves, whole fields of elk ran wildly in their attempts to avoid the flaming forests, alongside both larger and smaller predators and prey, old and young, healthy and infirm. No thoughts were given to their normal activities, like eating, sleeping, or establishing territories. They were all individually fleeing in fear, heading for any break in the flames that seemed to provide an escape. Most of them made it, but some of them died, overtaken by the faster flames or boxed in by bad escape route decisions, and many of the smaller animals were trampled underfoot by the larger ones.

Most animals ran south, around the east and west shores of Yellowstone Lake, where the flames were less fierce. Some, on the west side of the lake, followed the ridge line of the Continental Divide southward. Others, along the lake's eastern banks, ran down the Thorofare Trail, snaking through the paths used each fall and spring by the migrating elk.

Chapter Four

THE FRIENDS

John Reston had met Ellie Masters during the previous summer. He had been assigned to the park's busy south entrance, which was reached by taking the John D. Rockefeller Memorial Highway through Grand Teton National Park, which was reached either by driving north from Jackson or west from the all-but-invisible village of Moran. Ellie, a freshman at the University of Wyoming in Laramie, was working in the Hamilton Store at Grant Village, selling film and assorted photographic supplies to tourists for their once-in-a-lifetime snapshots.

Reston had made the twenty-two mile drive from the south gate to Grant to leave a couple of rolls of slide film for processing, and he and Ellie had hit it off immediately. A Bo Derek look-alike, although a bit taller, she had the same sharply chiseled face, the same large smoothly rounded high cheekbones, the same ice-blue eyes that seemed to make you want to look into them forever, and the same lanky ten-rated body, with all of the curves in all of the right places and nicely bronzed besides. He had made repeated trips to Ellie's counter in the following weeks and had bought a few more rolls of film from her than he thought he would ever be able to use.

The somewhat backward ranger had eventually built up enough nerve to invite Ellie to join him for lunch on a mutual day off at the Old Faithful Inn, and she had accepted. Ironically, she had never been to what was probably the most popular and well-known attraction in the park, had never heard the excited oohs and ahhs of tourists of all ages as the geyser shot steam high into the sky after making a few false stuttering starts, had never actually seen much of the rest of the park at all. She had enjoyed the lunch, and the sightseeing that had followed along the Fire-hole River, and they had spent most of their remaining days-off that summer touring the greater attractions of Yellowstone, and each other.

On a visit to Yellowstone's Grand Canyon, to look at the towering Lower Falls, Reston had commemorated the occasion by presenting Ellie with an official "Smokey Bear" park ranger hat—minus the Park Service emblem, of course—and she had worn it proudly on all of their remaining hikes. She had quickly found the hat's broad flat brim especially well-designed for keeping the sun out of her sensitive blue eyes, however protected as they already were by large dark sunglasses against the strong rays of the sun that stabbed through the thin air of Yellowstone's higher elevations. In return, Ellie had given John one of the small stuffed Smokey the Bear animals that they sold at the Hamilton store, personalized however with one of her own items of clothing that the Park Service would never have authorized.

At the end of the summer, Ellie had returned home to Denver, but the two had kept in frequent contact by telephone calls and letters, and had remained close friends. Reston had flown back to the nation's capital with a letter of recommendation from the park's chief ranger to work in the Park Service's headquarters, making potentially valuable contacts for the career that he hoped to build in government service.

Reston had asked to spend another summer in Yellowstone, basically because he loved the area and the animals (and at least one of the people), and his request had been approved. Ellie had also returned to northwestern Wyoming, this year to work as a waitress at Bubba's Bar-B-Que in Jackson, one of the most popular eateries in town. In talking to friends, she had learned that she could make far more money waitressing at Bubba's—as much as two hundred dollars a night in tips alone—than she could anywhere else (particularly in the park), and she needed the money for school.

Her position, and his, had brought them back to within sixty miles of each other, but the isolation of the Thorofare outpost meant that they were still no less than three days of hard hiking away. So while Ellie and John were able to remain in close but distant contact all summer long it had been a strictly platonic relationship.

Until now.

Reston's five-month stint at the Thorofare station was winding down, but Ellie's summer at Bubba's had already ended. She had quit waitressing a couple of weeks earlier than her managers would have liked, not only to get ready to go back to school but also to drive up to Yellowstone and backpack in to Thorofare where she could spend a couple of days with John. During the summer Ellie had become fast friends with her roommate, Donna, a waitress at the Mangy Moose in Teton Village. They had hiked together whenever they could in the beautiful country around Jackson—they especially loved the Jenny Lake area and its Hidden Falls trail—and had agreed to make the Thorofare hike together.

"Equipped for bear," the young women had driven up to Yellowstone in Donna's battered Isuzu Trooper, around the northern shore of the lake, had exited the park at its east entrance, and had parked their car at the Eagle Creek campground on U. S. 20. There they had shouldered sixty-pound backpacks filled with eider-down sleeping bags, camping utensils, extra clothes, fly-fishing gear, and a lot of dried food, and had set out on the trails that would take them thirty miles through Eagle Creek Meadow and Eagle Pass and down the

Mountain Creek Trail to its intersection with Thorofare Trail—only about six miles from the ranger station. They had not told Reston that they were coming (Ellie had wanted to surprise him) but they were sure that he would be happy to put up with their company for a couple of days.

Chapter Five

THE FOOD

The huge, eight-hundred-pound grizzly awoke from his afternoon nap with an appetite. All summer long he had barely been able to satisfy his hunger, and had found it more and more difficult to locate food in the valley as the weeks went by. First, upon rolling out of his hibernation den on the mountain in mid-March, he had scent-tracked few elk carcasses to quench his immediate need for protein. Instead, he had discerned signs that other scavengers—particularly those damned wolves—had beaten him to most of the winter-kill carrion, and had stripped almost all of the meat from the scattered piles of elk bones. Then, expecting to dine on spawning cutthroat from Mountain Creek and its tributaries, he had found that normal source of energy to be disappointingly less plentiful than in previous springs. Then, the following hot summer had not only kept him constantly uncomfortable, even with frequent dips in the seemingly disappearing cold water of the several streams that drained the mountain snowmelt, but had also dried up much of his succulent grasses-bushes-berries food supply. Soon, perhaps sooner than he would like, he would have to climb back up the steep slopes to his winter home on Eagle Peak, where he might at least find some whitebark pine seeds and moths to fill him up and provide the carbohydrate fat that he still needed to put on for the coming winter of hibernation.

But for now, the grizzly was going to do some more exploring in the valleys and their streams, foraging for whatever food he could locate. He would make a special effort to find fish in those shallow waters. But if he couldn't find any fish, he'd find something else. He really had no choice. If he couldn't find food, his all-controlling metabolism would not allow him to hibernate.

It had been one beautiful hike, thus far. The first day of trekking along the trail paralleling Eagle Creek had featured incredible views of the long valley, with the east and west mountains rising steeply from their base, and many small streams branching off to the east from the main creek. They had seen several mule deer and elk, and even a couple of moose in the shallow water, slurping up weeds from below the surface, and it seemed like the smaller animals were everywhere. Whenever they had stopped to rest, or to snack on their high-energy health bars, the long-tailed black-and-white magpies in particular would come right up to them, hoping to be first in line for any loose morsels of food that dropped to the ground. In one place they finally had to shoo a bothersome red squirrel away when it brashly began nibbling on the bottom of Ellie's backpack.

They had decided to spend the first night at the foot of Mount Humphreys, saving the climb to Eagle Pass for the next morning. That would put them on the trail down the other side of the mountain in the afternoon, when the heat would make any hiking most uncomfortable. They could then follow the trail along Howell Creek until it joined Mountain, where they would pitch their "two-man" pup tent and spend their second night. Reaching the ranger station after a fairly level hike at the end of the third day would be a mere walk in the woods.

- THE FOOD -

It was late afternoon. They had gone through Eagle Pass around noon, as they had planned, and had hiked downhill for the past several hours. Around three o'clock they had passed a lone fisherman, an older, grumpy sort of guy, wearing a fly-filled floppy cotton hat, who was headed north along the Mountain Creek trail. Grumbling to himself as he approached them on the trail, he was apparently disappointed with his fly-fishing efforts in the river-feeding creeks. They had chatted briefly with him as they all rested on a fallen tree along the trail.

The old guy, a retired executive from some marketing company in Los Angeles, had expressed great concern for their safety. To begin with, he was really surprised that two "young ladies" would even attempt such a long, dangerous hike by themselves (unaccompanied and therefore unprotected as they were by any masculine bodyguards, he implied). Then, he was flabbergasted that neither of them had ever even attempted to make such a long trip before, in rough country where bears roamed and broken bones from falls were a constant possibility. He took little comfort when they showed him their defensive cans of pepper spray, the bear whistles hanging around their necks, and their fully stocked first-aid kits. As a last resort, Ellie had also brought along her cellular phone, although she didn't know if it would work or not in these deep valleys. If so, and they needed help, she could call the number that she had written down for the park headquarters and ask them to radio John. Of course, that would spoil the surprise, but if they really needed help they wouldn't have any other choice. As for the fisherman, he himself had packed—unknown to the young park ranger at Thorofare, he boasted—a .45-caliber Smith and Wesson revolver. He was a card-carrying member of the NRA, and not even the government was going to tell him he could not carry a loaded weapon into Yellowstone Park to defend himself if necessary. That had not, in fact been necessary, but he had seen a couple of bears off in the distance while fishing, and his final say on the subject was to caution them to be careful.

"I'm hot," Donna panted, as they stumbled along. She was getting more and more weary by the hour. Her complaints about the heat were actually caused by the rate at which she was losing energy, not the temperature of the air, which was, however, oppressive.

"Me too," Ellie answered. "I didn't think walking downhill would be such an effort. We really shouldn't have attempted a three-day hike in this kind of heat at this altitude without more conditioning."

"Tell me about it. So why don't we just quit now, use your phone to call for a taxi, or a horse, or something, and come back when it's cooler? Like maybe December. We could rent a snowmobile. That would be good. Whose idea was this, anyway?"

"Oh, c'mon," Ellie pleaded. "You can make it. We're halfway there already. We'll be at Mountain Creek in another hour or so, and then we can set up camp. We might even run into some rain, from the sound of all of that thunder that we've been hearing in the west."

"I have to pee."

"Okay, we'll take a short break."

The trail was flat. To their left was Howell Creek, which sparkled in the afternoon sun, although the water level was clearly lower than normal, as evidenced by the dry rocks, exposed tree limbs, and other debris along its banks. They removed their backpacks, leaned them against trees, and Donna stepped off the trail to relieve herself. Ellie opened her canvas-covered metal canteen and took a swig of water, splashing several spoonfuls around the inside brim of her "Smokey" hat. In a couple of minutes, Donna rejoined her.

"Well, that was a relief. Doesn't that water look good?" Donna asked, referring to the gurgling, shallow stream.

"Any water would look good in this heat," Ellie replied, wiping her forehead again with a dampened red-and-white checkered handkerchief.

"I don't know about you, but I'm going swimming—or at least soaking. The thought of cooling my aching feet in that water is just too, too tempting."

"We should go on. Maybe we can take a dip in Mountain Creek after we pitch camp," Ellie said. Donna wasn't going to argue; she was already removing her shoes and socks.

"Too little, too late. I'm going in right now. It'll feel good in the cold water with the hot sun." She had already taken off her plaid cotton shirt, loosened the leather belt that helped hold up her faded blue jeans, and was now slipping her rather proudly pointed and fulsome breasts out of her bra.

"What are you doing?" Ellie exclaimed, subconsciously looking around for anyone else on the trail. "Soaking your feet is one thing, going skinny-dipping in a national park is another."

"So sue me! Who's going to see us, anyway, some horny moose or owl? That guy we passed around noon was the first person we've seen in two days—and I'm sure he wouldn't have complained. At least not much. Besides, if we're lucky, maybe a couple of good-looking guys with hot bodies will come along and join us." She was now fully naked, and was prancing gingerly across the trail towards the water. Directly above her navel, the sunlight sparkled off a silver ring, its pointed ends pinching a small sapphire bead. From each nipple similar rings were pendulant. Several inches below her navel a fourth ring completed the set.

21

"I already have my good-looking guy," Ellie responded. "If his body isn't hot already, it will be when we get there." But the temptation of a quick dip in the cool water soon lured her. "Oh, what the hell. The worst that can happen to us is that we'll get eaten by a bear. But I'm not coming into that water with you completely butt-naked. I'm keeping my "Smokey" hat on—just in case we get some company." She began removing her clothes. All except for the hat.

Chapter Six

THE ALERT

John Reston was bored. He had read every book in the ranger station at least twice, had run out of crossword puzzles to work, and had memorized most of the dialogue in the movies that were now barely playable on the station VCR that badly needed its heads cleaned. He had even begun to talk to himself, applying movie lines to backwoods situations that their writers had never imagined.

The one thing that he had never found boring was the eight-by-ten photo of Ellie, which he had mounted in a frame of four stocky aspen branches that he had painstakingly carved to fit around the photo exactly. He had snapped the picture with his Canon during their visit last year to Yellowstone's Grand Canyon. Ellie was standing at the edge of the low rock wall that protected tourists from a long fatal fall at Lookout Point, wearing the "Smokey" hat that he had given her. Behind her, the late afternoon sun was hitting the colorful canyon just right, creating deep shadows here, bright highlights there, and painting the steep walls of the canyon in an amazing palette of pinks, purples, blues, browns, reds, oranges, greens, and of course yellows. He could hardly wait to see her again in person—hopefully they could spend a couple of days together before she had to go back to the Laramie campus and he would fly back to Washington.

Reston had spent the morning catching up on the station's minimal amount of required paperwork, making official computer hard and floppy disk entries from his handwritten notes on the weather, visitors, wildlife sightings, and such. He had to chuckle when he recalled the old fisherman who had dropped by the day before. Some of them know what they are doing and some of them obviously don't, he thought. Some of them bring the right flies, and catch their quota of fish, keeping some to fry, releasing others; some of them bring the wrong flies, and have a long walk here and back for nothing, except maybe to enjoy the scenery. This old guy was in the latter category. Maybe he should have just pulled out the revolver that he didn't know John had seen and shot his fish. But then he really would have been in trouble, and John would have had no choice but to cite him and confiscate the weapon. As long as the old guy didn't mention the gun, or outright flaunt it, John could just pretend that he had never seen it. No harm done.

All morning long he had noticed the clouds building on the western horizon. Since he hadn't seen any cumulus clouds at all for months, only the wispy stratus and cirrus, they had quickly caught his eye. It seemed to him that these clouds were unusually thick and dark, and almost stationary, and he wondered if the park was at last about to get some of the rain that it so desperately needed. All of the creeks around Thorofare were slowly drying up, the normally marshy valley of the Yellowstone River was not even spongy any more, and on his recent jog outside the park to the south he had seen the level of Bridger Lake almost two feet lower than it had been on his first visit to the lake in early summer. The rain would be more than welcome. Any rain at all.

Even as he watched, the curiously motionless clouds— probably sixty or seventy miles to the west—all at once began rushing eastward, as though a giant vacuum was sucking them through the sky. Dozens of bolts of lightning, almost like they were being fired from a Gatling gun, began striking the ground. He began counting: one-one-thousand... two-one-thousand... in a long-ago learned crude method of attempting to estimate the distance of the strikes from the associated thunder that followed. But that quickly proved to be a futile enterprise, for once the thunder began it just rumbled on and on, the claps spaced so closely together that he couldn't even distinguish one bolt of lightning and its thunder from another.

Reston went outside for a better look and listen. The ground itself seemed to shake with the pounding the park was getting, like it was experiencing an endless series of the minor earthquakes that Yellowstone, a noted area of seismic activity, constantly encountered. From the radio inside, he heard himself summoned, and went back in to respond.

"This is Reston. Over."

It was Bill Williams, assistant to Park Superintendent Don Madison, calling from Mammoth.

"John, we've got a real problem on our hands. This lightning is setting dozens of fires. We're closing the whole park immediately. You heard right. On Don's authority. That means getting every last person out—now. You got any fishermen or backpackers running around loose down there? Over."

"Not that I know of. Last guy I saw left the day before yesterday. But I probably should look up the streams. There could be some people coming in that haven't made it here yet, or weren't planning to check in. Over."

"That's what we want you to do," Williams said. "The sooner, the better. Look, John, this is going to be really bad. If you run into anybody at all, and they don't want to leave the park immediately, just shoot them, bury them, and go on to the next guy. Well, you can't actually do that, but you gotta use every bit of your authority to get them out of the park. We're gonna have one hell of time with these fires. I've never seen anything like it. We can't have more people burned up than animals, and if we don't kick everybody out, that's exactly what's gonna happen. Over."

"No problem. I have the rest of the afternoon to check out the most popular streams—maybe as far as Mountain Creek—and I can cover an even broader area tomorrow. But what's going to happen to anyone that I have to boot out if the fires come through here? There's no way they can hike all the way back to the highway before the fires catch up to them. Over"

"Good point," Williams agreed. "But the thing is, John, once we get these people across the park boundary, they're on their own. Know what I mean?"

"Yeah. 'Hi. I'm from the government, and I'm here to help you. Just step across the dotted line and get out of our jurisdiction, please.'"

"That's about the size of it. Take care, John. We'll try to get a chopper down your way to pull you out if things get touchy. Keep some of those pretty smoke pellets handy for identification. Over"

"Got it. Tell them to look for me somewhere between here and the lake in the middle of what's left of the Yellowstone River. I'll be the one farthest down—the one with no fins."

After signing off, Reston hustled to his backpack, which he usually kept pretty much ready to go in case of an emergency such as this, tossed in a few edible items from the cabinet and the refrigerator, and considered what else he needed. Binoculars, for sure. Jacket, in case he couldn't get back to the station before dark. Flashlight. Spare batteries. Rifle? Well, he might need it, and his belted pistol. Anything else that wasn't already in his backpack he would just have to make do without. He was going to be pressed for time as it was; he had no more left to look for this thing or that.

Reston was already forming a basic search plan as he flew out the door and began hiking north. Escarpment? Well, that area was badly burned by the 1988 fires, and hasn't fully recovered yet. Few fish, probably no fishermen. But it's worth hiking upstream for a while. Cliff Creek? Also burned in '88, but probably also worth a quick look for a mile or so where it feeds the river. Mountain? For sure. Has both spawners and resident cutthroat. Joins Howell. Wasn't killed in 1988. Well, Howell was burned, but I don't have to hike that. Anyone coming down off Eagle Pass should be able to look west and see the forest burning and have enough sense to turn around and head back to the highway. If they get back through the pass, they'll be out of the park. Anybody who doesn't come down the Mountain Creek Trail follows the Thorofare Trail along the river. Should be able to see them. If they can make it back to the lake they should be okay, eventually make it clear back to the highway, and get help there. What if someone won't go? You heard the man. Shoot 'em! Yeah, right. That would earn me a quick trip to Washington. What about the animals? Some will die, but most will find their way out. Just like they did in 1988.

Chapter Seven

THE FIND

Reston saw no sign of recent human visitation up the first mile of Escarpment—Its steepest section, and rather than backtrack along its banks decided to hike over the ridge forming the middle tine of The Trident and follow the flow of Cliff Creek back out to the Yellowstone. This hike proved to be equally unrewarding—or completely worthwhile, depending on your point of view. His greatest success would be failing to find anybody at all in the area. His worst nightmare would be to find some young couple with three or four kids hiking in the area with no backcountry permit and no record, therefore, of where they were going or when they were supposed to be coming back. It was hard to convince some people that the Park Service wasn't really looking for more money when the rules were laid down that required all backcountry hikers to obtain a permit. If they got in some trouble, or didn't return when they were supposed to, the cost of the permit would be cheap insurance for having search or rescue parties sent in after them. But if the Park Service had no record of them they were on their own. One of the problems with Yellowstone was that it had only five official entrances—but a perimeter that measured almost 250 miles. It was impossible to control entry into the park along that entire periphery; the rugged terrain itself made it impossible to even patrol. It was even worse than the United States/Mexico border. All the rangers could do to encourage trail head registration for day-hikers and proper permitting for any overnighters was to warn them of the possible dangers. Unfortunately, in a place as wild as Yellowstone, when people failed to follow the rules set down for their own safety they sometimes didn't have to worry about getting caught or fined; they just plain died—or were killed.

By the time he got back down to the river valley Reston could both see and smell the acrid smoke. The sky was a sickly brown, in the west, towards the north, and to the south, for as far as he could see, as smoke from what had to be dozens or even hundreds of fires drifted eastward over the park. Now almost north of him, in the easternmost part of Yellowstone, the dark clouds that had launched the lightning attack were still throwing their spears from the sky at the ground. He thought it strange that such a huge storm front could pass completely through the park and apparently leave little or no rain, nothing but lightning-set fires in its wake.

Reston wasted no time in going north in the river valley on the Thorofare Trail. Again he met up with no hikers or fishermen. He had now come to the Mountain Trail junction. If anywhere, here is where he would find them, he thought. Anyone who is not now on the Thorofare Trail was probably on the Mountain, wondering what the hell was happening with all of this thunder and lightning and ground-shaking.

It was beginning to look like his assigned coast was all clear, when he noticed something floating down the creek. From a distance, it sort of resembled a little boat, except it was too round in the middle and too flat on the ends. As he hurried over to the stream to get a better look, the thing next appeared to look almost like a standard-issue "Smokey Bear" ranger's hat. When Reston managed to wade up to the slowly drifting object, and retrieve it with the forked branches of a dead tree limb that he extended, he discovered that the oddly shaped object was in fact just that.

Chapter Eight

THE HAT

A cold chill came over Reston as he removed the ranger's hat from the water, and he shuddered to think that it probably belonged to one of his friends. It just couldn't be, he instantly concluded, for he was supposed to be the only park ranger within twenty miles. The next nearest station was the gate at the east entrance. There was no way that this hat could have gotten from there to here. It was even unlikely that it could have floated all the way down from Eagle Creek campground. No, that was impossible. The hat would have had to come through Eagle Pass—not very likely. What am I thinking? Eagle Creek flows north, not south, so the hat certainly had to have started its downstream float on this side of the pass, probably somewhere along the Mountain Creek Trail, in either Howell Creek or Mountain. What would an east gate ranger be doing down that far? Some kind of search-and-rescue mission? No, he would have gotten some word about that. So this was probably not the hat of an east gate ranger.

Then who owned the hat?

The name of the hat owner was probably taped inside. When everyone's hat looked the same as everyone else's you couldn't tell whose was whose in a meeting without a hat rack, so they all had to be labeled. He turned the hat over and looked inside. Nothing obvious. Maybe something under the sweat brim. Still nothing. Strange. Wait a minute. He was missing something here. The hat itself was missing something. He turned it upright, and spun it around, so that he was looking directly at its front.

Thought so. The Park Service emblem. This hat didn't have one. Now why was that? No ranger would ever think of wearing his "Smokey" without the brass emblem that made it official. Where was it? Why was it missing?

He had to find out, and fast. If another Park Service ranger was in this area—and missing his hat—he was probably in trouble. A fall? Possibly. The trail was hazardous, but it also didn't run too close to the stream. How could this guy's hat get into the stream if he stayed on the trail? He had to have left the trail. Lost? Not likely. It wasn't even dark yet. What kind of a ranger would get lost in broad daylight on a trail that could be traveled by a fully loaded fisherman? A bear? Could be. He could have confronted a grizzly on the trail by surprise and then took off running to escape an attack. But all rangers were trained to not do that, since a bear can run about five times as fast as a man. What they were trained to do was back away slowly, discard any available items that might help to momentarily distract a charging bear (except a backpack that could help protect the back and neck), and as a last resort drop down, curl up, and play dead, shielding the head as much as possible. Maybe that's what had happened. Maybe the ranger had tossed his hat at a bear to distract it, and the bear had gone for the hat, carried it into the stream, and then lost it. That could explain the floating hat. But not the missing emblem. Any tooth marks on the hat? None on the brim, none anywhere else either. So how could a bear carry this hat without leaving any tooth or claw marks on it? And it had also removed the emblem without leaving any sign of having done so? No way.

So did this hat even belong to a ranger?

He suddenly shivered violently and uncontrollably in the hot sun, as another possible scenario struck him, one far more ominous than any ranger missing his "Smokey." He knew of only one person who was not a ranger and had one of these hats. But she was in Jackson. Wasn't she? What would Ellie's hat be doing here without her? He had a sudden thought. He had bought the hat for her specifically, and he still remembered its size.

Was this hat the same size? Please, God, no.

Reston turned the hat over slowly. He had to ask the question, but he feared to learn the answer.

Chapter Nine

THE BURIAL

John Reston ran. He ran faster than he had ever run before. He ran faster than he ever thought he could. He had dropped the hat, peeled off his backpack, and discarded anything else that would slow him down as he ran up the trail. Against all training and experience, he had even shucked and ditched the shoulder-slung rifle.

His only thought was that he had to find her. To find her injured? To find her broken and bleeding? To find her mauled by some half-starved grizzly?

To find her. Just to find her. And to hold her in his arms once more.

He would deal with anything else that he had to once he had found her. All he wanted now was to be by her side, to know that she safe, to tell her how much she meant to him and, yes, how much he loved her. But Ellie had to be in some kind of trouble. She had to need his help. She had to need him. Even more than he now needed her.

He slipped and fell twice on loose rocks, the second time twisting his right ankle badly. He tried to ignore the pain, thinking it would soon go away. It didn't. The ankle would be swelling quickly, were he not wearing the tightly-laced trail

33

boots. Even so, he knew that he would not be able to get the boot back on the injured ankle once he removed it. Not for hours. So he would simply leave the boot on, until the potential for swelling had subsided.

It was hard to run and to search the stream at the same time. He didn't even know if Ellie was in or near the water. He began spending as much time scanning both sides of the trail as he did looking for signs in the stream. There was nothing. Not a broken branch, not an obviously out-of-place rock, not a piece of torn clothing. Nothing. He was now almost to the fork where Howell ran into Mountain.

Should he stay on Mountain? Follow one of its three or four tributaries? What if she had started farther east on U. S. 20, and had hiked down through Fishhawk Meadows? That would have brought her over the ridge near the headwaters of Mountain Creek. There was a trail there—but it came almost straight west until it bowed north to join the Mountain Creek about halfway between his current position and Eagle Pass. Along Howell Creek. Why would she go through Fishhawk Meadows if she could have a shorter hike by starting at Eagle Creek Campground? Nobody would do that. Unless they had to.

Damn it! What was she even doing, hiking through this dangerous area by herself, without even telling him that she was coming?

So he now had narrowed his choices down to one—she was somewhere on the Mountain Creek Trail, where it paralleled Howell. He continued following that trail, keeping an eye over to his right, on the slow-flowing Howell.

Reston must have gone another two or three miles—and still seen nothing unusual—before he began to think that he had missed something. He had not been able to keep Howell Creek in view the entire time, at least not as closely as he would have liked, but he was fairly certain that he had not overlooked anything else floating on the water. So far. There were still stretches up ahead where the trail ran right next to the stream. He had lingering, anxious thoughts about turning back and searching the same section of the trail again.

But then he found it.

There was a black-and-red plaid shirt just off to the left of the trail. His worst fear was that the shirt had been ripped from Ellie's body by an attacking grizzly. With their much-reduced food supply this summer the few grizzlies in the immediate area would be out prowling for any food they could find, and could even be moving on up to the higher elevations already. Ellie could have encountered one of those bears on the trail, a bear that had found it easier to follow a beaten path to climb the mountain than to blaze a new trail through the brush.

Reston hesitated to pick up the shirt, but was relieved when it had no teeth or claw marks on it, nor—thank God—any blood. But why would Ellie have stripped off her shirt? Maybe she was wearing a tee-shirt, as he knew she often did—with no bra—with the plaid shirt's arms looped around her waist and tied in a loose knot. Maybe she had come across a bear and had thrown the plaid shirt at it to distract it. Maybe she was somewhere around here safe after all, taking refuge in a tree, too scared to come down.

"Ellie!" he shouted, hoping she would answer. He paused, and listened. No response.

"Ellie!" Again he paused. Again he listened. Again there was no answer.

Well, maybe she was farther up ahead. Maybe the bear had somehow picked up the shirt, come on down the path, and then dropped it. Or maybe Ellie just couldn't hear him yet. He continued hiking along the path, which still stayed in the valley but would soon get steeper as it approached Eagle Pass. His twisted ankle was beginning to hurt like a sonofabitch.

Reston thought he could smell something. Meat? The putrid scent of a bear? He couldn't quite place it. He couldn't even determine where it was coming from. Maybe from up ahead. Maybe from behind. He couldn't tell.

"Ellie!" Still no answer.

It was then that Reston saw something pale, something white, something irregularly shaped with jagged edges, at the edge of the trail before him. A piece of cloth? Maybe. There was a round silver ring, apparently jewelry, attached to it. It was...not cloth. Oh, God.

Reston approached whatever it was circumspectly, reluctantly. As he came closer he could see clearly that it was a sizeable section of human skin. There were long, red streaks—deep, bleeding gashes—raked almost completely across it, over what seemed to be a part of a person's chest or abdomen.

He retched, several times, until there was nothing else in his stomach to bring up. His eyes were tearing. His mind was confused. He was relieved to find her, but speared in the heart to imagine what she had gone through, and enraged at the bear and wanting revenge. But most of all he felt helpless, knowing that there was not a single thing that he could now do to bring Ellie back. He stared listlessly at the bloody mess lying there before him, his eyes refocusing on the shining object attached to the skin around the navel. Despite his distaste for doing so, he moved still closer, until he was right over the skin, and examined the shiny object close-up. It was a silver ring, with some kind of bead on it. Body jewelry. This woman had gotten her navel pierced.

Would Ellie have done that? Probably not without telling him about it. And she had not said a word, had not written anything about getting pierced in the entire time he had known her. Well, college students do stupid and faddish things, however painful, and lots of people are getting pierced in all sorts of places today—both men and women—but Ellie? She didn't need to have her navel pierced to make herself attractive, or to be considered "in" with the campus in-crowd. This mangled skin apparently belonged to a woman—but it did not belong to Ellie!

Then whose skin was it?

The answer had to be somewhere in the immediate area, something that would identify this poor girl, who had been wearing a plaid shirt, a ranger's hat of the same size as Ellie's, at least one silver body ring...and who knows what else where.

Reston began scouting both sides of the trail more closely, and soon came to more clothing, scattered all over the place— and two backpacks. So, he quickly concluded, this girl was hiking with her boyfriend. Either the guy had gotten away, or the grizzly had gotten them both. But as he looked through the strewn clothing it seemed like something was wrong. There were too many pieces that seemed to be something a woman would wear—and not a single piece of clothing that looked like it was made for a male. That was strange. So was this. There seemed to be two complete piles of clothing, hiking boots and all, as though both hikers had removed every stitch of the clothing that they had been wearing—shirts, jeans, shoes, socks, bras, panties, everything. Now why would two girls on a backwoods hike in bear country do that?

Reston investigated both backpacks—or what was left of them, after they had been raided by the bear for anything interesting to eat—sifting through their remaining contents. They both contained tampons, panty liners. Well, he was certainly no forensic expert, but he was now positive that both of these backpacks had belonged to women. This was no retreat for romance—at least not between a man and a woman. This was two women, apparently two young women, hiking together. Again his heart skipped a beat, as he realized that Ellie could very well have been the other young woman.

The stream—such as it was, at this time of year and being short the entire summer on snowmelt—was only a few yards away. As Reston looked left and right he suddenly saw in the stream a large object that he knew had to be another piece of a body. As hesitant as before he went down the bank, and saw the main portion of the woman's torso from which a large part of the front had been torn. Her face was staring right at him, or at least he was looking at one eye; the other was hanging out of its socket, apparently dislodged by a tremendous blow to the side of her head.

This woman, this poor girl, whoever she was, was not Ellie. He could not contain a sigh of relief, but at the same time realized that Ellie's life—or that of the other hiker, if she was not Ellie—might have been saved by this woman's gruesome death. While the bear was occupied with its attack on her, the other woman could have gotten away.

Reston thought about removing the remains of the body from the stream, and joining it with the missing belly alongside the trail, but quickly concluded that he had nothing, really, to cover her up with, unless he could find a ground cloth or two around the backpacks. But there was not much immediate need to cover this woman's body, other than to do so out of modesty and decency, and respect. It was more immediately important to locate her missing companion. He decided to leave the body alone.

Reston must have searched both sides of the trail for a couple of hundred yards in either direction for the next fifteen or twenty minutes, but he found nothing else to indicate that either woman had been anywhere else around the immediate area, except where he had found the riddled backpacks.

With the sun now behind Table Mountain, Reston realized that he was beginning to lose the daylight. He thought about crossing the stream and looking around in the little valley. Maybe the other woman had run in that direction, as the bear attacked her companion. Maybe she had been caught by the faster bear somewhere east of the stream. On the other hand, a smarter person would have tried to scramble uphill, in a desperate attempt to reach and climb a tree. She could have been overtaken there. He was leaning towards the tree theory, looking up the hillside, when he noticed a small mound of seemingly fresh dirt about thirty yards into the trees. Grizzlies are famous for burying their leftovers, he recalled, often digging huge holes to stow away a whole elk or a half-grown bison, and coming back later to finish them off. He had read one report about a grizzly that had half-dozed atop a partly buried elk carcass for several hours to protect it, while both hungry wolves and a brash young black bear, at separate times, had made darting but unsuccessful efforts to try and steal it.

Reston climbed over several large rocks and drought-stunted bushes, until he reached the mound, and saw that he was right. The bear had caught this one, too, had probably eaten on her until his immediate hunger was satisfied, and had buried the rest for later. Or had started to. Her left hand and arm—both covered with blood—were sticking straight up from the mound, like a grave marker for some unknown soldier. He had to do it. He had to know. He used his cupped hands to remove the loose dirt and other debris from the woman's badly mauled shoulder, and the her neck, until he uncovered her battered, bloodied face. The blue eyes, still open, and staring right at him as though she could see him, were lifeless.

"Ellie!"

Reston didn't have even a single minute—to breathe again, to vent his shock and revolt and remorse with a scream, or to pray that Ellie would sleep in peace—before he heard a rumbling roar, and the breaking of limbs and branches, and turned just in time to find himself looking straight at the fangs of an irate eight-hundred-pound grizzly. He had made a cardinal mistake, a really stupid, amateurish mistake, in getting too close to a grizzly's personal carrion stash, and now he was going to pay for it.

The young ranger never had a chance. The bear's first powerful swipe with its stiletto-sharp claws caught Reston's upraised left arm, severed it just below the shoulder, and sent it sailing towards the trail. The force of the blow was more than enough to knock Reston down, and his head smashed hard into a granite rock. He immediately lost consciousness. John Reston never knew that he was only minutes away from joining Ellie Maxwell in her temporary grave.

Chapter Ten

THE REJCUERJ

John Reston was repeatedly radioed at noon by park headquarters on the second day of the fire, in an attempt to get an update on the status of any Yellowstone visitors in his area, and for an up-close-and-personal report on any fires there.

There was no answer. This did not seem strange to Madison and the other park administrators, because they knew that Reston had gone out the previous afternoon to look for backpackers and fishermen. And since they were making similar calls to all of the other stations in the park, and were still occupied with fighting the fires, Reston's absence wasn't conspicuous.

At about two p.m. Williams attempted the radio contact again, and again there was no answer. Now Madison and Williams began to grow concerned. He should have been back to the station by now, knowing that they would be expecting some kind of update. Even a second-year ranger would know enough to remain in contact in circumstances that warranted such contact. If these circumstances didn't qualify, none would.

They checked the latest satellite photos, to see where the burn areas were in the park, as revealed by infrared imagery that cut through the massive amount of smoke and showed them where all of the hot spots were. There were hot spots everywhere, from one end of the park to the other, with few exemptions. One of those exceptions was the area around Thorofare Station, where the fires apparently got as far south as the headwaters of the Snake River but were halted in their eastbound shoes before they touched the west bank of the Yellowstone River.

That should have meant that the station was safe, unless it somehow had been one of the first buildings to burn and had cooled enough to not show up in the latest satellite photos. If not to direct lightning, then maybe the station had fallen victim to drifting sparks. In stiff winds, the high-flying embers from burning lodgepole pine could be blown for incredible distances, setting new fires when and where they landed. But even if that had happened at Thorofare, and Reston had been around, he probably could have gotten off a call for help before abandoning the building and the radio. Since no call had been received, and since none of the satellite photos showed any indication of the station's burning, Reston must not have been around.

All other stations had reported in. One had already burned to the ground, and a couple of the others had been seriously threatened, but the massed firefighting forces seemed to be holding their own. Most of the effort, of course, was concentrated around the park's major administrative and developed tourist areas—Mammoth, Old Faithful, Tower-Roosevelt, Canyon Village, West Thumb, Grant Village, the museums at Norris and Madison, and of course Lake Village, site of Lake Lodge, Lake Hotel, and the park's historic hospital. As in 1988, it had been necessary to sacrifice a few of the outlying buildings in those areas in order to save the more important ones. Overall, however, the quick and positive actions of the park administrators when the fires had first broken out appeared to have been the key to not only containing the hundreds of fires so far but even controlling them. After only a single day of fighting the fires the reports from several fire bosses were...glowing. In 1988, it had taken weeks of unparalleled effort to reach the same point, and the price had been paid in precious park resources.

If Thorofare hadn't burned, they wondered at Mammoth, then where was Reston? After the second attempt, the radio calls were made every fifteen minutes. When no answer had been received by two o'clock, they decided to determine why. It was apparent that something had happened to the second-year ranger, something that could only be bad.

It was decided to pull two rangers away from their temporary duties around Old Faithful, equip them with basic backpacks, and fly them by helicopter to Thorofare, where they could check out the situation, look for Reston and lend assistance if necessary, then hike back up to the highway along the lake trail or to Eagle Creek Campground. If they could use the station radio to report in, fine; but each of them was going to have a satellite phone with which to call home anyway. The park already had one ranger missing in action; there was not much need to have two more join him.

Bob Nelson and George Harris were the rangers chosen to go after Reston. Both were Yellowstone veterans. Nelson had been the park's bear management specialist for maybe a dozen years. Harris had served in the park even longer, in several capacities. They were experienced in both search and rescue and in fighting fires. They would be flown to Thorofare in a U. S. Army helicopter, which was warming up in one of the Old Faithful parking lots even as they found out about their assignment. Nelson and Harris had only minutes to pack, but that's all they needed. When the bird took off, both of them were on it.

The helicopter flew in almost a straight line towards Thorofare, making detours in the smoke-filled sky only to avoid collisions with other firefighting aircraft or to escape the rising columns of hot, hazy air that created considerable turbulence and reduced visibility. Once or twice Nelson asked the pilot to bank slightly to the left or the right, so that he could get a better view of the moving animals, particularly the bears, or make a rough count of the number of carcasses burned. A firm believer in using all available technology to help him in his bear management duties, Nelson often carried a Sony Hi-8 video camera with him to record animal activities. He had brought it along on this trip, and was recording almost constantly. If nothing else, the Park Service was going to have a lot of good fire footage when he got back.

They flew the last leg of the mission directly over the Yellowstone River, thinking they might get some clue to Reston's whereabouts in the valley, but got none. There were still many animals—mainly elk—headed south along the east edge of the river, and a few were spooked by the sound of the helicopter but there were no fires in the river valley. The fires seemed to have come to a natural halt up on the Continental Divide. Nor apparently had any fires broken out east of the river, around The Trident, or on the mountains to the north with tributaries flowing into the Yellowstone.

Nelson and Harris both sensed that something was wrong as soon as they saw the station. Even from a distance there appeared to be absolutely nothing out of place around the building. It had not burned. It had not been touched at all by any fingers of flame. So there was no apparent reason why Reston could not have responded to the repeated radio calls if he were around. It was obvious that he was not. The pilot landed the helicopter close to the building, and idled the engine a few minutes while they checked the station. Harris confirmed that the radio was operational by calling Mammoth and reporting in, and also let them know what they had discovered so far. He got an okay to release the helicopter for other assignments, and had Nelson relay that release to the pilot, who was to make a bee-line for the east entrance immediately, pick up a firefighter who had been badly burned by a falling tree, and fly him to the nearest source of complete medical treatment, the hospital in Bozeman, Montana. The pilot took only enough time to wave good-bye before he was headed almost directly north. He would fly back up the river valley, swing right at Mountain Creek, follow Howell to Eagle Pass, then head straight up the Eagle Creek valley until he reached the highway. From there he would be only about five miles east of the entrance.

Nelson and Harris checked all through the interior of the station but were unable to come up with any clues as to what had become of Reston. They had no idea how much food he should have had in the cupboards and refrigerator, so they couldn't say how much—If any—was missing. They did determine that Reston's backpack was gone, and maybe a rifle, but that was to be expected if he had left the station to search for strays. They called headquarters again, to see if Reston's last communication could give them any clues as to which direction he had gone.

What they got, in response, was a surprise.

The Army pilot, flying over Howell Creek, had radioed in to report that he had seen some colorful objects that had appeared to be strewn clothing along the trail as he looked down near the creek's junction with Mountain. He had seen no sign of life, although he had not had time to hover around looking. He did think he may have seen a person at the edge of Howell Creek, but whatever it was wasn't moving and he was only guessing that it was a person. He had continued flying north.

It wasn't much, but it was a lot more than they had found anywhere else, so they told headquarters that they would check out the pilot's report first, then look up and down the other streams. A few minutes later they were on the trail, walking north, being particularly careful to avoid the lanes of southbound traffic. They didn't want to disturb any of the animal pedestrians, least of all the bears.

Chapter Eleven

THE ARM

"George, I don't think I've ever seen animals in such bad shape as these," Nelson observed as they walked along. "Some of them are so weak they can barely walk. They might have made it even after the dry summer, but they sure as hell aren't going to survive now, after running for miles to escape the fires."

"Pretty bad," Harris agreed. "Looks like the elk have started their migration early. They'll probably lay up for awhile down in Teton Wilderness before going on down to the elk refuge."

"I bet a lot of 'em won't even make it that far," Nelson speculated. "See all of those carcasses along the trail? They're already keeling over. I don't think I've ever seen prey and predators all packed together like this, not even trying to hunt or get away. The meat-eaters are going right by the dead ones, like they're not even hungry."

"Hard to imagine," Harris agreed. "Most of these animals are nothing but skin and bones."

"Well, they'll eat when they get hungry enough, I suppose, when they stop in a few miles to rest. They'll soon figure out that they've outrun the fires, and everything will get back to normal."

"Down there maybe, but up here in the park it's going to take a bit more time to recover. First thing have to do is get all of these fires out, before they can run wild like they did in 1988."

"You see how them Army boys are digging right in?" Nelson asked. "Good troops. Tough. I saw one of them get hit on the shoulder by a falling tree. Got back up, brushed himself off, went back over and just kicked the living shit out of that tree! Like he had lost the battle but was sure as hell not going to lose the war!"

"We oughta be damned glad that we have all of this help," Harris replied, nodding his head. "Looks like we might actually have learned something in '88 about fighting fires. You gotta get to them while they're young—sort of like having a mountain lion for a pet. Once they grow up untamed you'll have one hell of a problem."

"You suppose that helicopter pilot really spotted John's body?"

"Wouldn't surprise me a bit," Harris said. "As you know, this is grizzly country, and they can be pretty grumpy about this time of year, particularly after going through a whole summer of always being short on food. John probably looked like a walking hot-dog to one, as he trotted along looking for hikers, and a grizzly probably surprised him. I expect we'll find him in pieces up there on Howell—if we even find him at all."

"Nice kid," Nelson sniffed. "Once told me he spent a lot of time at the Washington zoo when he was there. Liked animals."

"Well, it's beginning to look like one of them may have liked him back."

Nelson and Harris sped along the trails about as quickly as they could, bearing their backpacks and being cautious. They left the Thorofare at Mountain, and began a slow ascent, generally following the stream along the trail. It wasn't long before they came to what had to be Reston's backpack, his rifle, and a few smaller items.

"What do you make of this?" asked George, shaking his head slowly in puzzlement.

"You mean why would John get rid of both his rifle and his backpack, going against his training?" Nelson replied.

"Exactly what I mean. Not only did he discard his rifle in bear country, but he took off his backpack, knowing it would have given him some protection in a bear attack."

"Maybe he had to take off running," Nelson guessed.

"Away from a bear? Even a second-year ranger would know better than that! And why would he get rid of his rifle? Did he even fire it?"

Bob picked up the rifle, a .30/.30 Winchester lever action, and worked the lever. The shells came flying out the side ejector slot. He held the gun up to his nose and smelled it.

"Doesn't appear to have been fired recently," Bob announced.

"None of this makes much sense. Think we should call in yet?"

"I think we should look on up the trail. The pilot said he saw clothes. I don't see no clothes around here. I think we should try to find the clothes and see what we can make of them before we go getting headquarters all excited. Besides, all we got to tell them right now is that this boy apparently wasn't too good about following their advice."

They first found the torn piece of torso, apparently belonging to a woman who was, they immediately discovered, wearing a silver ring with a captive sapphire bead in her navel. Strange. They next found the clothes, in two fairly neat piles a feet away from the bear-raided backpacks. Most of the items that had been stuffed into the backpacks were now scattered about.

"Jesus," Bob spat. "What the hell happened here? One of these backpacks must have belonged to that girl back there. But that means we have another... apparently another girl, from the looks of all of these clothes that are scattered about."

"Something's not right about this, Bob," George quickly concluded. "Look at these piles of clothes. Imagine putting them all back on these two girls, a piece at a time. You get the impression that they were running around here buck naked?"

Bob studied the piles, obviously enjoying the challenge of mentally redressing two imaginary young females. But he had to agree with George that there were two complete sets of clothes, each belonging to a young woman. "Damned if I don't. You think Reston was out here chasing these ladies?"

"Well, right now I don't know quite what to think," George puzzled. "First we find John's rifle and backpack, then the torn-up piece of a female, and now two piles of clothes belonging, apparently, to two young women, one of which was probably the girl we found a piece of. No doubt we've had a grizzly attack—look at the torn backpacks. But where's the rest of the first girl? And where's the second? And where's John?"

"I don't know about you, good buddy, but I'm about to get my rifle into a more usable position. If we had a hungry grizzly chewing on all of these people chances are he now likes the taste, and he may still be around here. I don't think I want to be surprised by this sucker."

"Got that right," Harris agreed. "Look, why don't you head over to the stream and see if you can find anything along it. I'll take the other side of the trail, and look up in the brush. Yell if you see anything. If not, meet me back here and we'll go on up the trail as far as Eagle Pass."

Nelson headed towards the stream. Harris went up the bank.

"Hey, George!" Bob soon shouted. "I just found the rest of the first girl. Most of her chest is ripped off. My God! You don't even want to see this."

"Does she still have her left arm?" George replied.

Chapter Twelve

THE AIRLIFTS

The helicopters—all three of them—hovered overhead. On the trail, the search-and-rescue specialists loaded the remains of the first young woman into the basket that hung tightly from a cable, waiting to be reeled up into the first helicopter. The air and ground efforts were coordinated with walkie-talkies.

Up in the brush Nelson and Harris were hastily clearing an area big enough to carry out a similar airlift there—while two EMTs were doing the best they could to bandage Reston's several wounds and deep gashes, including the bloody stub of his missing left arm and a deep cut in his forehead. A few feet away the nearly nude body of Ellie Maxwell, or what was left of it, lay under an olive-brown wool Army blanket.

"I cannot believe this guy is still alive," the first EMT said to the second. "He's been like this for almost two days?"

"I think that ranger was right," the other EMT replied. "The bear must have knocked him over when he took off his arm, and the guy hit his head on a rock and passed out. In effect, he was playing dead, so the bear then let him alone, except to bury him with the girl."

"A real looker. Damned shame. I wouldn't have minded getting a piece of that."

"Yeah. I almost think I've seen her somewhere. She looks so familiar. Hold this IV a minute." He reached over, pulled the blanket down as far as the girl's midsection—somewhat farther than he needed to—and took another look at her bloody face. "I don't know. There's something about her eyes." His own eyes wandered on down her torso, pausing for a long moment at the shapely breasts. He sighed, then covered her back up.

The basket was being lowered from the second helicopter. Nelson and Harris were catching it, stopping its rotation, and guiding it to the ground.

"You guys have him ready to go?" Harris asked.

"All set," replied the second technician. "Bring that over here as close as you can get. Then help us lift him in it."

"You think he's going to live?"

"Well, he's lost a lot of blood—but not as much as he would have if he hadn't passed out and stopped moving. It helped to have the bear immediately bury him under all of this dirt and leaves. There must be something in the leaves and grass that acted as a clotting agent, helping to stem the flow of blood."

"How's his head? It looks like he took one hell of a blow."

"That's the main problem. We don't know how much damage was done to the brain until they do a CAT scan. He may turn out to be a vegetable for the rest of his life. Sorry, but you asked. I know he was your friend."

"Is, not was. Is our friend. Well, let's get him out of here."

John Reston didn't yet know it but he was still alive. Still unconscious, he made no noise as his bruised, bloodied, and battered body was hoisted into the helicopter, secured, and flown off into the approaching night sky to the west, first to Lake Hospital for the best treatment immediately available. Soon he would be transferred by Life Flight out of Jackson to Salt Lake City.

In the third helicopter the half-eaten body of Ellie Maxwell began the first of a series of flights that would eventually deliver her to her home in Denver, where she would be buried in another, more-permanent grave.

Chapter Thirteen

THE MOTHER

"Good morning. Bubba's. This is Barbara. How may I help you?"

"Rhonda, please."

"I'm sorry. Rhonda is not here right now. Would you like to leave a message?"

"Maybe you can help me. This is Mrs. Maxwell—Ellie's mother?"

"Oh, yes. Hi, Mrs. Maxwell. We met this summer when you came up to Jackson. How can I help you?"

"I'm trying to get in touch with Ellie."

"She quit work a couple of days ago. I thought Ellie was coming back to Denver to get ready for school. She isn't there yet?"

"I haven't heard from her in a couple of days. The last I knew, she was coming home But she hasn't arrived, and I can't reach her at her apartment. I can't even get her roommate to answer the phone. I think something has happened."

"I'd be happy to help you find her. Let me make some calls. What is your number there in Denver? I'll call around and get back to you. But it may be an hour or so. We're starting to get pretty busy. Lunchtime."

Mrs. Maxwell had the cashier her home number in Denver, had thanked her for her help, and was now sitting at her kitchen table to wait for a response. Over the rim of a fresh cup of steaming black coffee, she was reading the day's Denver Post. All during the summer, anything in the newspaper about Jackson Hole or Yellowstone National Park had caught her eye. In today's paper she was reading a story about the hundreds of fires in Yellowstone that had been started by lightning. The story mentioned the fact that thousands of animals had been displaced—and many burned to death—by the incredible number of fires that were being fought simultaneously all over the park.

Mrs. Maxwell thought about that young Yellowstone ranger that Ellie was seeing last summer, and wondered if he was okay. She knew Ellie had not been able to see him in person this summer but had remained in close contact with letters and telephone calls. They seemed to have something long-term going. She smiled, remembering her own days of dating.

Her next thought was about the displaced animals. She was an active member of the local Sierra Club.

"Those poor, poor bears," Mrs. Maxwell sympathized.

Barbara Whissel, the Bubba's cashier, while checking out a steady flow of lunchtime customers, tried all of the telephone numbers that she had at the front counter for reaching Ellie Maxwell. Nobody knew anything about her present whereabouts. The slim, competent, conscientious cashier began thinking about other possibilities. She knew that Ellie had roomed all summer in the tight Jackson housing market with another waitress. She couldn't remember where the other girl worked.

Maybe one of the other Bubba's waitresses would know. She would start by asking the ones working the current shift. She was about to go back to the kitchen to begin asking around when the telephone rang. Busy morning. She glanced at the wall clock. Well, so much for the morning.

"Good afternoon. Bubba's. This is Barbara. How may I help you?"

"This is the National Park Service calling from Yellowstone. Is there someone there I can talk to about your employees?"

"I'm sorry. The person you need to talk to is gone at the moment. Can I possibly help you?"

"Do you have an Ellie Maxwell who works there?"

It was too much of a coincidence, Barbara thought. First her mother, now the Park Service. She was immediately chilled.

"We did have, but she quit work for the summer a couple of days ago to go back home to Denver. Is something wrong?"

"There's been an accident, and Ms. Maxwell was involved. We need to reach her next-of-kin. The only information we have is that she apparently worked at Bubba's. We found a pay stub."

"Do you mean 'accident' as in injured, or 'accident' as in killed?" the cashier asked.

"I'm sorry, but we aren't permitted to say, at this point, except to close relatives. Do you know how we can contact Ms. Maxwell's parents?"

"I just got a call from Mrs. Maxwell about an hour ago. She's worried that something has happened to her daughter. She gave me her home telephone number in Denver."

"May I have that, please?"

The cashier relayed the telephone number that Mrs. Maxwell had given her. The Park Service woman thanked her, and immediately hung up. The cashier stood there in concern and disbelief, with the silent telephone handset still at her ear, as an anxious tourist asked for the third time to be checked out.

In a few minutes, Mrs. Maxwell received a telephone call at her home in Denver, dropped the steaming cup of coffee that she was holding, and immediately fainted. Her pet toy fox terrier, a spayed female, quickly came over and began licking up the dark brown liquid from the floor. But the dog soon abandoned that bitter liquid for the sweeter warm red fluid that was flowing from Mrs. Maxwell's forehead.

Chapter Fourteen

THE MEDALS

Not in the history of Yellowstone, nor even in the history of the world, had so many fires been fought and extinguished in such a short time. In less than a week the combined civilian and military firefighting force had, by actual count, put out 267 separate blazes, ranging in size from just a few trees to 432 forested acres. Not a single one of the fires had been allowed to get beyond its initial containment and flash across the forest until it eventually burned itself out.

It was a far cry from the way things had gone in 1988.

In the earlier fires, mainly administrative indecisiveness and just plain stupidity had increased the fire toll dramatically. Once most of those fires had gotten a head start the firefighters were completely outmatched by Mother Nature, unable to even slow—let alone stop—the advancing infernos. A lot of the weary firefighters had been lucky to escape with their lives, as the flames raced much faster than any of them had ever imagined possible through the trees and the underbrush. It was the great amount of underbrush, in fact, that made their efforts so difficult and added so much fuel to the fires. The federal government had long had a policy of putting out smaller fires before they could clear out the accumulating understory, thus preparing the way—through the irony of pulpwood paperwork—for even larger and fiercer fires in the future, a future that had arrived ahead of schedule in 1988.

Those fires, almost fifteen years ago, had not been entirely bad for Yellowstone, for they had superheated and popped open the pine cones whose seeds had allowed whole new forests of lodgepole pine to be born in the park. In addition to the standing trees, the fires had incinerated the understory slash—mainly wind-toppled trees—that looked so pretty to the tourists passing through Yellowstone but loomed so ominously to forest management specialists as potential forest fire fuel. The flames had instantly turned many dry meadows and parched grassy plains throughout the park into smoldering cemeteries of plant and animal death. But that death was also life for the countless new plants that had begun popping through the black mantles around the park as early as the very next spring. Some ecologists had been amazed. Others, perhaps more optimistic than their peers about the ultimate future of the planet itself—before or after a manmade disaster—had simply smiled at the way things changed as they always stayed the same.

In less than a week all of the present fires had been put out. That was such an astonishing achievement, and so widely reported across the country, that the entire Yellowstone Park administrative staff, once the park's gates had been closed for the winter, had been flown from the Jackson Hole airport (the only one located entirely in a national park) to Washington, D. C. on Air Force Two, welcomed by Vice President and Jackson resident Dick Cheney at National, and paraded up Pennsylvania Avenue to the White House, where they were each given an appropriate redwood-bordered plaque in a nationally televised ceremony by President George W. Bush.

"We owe these people so much more than medals," the President had said. "We owe these people, and the many other valiant firefighters who answered their calls and responded to their instructions, the very future of Yellowstone National Park, one of the country's most-precious natural resources. Without their instant grasp of the dangers of the situation, and without their tireless efforts throughout this long, terrible week, we may have lost all of Yellowstone, and perhaps much more."

The following day, in a much-applauded, also-televised appearance before a joint session of Congress, the same park staff was awarded the first Congressional Medal of Natural Resources Honor.

In Salt Lake City's Rocky Mountain Medical Center, the chief hospital administrator concurrently pinned the same shiny medal on the pillow of the young Ranger John Reston, who was resting comfortably but still unconsciously in his bed. Around the room, many doctors, nurses, and other persons applauded, including Dr. and Mrs. Alex Quincy Maxwell, III, of Denver, Colorado.

Chapter Fifteen

THE SANCTUARY

It seemed like they had been fleeing forever, like the flames were chasing them wherever they went. Half of the trails they took turned out to be fire traps—dead ends that were blocked by burning trees and blazing understory, causing them to back-track and look for another way out. The only safe trail seemed to be the one that went south, along the eastern shore of the lake, along the river that followed the path of the great herds of elk that left the park in the fall and returned in the spring.

So that was the trail that they followed, these Yellowstone grizzlies that normally kept miles between themselves and between the territories that they marked by reaching as high as they could up various trees around their perimeter, clawing off sections of bark as if to say, this is how big I am, if you think you're bigger, and stronger, then make a mark above mine and prove it. Beat this, or leave now.

They normally would have been fighting, so many bears thrust so close together. But this day was not normal. The sky had been dark, its jagged sparks had set fires everywhere, and the booming noise was endless, even rattling the very ground that they ran on. There would be time to fight later. There would be time to find and mark new territories, time to settle down, to fatten up, to dig in for the winter. Right now, they were simply running to save their lives.

As the bears ran, they joined or were joined by many other animals, nearly any of which would have been fair game under normal circumstances. But any feasting or evading, too, would come later, once they could all stop moving and rest. The weakened condition of these future prey, combined with the extra effort of escaping the fires, would cause the death of many of them. There would be carcasses littering the escape route. There would be no need to burn valuable energy chasing down fleeing food, no need even to bully the damned wolves away from their catch. Once the bears had found sanctuary, it would all work out. They would stop, rest, eat as much as they could stomach, eat some more, eat some more, and then find some place to turn in for the winter.

The mass migration flowed down the Yellowstone River valley and passed the silent Thorofare Ranger Station without even slowing. There was nothing in the dried-up valley that interested them. On the ridge to their right, on the Continental Divide, they could still see flames filling the early evening sky with soaring sparks and bursts of reddish light as new stands of trees fell victim to the leaping fires. They could still hear the crackling, popping, and snapping sounds of the burning trees and brush, the sudden explosions as the moisture in heated sap rose to the boiling point, expanded to the breaking point, and then broke through cambium layers and burning bark with a force that blew trees apart like they had swallowed live grenades. They could still smell the smoke that irritated their lungs and made it hard to breathe. They could still feel death attempting to lure them into making one wrong move, into taking one wrong turn, into staying one moment too long in the wrong place. They had to keep moving, until they had left the fire danger completely behind.

The migrating mass of animals found sanctuary just south of Bridger Lake in the Teton Wilderness. For whatever reason the fires seemed to stop at the Yellowstone Park border, reaching no farther south than the little Mariposa Lake, near the headwaters of the Snake River. It could have been a shift in the wind direction, it could have been a lack of fuel, it could have been a simple matter of fate. All that the animals needed to know was that they finally seemed to have outrun the fires. They seemed to be safe, in this valley at the juncture of the Yellowstone River and Atlantic Creek. They would stop here, rest here, eat and drink, and return their lives to normality as best they could.

It was not a bad place to do that. Right at the northeastern corner of Teton County, this Teton Wilderness valley was even more isolated and untraveled by humans than most of the areas in Yellowstone Park. A few hunters, an occasional fisherman, once in a while a curious backpacker—there were few human invaders of this natural retreat.

Now providing shelter for thousands of animals and dozens of species the valley looked like an American Ngorongoro from the air. Though not entirely encircled by steep hillsides like that Kenyan crater the valley still contained enough competing prey and predatory animals to merit the comparison, still seemed to be its own little ecosystem, with grasses for the ungulates, bushes for the herbivores, and of course plenty of meat on the table for the carnivores.

With winter coming on many animals—Including several of Yellowstone's bears—soon decided that they could take up temporary residency here, could roam--the surrounding mountains for ants and insects, bushes and berries, could find fish in the converging streams, could prey upon their less-fortunate friends, and could in the end find shelter against the soon-to-be-falling snow and cold temperatures. Other bears returned to the park, went back to their old stomping grounds— if they had not been destroyed by the fires—or found new places to live in the vast unspoiled areas that remained in the park.

Most of the elk, of course, felt the unseen arms of long tradition pull upon them to leave the valley, to continue the migration that they had already started because of the fires to the south. One by one, then in small herds, then in groups of so many animals that they could not even be easily counted the elk slowly began leaving the valley, working their way along Atlantic Creek, over Two Ocean Pass, and down Pacific Creek to its juncture with the Snake River near Moran. Along the Snake to Antelope Flats, along the east side of Blacktail Butte, along the dry brushy banks of the Gros Ventre (*grow-vaunt*) River. Arriving, finally, in scattered herds throughout the whole month of October, at the fenced-off National Elk Refuge that borders the town of Jackson, where they would find milder conditions, enough grass to hold them throughout the winter, or humans to bring them pelleted hay if it were needed to see them through the next three or four months, when they would ease their way off the refuge and follow the old trails north, back to Yellowstone Park.

Along with the elk, some ten-thousand strong, came a couple of returning mountain lions into the refuge, a lone family of wolves, and four hungry grizzly bears, who had had just about enough of all of this damned fool running around.

Chapter Sixteen

THE REFUGE

Just north of Jackson, Wyoming, occupying an area of almost 25,000 acres, is the National Elk Refuge—one of over five-hundred such animal sanctuaries in the National Wildlife Refuge System in the United States.

Created by an act of Congress in 1912, the elk refuge is administered by the U. S. Fish and Wildlife Service, which also has a national fish hatchery at the western edge of the refuge where up to a million native Snake River cutthroat and lake trout are given a head start on life each year, then dumped in various area rivers and stream to either eat or be eaten, catch or be caught.

The fish hatchery is just north of the National Museum of Wildlife Art, which is located off the refuge on the highway in a relatively new exhibition building that is sided with irregularly shaped rock. So well-hidden is the museum on the slope of a hill that its planners were forced to mark the entrance with bundles of burnt trees from Yellowstone, wrapped tightly with wide, natural-looking bands of rusting steel.

On the east side of the huge field that is home to some seven-to twelve-thousand elk each winter there is almost nothing civilized, only a few homes for government employees, a scattering of other homes belonging to regular people, the Twin Creek Ranch, and mountains and forests. Only one gravel road leaves the town of Jackson at the south-eastern corner of the refuge and winds through its eastern side until the washboard road branches into less-maintained trails that turn into even smaller paths that eventually disappear altogether.

On the west side of the refuge, which is half-bordered by the combined U. S. Routes 26, 89, and 191, and fenced high to keep the pickup trucks and SUVs out, are the typical enterprises that one would expect to find alongside a National Elk Refuge: a motel with the words elk and refuge in its name, a gas station, an art gallery, a few private homes, and, as already mentioned, the well-hidden National Wildlife Art Museum.

At the very south edge of the refuge, where its administrative headquarters is located in a complex of several forestry-looking buildings, is the town of Jackson. Settled in the late 1800's and incorrectly known by most tourists as "Jackson Hole" ("hole" being the mountaineer term for a broad flat valley surrounded by mountains), the town is a hub for sightseers (Ripley's Believe It or Not!), skiers (Snow King Resort), moviemaking (*Shane, Rocky IV, Any Which Way But Loose*), imbibers (the Million Dollar Cowboy Bar), internationally known law offices (Spence, Moriarity and Shockey—formerly Schuster), and an increasing number of residents trying to cope with the highest cost of living in Wyoming (you don't even want to know).

Along the northern edge of the refuge runs the Gros Ventre River, some small tributaries of which, including Flat Creek, trickle down through the most marshy section of the refuge and account for some of the most difficult catch-and-release fishing around Jackson Hole, commencing in the late summer. Farther north, but still bordering on the refuge, is a whole hilltop of private homes, and the little town of Kelly, where the most prominent buildings are several circular Kurdish yurts that look like they immigrated to Wyoming from somewhere up in the Himalayas.

North of Kelly's yurts, and thus removed by a few miles from the refuge, is Antelope Flats, which probably has more bison wandering around its sagebrush-covered plains than pronghorns. (Fenced in a field to the northeast of Kelly are pastured hundreds of lanky longhorn cattle, apparently someone's local tribute to Texas.)

When the elk annually migrate south to the refuge, and leave again in the spring to summer in or near Yellowstone, they pass through Antelope Flats or trickle in through the tougher, steeper trails in Bridger-Teton National Forest.

And when the elk finally arrive in the big field north of Jackson they become instant celebrities. From late fall to early spring tourists from all over the world, and would-be hunters from there and everywhere else, crowd the high woven-wire fence on the west border of the refuge, armed with high-powered binoculars, camera lenses, and spotting scopes, to view individual members of the many herds of elk that graze on the weeds and grasses, rest and ruminate, participate in a little hanky-panky here and there, knock heads with their neighbors, and flaunt their huge racks of antlers right before God, each other, and the drooling eyes of would-be hunters.

Once winter dumps enough snow on the refuge, around December or January, the refuge managers okay a private company to begin giving close-up tours of the elk, using horse-drawn sleighs that are pulled around and even through the now detached herds in a set pattern sort of resembling a county fair pony ride. The open-sleigh tours are conducted only when the wind-chill factor on the refuge approaches -200 degrees, which is almost always. Only while participating in the tours are members of the general public allowed to be out on the refuge when the elk are wintering. Towards the end of the winter, if you are lucky, and take the right tour, you can watch the elk get fed some of the thirty tons of hay pellets that they have come to expect and now need in order to survive the winter.

This particular fall, in addition to the thousands of elk that they came to see, the eyeballing elk hunters spotted something previously unseen in their scopes. They saw bears. Not just regular bears, but grizzlies. Four of them.

As in past years, Jake Mercy, Bob Crewson, and George Neuman were standing along the elk refuge fence, trying to get a line on possible targets for this year's annual elk refuge hunt. There would be far more elk trickling in by the time the hunt actually began, so their scoping was really just an exercise in wishful thinking and futility—more like an effort to reassure themselves that the elk would actually be there when the gates opened than any attempt to identify particular targets. As always, the elk were scattered about the big field, in herds of assorted sizes.

"What in the name of hell?" Crewson asked himself, in confusion.

"See a big one, Bob?" Neuman questioned.

"Yeah," Crewson replied. "I see it. I just don't believe it."
"Bull or cow?"

"Well," Crewson puzzled, "with grizzlies it's kinda hard to tell."

"What are you talking about? You mean you see a bear?"

"I mean I see a bear," Crewson asserted. "No. I see one...two...three...four of them. And they are all grizzlies."

"Grizzlies. Right. What the hell have you been drinking?"

"Take a look," he invited, handing Neuman the binoculars. "Towards the south end of the butte, about halfway up, in that clump of trees."

Neuman quickly grabbed the binoculars, and aimed them at Millers Butte. "Damn! Are you kidding me! There *are* grizzlies up there! I wouldn't have believed it!"

"No one I know of has ever seen grizzlies on the refuge," Crewson said, excitedly. "Or any other bears, for that matter. They must have followed the elk down from Yellowstone. Probably got burned out of other food by the fires."

"That'd be my guess," Neuman agreed. "Apparently nobody else has seen these bears before us, or there'd be a lot more excitement."

"Probably not," Crewson said. "But they won't stay a secret for long."

Mercy, who had been farther down the fence line, walked up to them.

"You boys about ready to roll?" Mercy asked. "I think I seen just about everything worth looking at out there."

Crewson and Neuman both laughed.

"I seriously doubt it, Jake," Neuman said. "Set up your spotting scope and focus it about halfway up Millers Butte, where those trees are."

"What would an elk be doing up there?" Mercy questioned, positioning his tripod-mounted scope firmly on the ground.

"Staying the hell awake, if he knows what's good for him!" Crewson laughed. Mercy looked over at him like he should have left the bar about two hours sooner the night before. He half-stooped, and peered through the scope.

"Shit." Mercy said, flatly. "I been doing this too long. I'm starting to see things that aren't even there."

"Like maybe four big grizzlies?" Crewson asked.

"...three...four," Mercy completed counting. "Tell you boys one thing. I'm going to be thinking real hard about putting my name in the hat to go out there on the refuge for this year's hunt."

Crewson and Neuman laughed again.

"They may have to add a new bag category this year," Neuman joked. "Hunters."

"Yeah," Crewson added, "Grizzlies are still on the Endangered Species list, so you can't legally shoot them. But they sure as hell can come after us!"

From on down the fence line loud shouts went up from other onlookers, who had obviously just discovered the bears. There was also a lot of commotion, as everyone hurried to look through their high-powered helpers before the bears could drift out of view.

"Well," Crewson said, throwing up his arms. "So much for our little secret."

Chapter Seventeen

THE MANAGER

"So. What are you going to do about these grizzlies, Johnston?"

The questioner was Jackson's plump, middle-aged mayor, Elvis Ashton, and the questionee was Dan Johnston, betroubled manager of the National Elk Refuge.

"Well, frankly, Mr. Mayor, we're waiting for instructions from Washington. We could just go out and shoot them, I suppose, but that probably wouldn't go over too well with wildlife protectionists: 'Refuge Riflers Slaughter Grizzlies to Satisfy Jackson Mayor.' You want that?

"We could also try to trap them. But when they've got so much meat running around on the hoof I doubt they'd even give our baited boxes a second glance."

"Couldn't you just drug 'em?" Ashton asked.

"Maybe drugs would work, fired from rifles. But how are we going to get four bears down all at the same time and load them up for relocation back to Yellowstone? I sure don't want to be one of the guys on the firing line if half of those bears decide they would rather attack their attackers than take a snooze.

"See the problem?" Johnston tried to relax, and rocked backwards in his big leather chair, one of the few office fineries that he had been permitted by the stingy Fish and Wildlife Service.

"Well, you have my sympathy, Johnston," Ashton offered. "But that still doesn't answer my question. I've got people coming into my office—as they have every right to do—concerned about their own safety, and the safety of their kids, saying I should be doing something to protect them. It's not my job. It's yours!" The mayor was so antsy that he couldn't even sit down. He repeatedly paced back and forth before the desk.

"I know," Johnston conceded. "And that's exactly why we've sent a situation analysis in to headquarters, to see what they want us to do." In spite of that, Johnston had no doubt that the ultimate decision—the one for which lower-ranked managers could and would be held fully accountable—was going to be his. That was simply the way Washington worked—survival of the highest. But he had to play by the rules of the game. "Until we get some guidance, our hands are tied."

"What if they weren't?"

"What if who wasn't what?"

"What if your hands weren't tied?" Ashton asked. "What would you do then?"

"Off the record?"

"Okay, off the record."

"I'd shoot every last one of them. Today. Right now. As soon as I could load a rifle. To hell with the headlines. Bears don't belong on an elk refuge. Black or grizzly. They should have stayed in Yellowstone. Coming down here was their mistake. What we have here is a disaster movie in the making. Sure, there's plenty of food on the refuge for the grizzlies to eat—and there will be all winter. But sooner or later these goose-guzzlers are going to want to hibernate. It's the nature of the beast. They aren't going to hang around the refuge all winter, eating an elk whenever they feel like it, and then just hike back up to Yellowstone in the spring. Before long, they're going to start looking around for places to sleep. And that's when we're going to have bears bumping into people. I don't have to tell you who's going to lose. We either shoot them now, or we shoot them later—after we start losing people."

"What about Millers Butte? Or Blacktail?" the mayor suggested. "Any way you could get them to hole up there until the spring? Keep people away from those places?"

"Not very likely," Johnston responded. "First, I doubt there are enough places good enough on those buttes—certainly no caves—to accommodate four grizzlies. Second, it would be hell on wheels trying to herd them up there. Third, we'd have to evacuate all of the people who live along the adjacent roads— and maybe everybody in east Jackson—In case one of the bears woke up, found himself in need of a snack, and decided to go looking for a restaurant. And finally, you want to be the one to tell Judge Ranck that he has to move out?"

"Well, you've just got to do something about this. And soon. Or I won't be held responsible for what happens to my vo... to the residents of Jackson." And with that warning the mayor stormed out of the office. Johnston arose and went around to the front of his desk to look at the floor where the mayor had been pacing.

He was going to have to have the boards rewaxed.

Chapter Eighteen

THE CIRCUS

It had started on a Saturday. In the cold, early morning mist on this day in late October cars, trucks, and (of course) recreational vehicles emerged en masse from the fog that followed the general course of Flat Creek, all headed for the same destination.

The National Elk Refuge.

First dozens, and then hundreds of sightseers left their vehicles parked unsafely and illegally along the highway, having already filled to capacity the two or three pullover areas, to squeeze up against the woven-wire fence of the refuge. Teton County Sheriff's Office cruisers were everywhere, all with lights flashing, as deputies both on foot and in their cruisers were trying to keep traffic moving, and investigating several fender-benders. So far there had not been any serious accidents, at least none with injuries. In one incident a gawker from Utah had slowed to look and was hit from behind by a Suburban, which was hit from behind by an Explorer, which was hit from behind by a 26' RV, which was narrowly avoided by one of the new VW bugs, which had run off the highway into the ditch but would have folded up like an accordion if it had plowed into the RV. The young woman in the Volkswagen had escaped without a scratch.

"Where are the bears?" an old woman challenged a camouflage-suited hunter. "I came to see the bears."

"Anybody seen the grizzlies?" asked a young man a few yards north, of a crowd already wondering the same thing themselves.

"I don't want to look at no bears," a small scared girl pleaded with her father. "I don't want to look at no bears." Since she was in his arms, she was going to look at the bears anyway—if they could be seen.

Hundreds of yards out on the refuge only ghostly images of grazing and reclining elk could be discerned through the fog. There were no bears to be seen, even if anyone could see them.

"What a rip," a bearded and tattooed biker told his "old lady." "There ain't no fucking bears here!" Nose-pierced and also well-tattooed, she sniffed and replied, "Telling me, dude. Let's split this two-bit town and head on over to Sturgis." She had absolutely no interest in seeing any bears, any elk, or anything else. All she wanted to do was ride—or be ridden.

For the past two hours the sun had been trying to poke through the fog, sneaking over the famous Snow King Mountain. Site of the steepest ski slopes in the country, in recent years the mountain had become almost equally noted for its spring Hill Climb, an event in which otherwise normal people tried to top the crest of the mountain's longest and most vertical ski slope riding highly modified snowmobiles. Until machines with more horsepower were developed in the late 1980s nobody had ever made it near the very top, let alone gotten over the final rise. Now, so many were succeeding that it had become more of a timed event, to see who could do it the quickest—usually the ones with the corporate sponsors who had the deepest pockets. Still, enough hill climbers would fall off their machines halfway up the mountain or the machines would rare up and tilt over backwards to cause all sorts of mischief that people were coming from all over the United States to spectate. The average concessionaire at the base of the mountain was making a fortune, by selling anything that didn't move. If he hadn't already retired, one day Warren Miller would have put it all on film.

But now the sunlight was not climbing Snow King Mountain but simply edging over it, bringing a certain amount of clarity to all of the elf refuge bear hunters. As the sun continued to rise the fog continued to clear.

"Look! There's one! See? Over there by that big herd. Whoa, look at them boogers scramble!"

"He got one! He got one!"

"Give me them binoculars! Dammit, give me them binoculars!"

"Okay, okay! I just wanted to see!"

"Oh, my God, he's eating it!"

"You expected him to do something else with it?"

"Oooh. I can't watch this! Yuck!"

"Man, this is so cool. Don't you think this is so cool? This is just so cool."

"Can we go now? I want to go home!"

They had all seen a bear—one of the soon-to-be-famous Elk Refuge grizzlies.

And by the side of the highway they could commemorate the occasion with an extra-large-only black cotton tee-shirt, featuring one local artist's concept of a raring grizzly, its eight-inch fangs crimson with drip-ping blood, its great six-inch claws accurately portrayed in glitter nail polish, its green eyes able to glow in the dark when exposed to UV light.

Only $18.95, plus six per cent sales tax. Cash or checks accepted. Buy two, get one free. UV lights also available, at extra charge.

By the middle of the following week there were so many tourists in Jackson that all of the 49,000 hotels and motels in the immediate area were showing "No Vacancy" signs. Up along the elk refuge fence, near the naturally hidden Wildlife Art Museum, you couldn't tell the players without a souvenir program—which, incidentally, had been conceived, written, edited, and printed in less than two days (only $4.95, plus six per cent sales tax, special protective mailing envelopes available, at extra charge).

"Grizzly Adams." The one everybody recalled seeing on TV.

"Hairy Harrison." Particularly unkempt.

"Benny Bear." Big nose. Probably Jewish.

"Bearfaced Lionel." Can't believe a word he says.

The great circus had begun.

Chapter Nineteen

THE TURNAROUND

All summer long the Jackson Hole economy had been in the pits. Largely based on tourism (to a greater extent than some community leaders cared to admit), the area had suffered substantially from the heat and drought.

The hot sun that had scorched the land in Yellowstone and had set up the park for the lightning attack had also had a dramatic impact on the number of park visitors. In a good year, on any summer day, the five Yellowstone entrances could expect to pass through more than fifty-thousand tourists. This year, a less-comfortable one in which to engage in the many outdoor activities that had made the park popular, the daily average was down to about thirty-five thousand, although there had been a few spike days over forty.

To the south, Grand Teton National Park had also sustained a similar percentage hit in its visitation numbers. And the trend had continued, of course, right on down to Jackson, where the hotels, motels, restaurants, gift shops, and other retail outlets were equally affected. West of Yellowstone the tourism fall-off had impacted West Yellowstone, Montana. North of the park the heat ax had fallen on Livingston and Bozeman, Montana. Eastward it had been Billings, Montana, and Cody, Wyoming, where the normally popular Buffalo Bill Historical Center had recorded its lowest August visitor count in nine years.

As went Yellowstone, so went the entire surrounding area.

Some sharp Jackson entrepreneurs, knowing that they were running out of summer season days to add to their personal income, actually perked up when they first read about the Yellowstone fires. Remembering how it had been in 1988 they immediately realized that the fires could be extremely good for the local economy, if they held on long enough, for all of those firefighters had to be supplied and resupplied, and Jackson's businesses were just the ones that could do it. The cheers turned to frowns, however, when within a week the fires had been extinguished unexpectedly—along with the hopes of the entrepreneurs for any help with their financial problems from the federal government.

But when the bears entered the elk refuge and all of the sightseers started coming the entire local economy turned around. All of a sudden there was not an empty lodging bed to be found, you could not get a quick seat in a local barbeque restaurant if your name was Maria Shriver, and tourist-attracting trinkets started jumping off store shelves. Jackson's sidewalks were packed with pedestrians, as were the streets, and it typically took forty minutes to drive through town (even if you knew all of the shortcuts)—about eight times longer than normal.

All of a sudden everyone had to have his or her picture taken under one of the four elk-antler arches that cornered the town square, or had to sit astraddle the real bar-stool saddles in the Cowboy Bar. The town's six o'clock fake "Shoot-Out" on the town square, which had already ended its daily performances for the summer, was reactivated, with a new script to adapt the act to the visiting grizzly bears and to the unusual obstacle of slick and icy paved streets as winter approached.

Nearly every business in the town of Jackson was now profiting from the bear traffic, and since nearly every resident of the town of Jackson was unexpectedly benefiting from those profiting businesses, everyone was happy. Except maybe Dan Johnston.

Johnston still had not received any response from Washington to his urgent request for guidance about the bears, so he remained essentially stifled. Moreover, the mayor was back. Damn, Johnston thought, as he watched Elvis Ashton stroll into his office, I just had the floor rewaxed.

"How's it going, Dan?" the obviously happy mayor opened the conversation.

"Pretty much the same, Elvis," Johnston answered, picking up on the mayor's out-of-the-ordinary attempt at familiarity and congeniality. "I guess you're here to see what we're doing about the bears."

"Oh, no, no," the mayor said quickly. "Nothing of the sort. The bears are doing just fine. Minding their own business. Everyone is happy. No one has been coming in to complain. What I was wondering about are sleigh tours on the refuge when there's enough snow."

"Sleigh tours? You mean as in taking people out onto the refuge to get an even closer look at the bears? Are you out of your friggin' mind, Mr. Mayor?"

"Well, now don't get on your high horse about it. I was just thinking it might be possible," the mayor hastened, mildly rebuked and embarrassed.

"You think the bears would rather eat people and horses than elk, right?"

"Who said anything about horses? Haven't you ever seen those motorized tundra buggies up in Alaska where they take people right out with the polar bears? They have doors, windows—everything. Why couldn't we bring in one or two of those? Nobody would get hurt, the people would stay warm, and the bears couldn't reach them. You could even use them to haul in your hay pellets for the elk!"

"My wife told me I should have accepted that offer to go to Alamosa last year," Johnston said. "Do you hear what you're saying?"

"Well, what's wrong with capitalizing on our accidental good fortune?" the mayor asked. "Nobody's afraid of those bears any more. Just the opposite. People are coming from all over the world to see them! You know, I think there should be a way the Fish and Wildlife Service could benefit from this. Maybe you could increase the charge for the tours by a little bit, and use the money to buy your hay. I'm sure people would pay it. What about that? Don't you think your superiors in Washington would go for that idea? I think it's a great idea. Why don't you send them a message, give them a telephone call, or do whatever you do to contact them?"

"Why don't I just tell them that I'm the biggest idiot in Wyoming for even suggesting the idea?" Johnston was beginning to get irritated. "Have you forgotten, Mr. Mayor, that those bears haven't yet started looking for places to hibernate? Have you completely forgotten the people problems that we're going to have when that happens?"

"We don't have to keep the tours going forever!" the mayor shouted. "Only until the bears start to hibernate! And then you can shoot 'em, or drug 'em, or do whatever you want to do with them. Feed their mangy asses to the wolves and the mountain lions, for all I care. All we need is a little more time!"

"What you really mean, all your retail constituents need is to make a little more money because of the bears, while the getting is good!"

"What's wrong with that?" asked the mayor, offended. "What's wrong with them taking advantage of this golden opportunity to recover some of the money that they didn't make this summer because of the drought?"

"Nothing at all," Johnston replied, "as long as they don't expect to make their money on the blood and guts of bear-mauled tourists lying all over town. That isn't going to happen on my watch!"

"Be reasonable, Johnston!" the mayor pleaded. "Just 'til people start shopping for Christmas! That's all we ask! Two or three weeks! No more than a month!"

"I'm not going to allow this circus to go on ten minutes longer than it has to," Johnston responded. "The moment Washington says shoot, those bears had better duck! Don't you get it? This is a dangerous situation! Grizzlies and people in a concentrated area just don't mix!"

Irate, the mayor stared for a moment at Johnston, digesting his defeat, then spun sharply on his heels, and left. Johnston arose from his chair, went around his desk, and looked down at his freshly waxed wood floor.

"Damn!"

Chapter Twenty

THE PHOTOGRAPHER

For as long as most readers could remember, two weekly tabloid newspapers had shared the Jackson Hole market. Each was published on Wednesday morning. Each had recently kept its readers fully informed for the remainder of the week, except on weekends, with small daily editions.

The two newspapers were highly competitive, and both staffs took an excessive amount of pride in the various awards they regularly won in annual Wyoming competition for newspapers of their size, for general content, editorial and advertising excellence, news, features, and sports reporting, and photography. It was beside the point that in such a sparsely settled state as Wyoming the two newspapers had virtually no competition other than themselves. So whatever award one of the news-papers failed to win in any given year, the other usually succeeded in winning.

There was a fierce rivalry between the two staffs, in particular, to be the first to report "breaking" news. Such major stories were usually self-assigned by each newspaper's editor-in-chief, and the results were usually copyrighted—specifically to force the competing staff to give in-print credit to their competitor if they chose to hop on to the story the next day. It was a small, trivial pursuit, a game of one-upmanship, but it was unusually well-played.

One day in August, 1996, at the end of a visit to Jackson Hole by President Bill Clinton, an entourage C-130 cargo plane had taken off from Jackson Hole Airport, had made the mandatory eastern banking (too soon and too low) to minimize ground noise, and had smacked straight into the side of Sleeping Indian Mountain, killing everyone aboard. Before anyone else could get the gory details of the accident, a photographer from the *Jackson Hole Guide* had hiked up the mountain for on-site coverage. The "beat" story was front-page news next day, of course, being noteworthy not only nationally but even locally. Since that day the rivalry between the *Guide* and the *News* had seemed particularly fierce.

Now, with national attention again focused on Jackson (and not just for a Presidential vacation or a question of vice-presidential residency), a couple of young staffers on the *News* decided that it was high-time to return the irksome "beat" favor, and maybe pick up another one of those career-boosting state awards at the same time.

It was as dark as the inside of an elk's stomach on the Refuge, although the solid darkness was intermittently interrupted with dim light when the thick clouds parted long enough to reveal a sliver moon. At the eastern edge of Jackson, in an old inconspicuous Toyota Corolla with all lights off, sat Joe Dean and Cindy Mason. Joe was the ace photographer at the *News*. Cindy was its features editor.

The elk refuge road straight ahead of them had been closed to all traffic except a few homeowners living east of the refuge (including Judge Bob Ranck), who had opted to remain in their homes at their own risk and had even signed liability waivers. All government employees who lived along the road in government housing had been evacuated. In the best interest of the recalcitrant residents, however, the Teton County Sheriff's Office had decided to make regular patrols of the graveled road each night, every hour on the half-hour, from dusk to daybreak.

With the narrow gravel road still open, at least to the waivered homeowners, there was no physical barricade to prevent any other vehicles from traveling along it; a hastily printed sign simply stated that the road was closed on federal authority to all "non-residential" traffic, and said there would be prosecution and a hefty fine for any violations. A cartoon had appeared on the previous week's editorial page of the *News* parodying that poster, proclaiming "ALL VIOLATORS WILL BE EATEN!"

It was one o'clock.

"Okay. Let's go. No lights. No unnecessary noise. High gear as soon as possible. No braking. Let it idle." Joe had spent a lot of time planning the details of the surreptitious nocturnal mission.

"Are you sure you want to do this?" Cindy asked one last time. She would be writing the story, even though it would be a joint by-line, because Joe would be getting not only his photos but her facts. She would simply be driving the car, then taking Joe's information and shaping it into some kind of story.

"Positive. This photo-story has prize-winner written all over it! Let's roll."

Cindy looked around to be sure that there were no other vehicles coming down East Broadway, checked each side of the street for prying eyes, and flipped the ignition key. The engine started immediately. She began moving the little gray vehicle in low gear, soon shifted to second, then to third, and quickly found high. She let the car idle through the elk refuge gate, thereby turning an innocent newspaper assignment into a federal crime.

"Remember, once we get to this end of Millers Butte I'm going to bale out while you're still moving. Go all the way up by the government houses to the sharp left, turn around at the cattle gate, and come back here—but don't stop moving. Understand? Under no circumstances are you to stop this car. And don't go any faster than idle. I figure I'll have maybe ten or twelve minutes to run around the butte, locate a bear with these night-vision goggles, shoot a whole roll of film, and get back to the road by the time you return. I won't have any trouble seeing the car. If you're only idling, I'll be able to catch you, open the door, and jump back inside. Piece of cake."

"I'm beginning to think this wasn't such a good idea," Cindy admitted, "even if Jeffries did approve it. Maybe we should just turn around and go back. Aren't we breaking some kind of federal law?"

"Federal laws were *made* to be broken. This is going to be like shooting photos of bears in a barrel, Cindy," Joe boasted. "I have it all figured out. The only thing that can go wrong is if we get stopped by somebody on patrol—and we'll just tell him that we were on our way to Idaho and took a wrong turn. C'mon, Cindy, no guts, no glory!"

"I just think this is a bad idea, a really bad idea. But it's your ass. If you want to get it chewed off by a bear, who am I to argue? It'll be the Page One lead."

"Great. So drive."

The Corolla rolled slowly along the gravel Elk Refuge Road. Even in the nearly constant darkness Cindy's eyes had adapted enough that she could easily keep the car on the road and her foot off the brake. She thought she would have to give the little car a bit more gas as it inched up the small grade by the old Miller house, but it had enough power to pull the rise easily, and even picked up a slight bit of speed as it rolled down the other side of the gentle slope and came to the south end of Millers Butte.

"Well, here goes nothing," Joe said, as he opened the passenger side door. "See you at the podium when we pick up our Pulitzer." He hopped out of the rolling Toyota and eased the door closed. As it continued idling down the road, with no lights on to reveal its presence, he ran for the end of Millers Butte. Cindy pulled a microcassette recorder out of her purse and began dictating notes into it.

Joe Dean's night vision, thanks to the special goggles, was perfect—so long as he didn't mind seeing everything in light or dark shades of green. The newspaper couldn't afford to pay a couple of thousand dollars for the latest, Generation 3 equipment that would give him the greatest clarity, or even Generation 2, but the first generation fuzziness and dimmer image was okay for his purpose. Especially since he hadn't expected Jeffries to approve the purchase to begin with. He had also ordered, over the Internet, special high-speed film for his Canon EOS. Even using his longest, most-light-sucking telephoto lens, he figured that he could still pick up decent images—with the camera steadied on the extendable monopod—at one one-twenty-fifth of a second. He would push the film during processing to increase the speed, and make any contrast compensation necessary with filters and polycontrast paper during printing. He had it all figured out.

A whole roll of sleeping grizzly bear photos, with a lot of elk in the background would make a good photo-feature; thirty-six frames of a galloping grizzly chasing down some terrified elk would be even better. He would be willing to settle for the former, but he was certainly hoping to get the latter.

Joe crept quietly around the end of the butte, looking for a bear. He thought he saw one over by a herd of maybe two or three hundred elk, almost all of which were not only awake but alert for any danger. Even the ones that were asleep would be ready to run on a moment's notice. The game they played with the grizzlies was called survival, only in this version the losers didn't get booted off any island, but eaten. This is exactly what I want, Joe thought. If the bear holds off his charge until I get a little bit higher up—maybe up there on those boulders—I'll be able to get the whole herd running, with the bear taking one of them down right up front.

Joe climbed the boulders, slipping a couple of times in his eagerness to get up on the rocks before the bear charged, but found himself in as perfect a position to get the photos as he had hoped. As he unsnapped the sections of the monopod under his camera, and extended it to the ground, the bear attacked.

Joe's motorized shutter tripped off all thirty-six frames as it landed on the granite boulders. Unfortunately, not a single one of those frames was in-focus, since Joe had spun the barrel of the lens around to set the focal distance on infinity, not to take close-ups at a distance of only five feet.

In a few minutes Cindy came back down the road in the Corolla. As she approached Millers Butte she tried hard to see Joe running towards the road from her right, but saw nothing. In direct violation of his instruction to keep the car rolling she decided to stop and wait for him to appear. In a few minutes she saw a shadowy figure coming around the end of the butte, and thought about yelling to tell Joe where she was, but remembered that he was wearing the night-vision goggles that would let him see her far better than she could see him. As she watched the shadowy form approach it seemed to get not only bigger, and bulkier, but lower to the ground. Why was Joe crawling? Had he twisted an ankle, broken a leg? And why was he apparently going in front of the car, not getting in? In a few seconds the inquisitive news editor had the answers to all of her questions, when the shadowy image became a large bear, with Joe's lifeless body in its jaws. Only half-realizing that she had even started the Corolla rolling, and was accelerating faster and faster, less than a minute later Cindy reached the end of the refuge road, where she attempted to turn right onto East Broadway. The speeding gray Toyota without any lights on immediately head-ended the white-and-yellow Ford Expedition of a Teton County Sheriff's deputy who was about to begin his regular patrol of Elk Refuge Road.

Chapter Twenty-One

THE ACCIDENT

"Anybody know who she was?"

The deputy sheriff's question—to anyone who cared to answer—seemed strangely uncalled-for, oddly insensitive, and almost unsympathetic. Around the still-smoking Toyota the perfunctory question got no response from any of the volunteer firemen who had extinguished the blaze, nor from any of the EMTs, nor from anyone else in the amazingly large crowd that the accident had attracted so quickly. He decided not to ask the question again.

Right now, Dave Hamilton could simply look for any clues as to why the accident had happened. He stood in silence as his shaken fellow deputy, the driver of the Expedition, was loaded into the squad for transportation to St. John's Hospital only a couple of blocks away. The investigating officer was certain that his friend would be okay. The victim deputy had been wearing his seat belt and shoulder strap combination in accordance with standard procedure (and Wyoming state law), and those safety devices, combined with the expanding air bag, had stopped his forward motion immediately—and had probably saved his life.

The woman in the much smaller car had not been so lucky. From the exploding pattern of cracks in the Toyota's windshield Hamilton guessed that she had probably been killed instantly— at least knocked unconscious with severe head wounds. When the car caught fire, the woman had either died already, or was about to. By the time the shaken deputy had extricated himself from his own vehicle, and had wobbled over to assist her, the flames had already sealed the woman's fate. There was nothing he could do but watch. The tremendous impact had awakened an East Broadway resident, who had looked out her front window, seen the flames, and quickly dialed 911. The fire trucks and EMT vehicles had arrived a few minutes later.

Dan Johnston and his wife Jane were asleep, his front to her back in a fetal position, when the irritating telephone on the nightstand awoke them with its first ring. Johnston raised his head, opened his eyes, and looked at the red digital display on the clock-radio.

"What time is it?" Jane asked, groggily.

"A little after two," Dan replied. Jane lay with her eyes half-open, to see if she could determine who was calling as Dan picked up the corded telephone handset.

"Hello?"

"Hi, Dan. Jack Wilson. I think we might have a problem that involves the elk refuge. Sorry to wake you up."

"Don't worry about it, Jack. I was asleep anyway," Johnston joked. "Although it does seem to be a little late, or a little early, depending on how you look at it. What's up?" Wilson, now the Teton County Sheriff, had been a good friend of Dan's for many years, way back when he was still a deputy and Dan had just arrived in Jackson to work at the refuge. The sheriff's appearance and talk had always reminded Johnston of the great westerns actor Richard Farnsworth.

"There's been a vehicle accident at the end of East Broadway," Wilson said, "Bob Thomas was gettin' ready to turn onto Elk Refuge Road to make his reg'lar patrol when his vehicle was hit head-on by a woman drivin' an older Toyota."

"Anybody hurt?" Dan asked, suddenly wide awake.

"Well, Bob was pretty well shook up, and was taken to St. John's for examination, but we think he's gonna be okay."

"What about the woman?"

"She was killed. Probably right out. Went into the windshield, but not through it, and either died from her head injuries or was burned to death."

"There was a fire? Isn't that a bit unusual for two vehicles going slow?"

"Well, you see, that's the thing. Bob was goin' maybe twenty or twenty-five. The woman must have been goin' seventy or eighty."

"Wow! Wait a minute. You said this was at the end of East Broadway? You mean she was coming off the Elk Refuge that fast?"

"You hit it. Why was she comin' off Elk Refuge Road goin' seventy or eighty miles an hour when she knew she had to make the sharp right turn onto Broadway?"

"Sounds like she was in one hell of a hurry."

"Either that or drunk. But we haven't found any cans or bottles in the Toyota. And she apparently doesn't live up that way."

"Have you identified the body?"

"We think we have. Everything in the vehicle was burned beyond recognition, but Dave did a tag check, and we think we know who she was. But that'll have to be confirmed through dental records or DNA tests or somethin'. If she was who we think, she was Cynthia L. Mason, age 22, a local."

"Cindy Mason the features editor at the *News*? I know her. What would she be doing on the Refuge at this time of night—or at all, since it's closed off?"

"That's what we have to find out. This might have somethin' to do with your bears. That's why I called you. I think maybe you and I need to talk about this."

"Can it wait until morning?"

"I don't know. How hungry are your bears?"

Johnston hung up the telephone, gave his wife a brief summary of the conversation with the sheriff while he was getting dressed, and left the house to drive over and meet Jack Wilson at his office on South Willow.

Chapter Twenty-Two

THE MEETING

"Cuppa coffee?" Jack Wilson asked, as Johnston walked into his office.

"At least one," Johnston replied. Wilson went over to the coffeemaker as Johnston sat down on the straight-backed, hard-seated wooden chair across from his desk. "Two sugars, no cream."

"You think after all of these years I don't know that? Wouldn't be a good investigator if I didn't pay no attention," the sheriff sniffed.

"I can't even remember how Jane takes hers half the time," Dan replied. "Must be getting old. Coming up on forty-three, you know."

"You're almost over the hill," laughed the considerably older sheriff. "How's Jane doin' after her operation?"

"She's doing okay. Hell of a thing to lose a breast to cancer."

"Do they think they got it all?"

"Yeah. Looks like they got to it in time to stop the spread. But who really knows?"

"Tell her Edna and I are thinkin' about her, and hope she's gonna be alright. Tell her to let us know if there's anything we can do.

"Thanks...byuch! What'd you make this coffee out of—ground up cow patties?" Dan sat the cup of coffee on the sheriff's desk, as though it were untouchably hot. He had all but given up on the idea of taking a second sip. "So, what do you think Cindy was doing on the Elk Refuge?"

"Well," Wilson said, as he thought again about it, "the only thing I can figure for her to be headed off the refuge that fast was if she was bein' chased."

Dan chuckled. "By another car, maybe. I don't think grizzlies chase cars—particularly at eighty miles an hour. Hard for me to picture one running along like a dog, snapping at a Toyota's wheels."

"Not what I mean. I think she must have been out on the refuge, got chased by one of the bears, hopped in her car, and beat it out of there."

Dan pondered the possibility for a moment before responding. "That would explain the speed, but it doesn't do much to answer the main question, which is why she would be out there in the first place. After one o'clock in the morning?"

"Near as I can figure, she must have been out there to get some sort of story."

"She would have to be really stupid to be out dancing with those bears in the middle of the night just to get some facts for a story," Dan said. "I don't believe she was—that stupid. But why would she be snooping around the refuge at night? What kind of facts would she be looking for then that she couldn't get in broad daylight?"

"You tell me," the sheriff replied. "I don't know what bears do at night. That's why you're here."

"Pretty much the same as they do during the day, I would think. I'm no bear expert either, but I'd guess they must roam around looking for food. They can see far better than we can at night, like most animals."

"Okay," thought the sheriff. "If the main thing they're doing at night is prowlin' around lookin' for food, she must have been out on the refuge tryin' to see them do that."

"Why would a bear's night eating habits be any different than the way it eats during the day? If all she was trying to do was see one go after an elk and eat it, Cindy could have joined everyone else in the world along the highway fence during the day."

"Unless she was tryin' to get closer," Wilson said. "Unless she was tryin' to get a better look." They both paused to think a moment.

"That brings up an interesting thought," Johnston offered. "How could she see any better at night than she could in broad daylight? Was she using the Toyota's headlights? Not likely. Too far from the road to the field. Did she use a flashlight? That would be a stupid idea—attract the attention of the bears by shining a light on them. But if she couldn't see them, why was she even there?"

"Maybe she was gonna take pictures, and not use any flash."

"She would have to have awfully fast film in the camera. It's still almost pitch dark. Without a flash, the camera wouldn't have gotten anything, particularly at a long distance. Did Dave find a camera in the car?"

"Didn't say anything about it, but his report won't be done 'til at least noon."

"Hmm. I just remembered something," Dan said, getting a sudden thought.

"What's that?"

"I don't think Cindy even knew how to use a camera. The first time she came to my office to do a feature story on me she had a photographer with her to take the pictures. His name was... Bean... Lean... Mean... Dean. His name was Dean."

"Maybe that was just for convenience. Maybe she didn't wanna take notes and take pictures at the same time."

"I don't think so," Dan tried to think back. "The photographer just sort of hung around while she was asking her questions, then we all went out to by the fence to get some shots of me with the refuge in the background."

"You think maybe she had a photographer out there with her tonight? If so, where's the body? It wasn't in the burned up Toyota."

"Maybe we need to look around the Refuge," Dan suggested.

"Maybe *you* want to do that in the middle of the night," Wilson added. "But there ain't no way that I'm gonna send any of my people out there in the dark with a bunch of bears to look for a photographer who may or may not even be missin'."

"Okay. I agree. So let's wait until morning, maybe start by calling the newspaper and see if all of their photographers are accounted for. If they aren't missing one, then that's one that we don't have to worry about. If they are, then we can go out looking in SUVs, maybe even borrow a helicopter to fly over the

Refuge. You know anybody around here who's got a helicopter for hire?"

"Well, not for hire. The only one that might be available, which he's loaned us many times for search-and-rescue, is my friend Harrison's. He's got a Bell JetRanger that he parks in a field by his house. We could give him a call, if he's not out shootin' space invaders or somethin', to see if he would be interested in flyin' us around."

"We could we call it Elk Refuge One."

Chapter Twenty-Three

THE EDITOR

Jenny Jeffries, editor of the *Jackson Hole News*, was an early riser. And a go-getter. She had a Type One personality, which basically meant that she was the closest thing to perpetual motion in Jackson Hole. Ever since she had arrived in Jackson, some six years earlier, she had been seen everywhere, had done everything, and knew all there was to know about the town and its people. There were those who thought she even knew a bit too much for her own good.

Jeffries had known all about Cindy Mason's stupid scheme to get the bear feature, and to take Joe Dean with her to get photos, and she had not vetoed the idea. Fully aware of the risks involved, she had even gone so far as to authorize Joe's purchase of the super-fast film and those bug-eyed night-vision goggles. If anything happened to them, she thought now at six a.m., as she stripped off her nightie for a shower, she was going to feel somewhat responsible. She probably shouldn't have allowed them to do it. It probably wasn't worth the risk, just to score one on the *Guide.*

The scalding-hot shower had felt good, and had perked her up. Before going through the rest of her morning toilet routine she wrapped a towel around her and went back into the bedroom to check the time. She had a six-thirty breakfast meeting with the town's planning director, to hear his latest ideas regarding ways to get Jackson area developers to provide more affordable housing. She wasn't particularly looking forward to the meeting. Affordable housing was one of those political conundrums that everybody had an answer for, but nobody really knew how to solve. She checked the clock. Six-ten. Making good time. Moving right along.

The clock was one of those with the built-in radio that you could have wake you up instead of that maddening buzz. It also had an integrated corded telephone, apparently so you could call the radio station when they said the first person to call in with the correct answer to some dumb question would win a million dollars or something. Right now, however, the handset wasn't even in its cradle, but hanging alongside the bed. At some point during the night she had apparently rolled over in her sleep and had knocked the phone off the hook. No wonder she had slept so well. She replaced the handset, and began to go back into bathroom.

The phone rang.

"Hello?" she asked, somewhat surprised to be getting a call immediately.

"Oh, Jen, I just heard. I am so, so, sorry!" It was Ben Jacobs, editor of the *Jackson Hole Guide.*

"What do you mean?" she asked. "What do you have to be so, so sorry about at this hour of the morning?"

"You mean you don't know yet?"

"Know what? Look, Jacobs, what the hell's going on? I just woke up! Tell me what you're so so sorry about!"

"Oh, I thought you would be one of the first to know," Jacobs half-chided, not really trying to conceal his delight in having obtained his information about the tragedy well before his peer. "Cindy was killed in an automobile accident last night."

"Cindy?" she asked, feeling all of the blood in her body sink to her toes. "Our Cindy?"

"Your Cindy. Cindy Mason. She was apparently coming out of the elk refuge in her old Toyota when she ran head-on into one of the sheriff's cars driven by Deputy Bob Thomas. He was just shaken up, but she was killed. She may have died in the fire."

"There was a fire?"

"As soon as they hit. Apparently, Cindy was going pretty fast. The sparks must have set her car on fire and she couldn't get out, or was already dead."

"My, God. I didn't know. Has anyone told her parents yet?"

"Don't have a clue. We actually didn't know about this until a few minutes ago. Someone at the sheriff's office is probably trying to get in touch with them." He paused a few moments, for something that resembled true sympathy. "I really am sorry, Jen."

"I know. And I'm sorry I yelled at you. I wasn't awake yet. Thanks for calling. I have to go now. Bye."

She placed the handset timidly in its cradle, as though she was afraid that it would ring again, sat down on the bed, and just stared straight forward, not really seeing anything, and trying not to feel. It was easy to do the one, but so hard to do the other. Her tearing eyes soon found and remained locked on the small, furry bear on the nightstand. It had been a gift from Cindy, given to her on the very first night that they had spent together, in this very bedroom.

The offices of *The Jackson Hole News*, on Maple Way across the street from K-Mart, Big-K, or whatever the company is calling itself today in order to compete with Wal-Mart, were a beehive of activity when Jenny Jeffries arrived at six-twenty-five. That was highly unusual for a Tuesday. Although the paper came out on Wednesday, not much needed to be done on a normal Tuesday, except put the final touches on the first section, print it, and then collate all of the sections into an actual newspaper. But this was not a normal Tuesday.

Almost everyone on the paid newspaper staff, and most of the volunteer contributors, was walking around the aisles and offices, either working on stories or commiserating with everyone else. There were a lot of tearful eyes, and a lot of eyes shedding tears. Jenny really didn't want to go through with this—It was simply not a part of her character—but she knew that something like it would be expected of her.

"May I have everyone's attention?" she said, as she walked to the center of the room. "May I have your attention, please?" The room went silent, and all eyes were on the young editor.

"As I am sure all of you know, or most of you wouldn't be here right now, we lost a good friend and co-worker a few hours ago. Cindy Mason was a good news editor, and she was going to have a great future. I know we are all going to miss her. I will miss her most of all, for reasons that I will not go into right now.

"Cindy is gone, and we can't bring her back—as much as we all would like to—but we can carry on her work, and put out the best damned paper that we can. Not just this week, but every week. Cindy was devoted to *The News,* and to newspaper journalism everywhere, and I want this issue to be a tribute to her memory.

"To begin with, I'll meet with each of you about individual story and photo assignments having something to say about Cindy. We might dig into the files and pull quotes out of some of her stories. We'll talk to some of the townspeople she interviewed, and have a story with their tributes. I want a big black border around the whole front page. Cindy was one of our own, and I want to show everyone that *The News* takes care of its own.

"Any questions?"

Any questions that anyone had could be saved for later. Right now, the whole room was in tears, and Jenny had joined them, for reasons that she did not care to go into right now, after calling for a moment of silence.

"Has anybody seen Joe Dean yet this morning?" Jenny asked, drying her tears and trying to sound disinterested. She had soon confirmed his expected absence, and already knew why he was missing.

"I saw him out at the Moose around nine last night," Jenny's sports editor reported. "He was there for about a half-hour, but I haven't seen him since." That was the last time that any of the newspaper staff had seen their ace photographer. It would be the last time any of them ever did.

Nobody knew anything about Joe Dean's present whereabouts. There was no answer when Jeffries had later asked a staffer to try and reach him at his apartment. There was no one at home when one of them then drove by to see if he, too, had gotten into some kind of accident. And none of his neighbors had seen him come or go. Inexplicably, Joe Dean had simply vanished.

Only one person in the entire world had some idea of what had become of Joe Dean. And she wasn't about to share that information, for reasons that she didn't care to go into right now.

Chapter Twenty-Four

THE MOURNING NEWS

"This is Jenny."

She had just gotten settled down in her office, with the first of many expected cups of coffee that day, when her office telephone rang. It was going to be a long day, and she had not yet figured out exactly how to get out of it.

"Sheriff Wilson, Miss Jeffries."

"Aren't we being a bit formal this morning, Jack?"

"It's a formal occasion. I called to officially tell you what I'm sure you already unofficially know."

"I didn't until about an hour ago. Ben Jacobs called me at home and told me about it. Have you been able to reach her parents yet?"

"Just got off the phone with them. As you might expect, they were pretty broken up."

"Cindy was a darling girl. She had a great future ahead of her. Thank you for calling to inform...."

"That's not the only reason I'm callin'," the sheriff interjected. "All of the facts in this case suggest to me that we don't have all of the facts in this case."

"What do you mean?" she asked, already suspecting that she knew the answer.

"Well, as you probably already know, Miss Mason was turnin' onto East Broadway from the Refuge Road when the accident occurred."

"That's what I heard. So?"

"So she seems to have been travelin' at a very high rate of speed, if she was plannin' to negotiate the right-hand turn."

"She apparently was in a hurry."

"That's what we think. We think she must have been in one heck of a hurry to leave the refuge."

He's playing games, she thought. He knows. Or at least he suspects. He's trying to trip me up, to get me to admit that I sent them both out there. Play along. How would he know that I was the one who gave final approval to this misadventure? "Isn't the road now posted for resident use only?"

"It is."

"Well, maybe she started to go into the refuge for some reason, thought the better of it, and figured she had better leave as quickly as she could, before anyone saw and reported her."

"I suppose that's possible," Wilson conceded, "but I don't think that's what actually happened. What I think actually happened is that she, and maybe another member of your staff, thought there might be a good story to be found on the refuge about what the bears do at night, went out to get that story, and got themselves into trouble. I think they must have had to run for their lives. And at least one of them didn't make it."

"Don't you think that's stretching a simple automobile accident pretty far?"

"Well, at first I did. But then I got to thinkin' how competitive your people and the *Guide* people are, how much they want to beat—Is that the right word?—the other guys to a story, how extremely proud you all are of winnin' awards, and all of a sudden everything seemed to make sense. This was a mission to scoop the competition."

"So you think Cindy, and maybe someone else on my staff, went out onto the refuge, in the middle of the night, in direct violation of federal law, and facing a possible fine, left the road, chased after some bears that they couldn't even see, got the bears to chase them, and had to hurry out of there to save their lives, all to get a few photos and paragraphs that they could flaunt in the face of their *Guide* competition?"

"That's about it," Wilson agreed. "Except I don't recall sayin' anything about any photos."

Shit. That was a mistake. "I think you are—forgive the mixed-metaphors expression if it reminds you of bears—barking up the wrong tree, sheriff."

"Well, I certainly hope you're right, but I strongly suspect that you're wrong. I guess we'll just have to wait and see."

"I guess we will. You know, I really resent the implications of what you're saying."

"Sometimes I have to say things in this job that I don't particularly like. By the way, do you have any missin' staff members this mornin', other than Miss Mason?"

She tried to hide her momentary telephone silence. He knows. Damn it, he was just setting me up, and I fell right into his trap.

"Uh, no. I don't think so," she lied. "But I could certainly check around."

"You oughta do that, Miss Jeffries," the sheriff urged. "I think you'll find that you may be missin' a photographer. And I wouldn't count too much on him comin' back to work. Well, good-bye." He hung up.

Jenny Jeffries placed the telephone handset back in its cradle and reached over to pick up the cup of coffee. Her hand was shaking so badly that her fingers missed the handle, and she knocked over the cup, spilling its hot contents onto most of the many papers that were cluttering her desk.

"Shit!"

Chapter Twenty-Five

THE SEARCH

It looked like a convention of Ford and Firestone Tire executives. Almost all of the Teton County Sheriff's Department's off-road force—most of the vehicles new Ford Expeditions—were assembled at the East Broadway end of Elk Refuge Road, waiting for the word to start rolling. A cold fog filled the air, although the rising sun would soon lift it.

Jack Wilson was standing by the elk refuge entrance, talking to Dan Johnston.

"All set?" Wilson asked.

"Any time you're ready," Johnston replied. "We'll all be on the same frequency, so there's no reason anybody has to get out of his vehicle to do any communicating. As long as everyone remains inside, and drives slow, we should have minimal impact on the animals. The elk are used to vehicles, and the bears probably won't panic. But I don't want anyone outside their car unless it's me."

"I don't think you'll have to worry about that," Wilson smiled. "Most of these guys are havin' second thoughts about goin' out there even inside their vehicles. I'm sure half of them already have their pistol drawn. Okay, let's move 'em out."

The caravan started rolling along Elk Refuge Road. The idea was for everyone to drive the three miles to the sharp left (the beginning of private property), turn there, and go straight north for about a mile until reaching the "unimproved" section of the road. At that point the caravan would split into three units, one of which would cross the field until halted by Flat Creek near the fish hatchery, follow the creek south as far as the marshy surface would allow, then swing around the south end of Millers Butte and rejoin the main road. The second group would make a shorter but slower circuit in the same general direction, but would keep much closer to the butte, and use binoculars to check out as much of the west side of the butte as possible. The third group would turn around on the road, and go back the way all had come in, except these vehicles would swing in to the government housing along the way, check those areas, use binoculars to scrutinize the east side of the butte, then check around the old Miller house and the other buildings there. Johnston, in his Fish and Wildlife pickup, would lead the second group. Wilson would lead the third. Dave Hamilton was placed in charge of the first.

The caravan disbanded at the designated point and each of the three smaller units began their assigned search patterns, maintaining periodic radio contact. The Hamilton group had almost nothing to report—a lot of elk, some standing, some lying, all apparently wary of the unusual parade of vehicles, a few scavenging coyotes, the normal assortment of blue heron, Canada geese, whooping crane, egret, and other water fowl. Johnston's group, more focused on the side of the butte, also uncovered nothing particularly useful, although they all saw what was probably the same two mountain lions that, in the winter of 1999, had been the first ever spotted on the elk refuge. For more than a month this pair—a male and a female—had been the talk of the town and the object of many prying eyes, until finally leaving the refuge in the spring with three cubs. Although Wilson's group saw several signs of half-hearted attempted break-ins around the buildings used by the government employees until their evacuation, apparently none of those efforts had been successful.

All three of the search units had rejoined on the refuge road after their assigned patrols, and had remained stationary with idling engines while exchanging notes and comments—by radio. No one, even on the open road, was anxious to leave the relative safety of his vehicle.

One thing all of the reports had in common became immediately apparent. The several searchers had spent more than an hour rolling through a sizeable part of the refuge, and nobody had seen a single bear, let alone the bloody body of a foolish photographer.

"So what'dya think?" Wilson radioed to Johnston.

"Well," replied Johnston, "either we are completely wrong about why Cindy was getting out of the refuge so fast, and also way off-base about her being accompanied by the photographer, or Elvis bear has left the building."

"That's just what I was afraid of," sighed the sheriff. "Well, there goes the neighborhood."

Chapter Twenty-Six

THE LIBRARY

Dan Johnston had no idea what had become of the bears. In fact, the refuge manager immediately realized, he had few actual facts in his possession about the comings and goings of grizzlies, their habits, habitats, or lifestyle. Until now, he suddenly realized with some regret, he had been a member of the usual bear observing public—perfectly content to catch occasional sight of one from afar. As long as they stayed on their side of the fence, he would stay on his, and everybody would get along just fine. One thing Johnston did know was that he had very little chance of determining where the bears had gone unless he could come up with some idea of why they would go there. He was going to need some facts.

Using his office computer, Johnston did a quick search of the Internet, finding only about five billion sites involving bears, and checked out only a few of them before deciding to take a more-traditional route. There were so many roadside references to bears on the electronic highway that the four elk refuge bruins could die of old age before he actually learned anything useful about them. He needed to narrow the information field down a bit.

Johnston passed through the automatic glass doors of the Teton County Library, turned left at the stone and brass wall displaying contributor names, and approached the main desk in the next room. Several paid and volunteer staffers were going about their various tasks.

"Excuse me?" he asked of the first woman passing by. "Could you help me, please?"

"Certainly," the pert young librarian replied. "How can I help you?"

"I need a book on bears—specifically grizzly bears," Johnston requested.

"Bear books would be in 599," she concluded, after giving it a moment's consideration. "If you like, I would be glad to show you where that is."

"Could you do that, please?" Johnston asked. "I have no idea what you are talking about."

"No problem," she smiled, a bit condescendingly. "Follow me."

He followed the young woman past several desks with modern computer keyboards and big screens only about two inches thick, and was amazed at how technologically advanced the local library appeared to be. Most of the desks, and similar ones that he could see throughout the well-illuminated room, were occupied by busily typing library users of all ages, doing research. They came to the beginning of the banks of bookshelves, all neatly numbered and organized so that – if you knew the system—you could find a book on apparently anything in the world. There were tens of thousands—maybe more—and if this library didn't have the book you needed, you could use the computers to borrow it from another one somewhere else in the state.

"Five-ninety-five, five-ninety-six, five-ninety-seven, five-ninety-eight, aha, five-ninety-nine," the woman said, confirming her knowledge of section contents. "All sorts of bear books. Grizzlies, right?"

"Right," he replied. "Yellowstone grizzlies, if possible."

"If it's here, we have a book by Paul Schullery that should tell you everything you want to know about Yellowstone grizzly bears. A lot of people check it out. Here, 599.74, *The Bears of Yellowstone*. I believe this is the third edition. You can scan through this, if you like, to see if it has what you are looking for. If not, please put it back on the shelf in the same place, and try another book. As you can see, there are several titles here. All we ask is that you try not to mix them up. If you find a book you like, and want to take notes, feel free to use any open desk. And if you would like to check out a title, simply bring it up to the desk, and we'll be glad to process it."

"Thank you very much," Johnston said, accepting *The Bears of Yellowstone* book from her. He scanned the index of chapters, finding some on black bears, some on grizzlies, and thumbed through a few of the pages about grizzlies. They appeared to contain the type of information he was looking for. He decided to take the book over to one of the nearby desks for additional study.

Hmm, Johnston thought, reading through the introduction and the author's biography at the end, this guy Schullery has written several books about Yellowstone's bears, works for the park's Research Division, apparently spends most of his time out in the field observing them. Oughta know what he's talking about.

Lot of pictures. Look here, President and Mrs. Coolidge at Tower walking with bears, 1927. Secret Service guys seem to be a little edgy. Interesting. Both Coolidge and Harding visited in the 1920s, Teddy Roosevelt in 1903. Gerald Ford worked as a ranger in Yellowstone in 1936? Didn't know that. He "rode shotgun on bear-feeding grounds," and came back for a visit as president in 1976. Probably brought his clubs with him to play golf in Jackson. Wonder if he beaned anybody.

Here we go. *'The Grizzly Bear: Food Habits.'* "Bears will kill and eat an extraordinary number of fish; one adult female averaged about 100 fish a day for several days.... Usually the trout have returned to the lake by the middle of August and bears have moved on to other foods.... In August berries start to assume a more important role in bear diet.... some years bears benefit from sugar-rich strawberries, huckleberries, buffaloberries, and grouse whortleberries... By September and October, with the decline of succulent vegetation and the increased availability of pine nuts, grizzlies concentrate on the latter.... The pine nuts are very important to the bears, not only for the fat that will help prepare them for denning but because in years when the pine nut crop fails the bears amble off to find other food and frequently get in trouble with people.... The fires of 1988 burned something more than 20 percent of the whitebark pine in Greater Yellowstone."

Page 58. *'The Grizzly Bear: Denning.'* Dens observed at elevations from 6,500 feet—three hundred feet higher than Jackson—to more than 10,000 feet—top of Rendezvous and higher. Most fall between 8,000 and 9,000 feet. Snow King or Sleeping Indian.

Page 69. *'The Grizzly Bear: Lifestyle.'* "Grizzly bears spend almost all of their waking time searching for and consuming food. Though to the casual observer the bear's feeding behavior may appear random, it is not. Yellowstone offers the bear many foods in many places and at many times, and all the offerings vary from year to year. A mild winter means fewer winterkilled elk. A dry summer means a failed pine nut crop or a poor berry crop. Bears, through a combination of experience and instinct, have adapted to take as full advantage of their varying menu as possible."

Page 75. "Here again we see the bear's commitment to edges. Whether in the timber or not, the bears were usually close to the forest-nonforest boundary."

Johnston sat at the desk a few minutes more, mentally reviewing what he had read and flipping through other pages, then closed the book, took it back to the shelf, repositioned it, and left the library, waving his thanks to the staffers at the main desk as he went by. He returned to his office on East Broadway.

Chapter Twenty-Seven

THE WORD

It was a fax, just a fax, not even an official communique in an overnight Federal Express envelope with a telephone call saying it would be coming.

"You are hereby authorized to employ any and all immediate discretionary measures to dispatch as many as four (4) grizzly bears (*americanus horribilus*) now occupying the National Elk Refuge at Jackson, Wyoming without further specific direct or non-direct authorization in order to ensure the public safety and to protect members of the resident elk herd and the local populace against any potential dangers associated with the presence of said grizzly bears."

That was it. That was all it said. What the hell did it mean?

"Discretionary"? Oh. If I "employ" the wrong "measures," I'm history, which I probably am anyway.

"Without authorization"? Like the bears had not submitted the proper paperwork to "occupy" the elk refuge. No doubt that makes sense to some bureaucrat.

"Resident" elk herd? What about the ones that are just visiting?

They even got the Latin wrong. Twice.

Well, someone in Washington is gonna go through the roof when they learn that all of the bears—with or without authorization—have already left the refuge. Apparently. We really don't know that for certain, since we didn't actually climb the butte and search through its rocks, bushes, and trees. There could still be one or two up there. Maybe we just didn't see them.

According to his library research, grizzlies seem to spend most of their time following their food supply. Wake up from hibernation, dine on winterkilled elk, deer, and bison. Then spawning trout. Then the "succulent" bushes and berries. Then pine bark nuts. Then it's back to hibernation—unless you've had a long hot summer that dries up your supply of fruits and then have to face fires that kill your chances of finding any pine bark nuts. In which case, you go with the flow and follow the elk to Jackson, and stick "around the edges." None of those bear "edges" on Millers Butte. Not enough trees.

Okay, so what happens after you get your fill of elk, and begin to feel a little bit tired? Can't hole up on Millers. Too small. Go clear back to Yellowstone to hibernate? Not likely. Somewhere around here. Sixty- five-hundred to 10,000 feet, mainly at eight- and nine-thousand feet. He began poring over the office's topographic maps, looking for those specific elevations.

He started with Millers Butte. At the most, the butte reached an elevation of only seven-thousand feet. Very little cover. No place for bears. Snow King Mountain? Close to eight-thousand feet, a lot more trees, a lot more cover. Could be. Always wake up and snack on skiers. That'd create a hell of a lot of excitement. Bears chasing skiers up and down the mountain. Make a good marketing slogan, though: "Glide With the Grizzlies, Only at Snow King Ski Resort." Enter a race, last person to avoid getting eaten wins. Look here. Jackson Peak, 10,707 feet, go right up the side of the mountain from the refuge. But maybe too close to civilization, and a little higher than the book said. Same for Sheep Mountain—Sleeping Indian—10,772 feet. But that's at the top. They could leave the refuge, follow Flat Creek Canyon, make an easy climb right off the refuge, go as far up the mountain as they want until they find a cave, a place to dig a hole, good pile of brush to protect them. Probably a lot of places up there like that where they could bivouac. Come back down the same path in the spring, and pick up some easy winter-kill meals. If I were a grizzly, that's where I'd go for my winter vacation. Sleeping Indian.

What's to the west? The Tetons, of course. The Grand, at 13,770; the South, 12,514; lesser peaks of Buck Mountain, Static, Prospectors, Hunt. Could go as far south as Rendezvous. But how would a bear get there? Have to cross the highway, go across this pasture land, cross the Snake River, Lake Creek, Fall Creek, then climb almost straight up. Too far to go, and too much work, even for a grizzly.

Has to be Sleeping Indian, Johnston concluded. They went north last night, headed up Flat Creek Canyon, and are probably working their way up the side of the mountain right about now.

All of them?

Chapter Twenty-Eight

THE JHERIFF

Jack Wilson was not a happy camper. To begin with, he had a pretty good sense about whether people were telling him the truth or telling him lies. Jenny Jeffries was telling him lies, and that did not make him a happy camper.

He couldn't figure out why she had lied. Why would a newspaper editor want to conceal the fact that one of her staff members—a photographer—was missing? Was she trying to hide the fact that Joe Dean was missing, or that the photographer was missing? Was he even missing? Maybe she knew Joe Dean the photographer or the photographer Joe Dean was out doing something that he wasn't supposed to be, and she was trying to cover it up. Or maybe she was trying to buy time, until Dean could get back from that mysterious mission. Or maybe she knew he would be coming back soon, so he really wasn't missing at all.

He hated it when some crime perpetrators did that. It was like a game to them, like they were presenting him with a maze to solve, and he had too many choices and not enough time to do it. Make the wrong move and you have to go back to square one and start all over again, take a different route, use a different tact. Catch me if you can. Wilson felt that Jenny Jeffries knew a lot more about the unannounced absence of Joe Dean than she was willing to tell him. Why was that?

Wilson had not needed to uncover Dean's absence in the telephone call to Jeffries about Cindy Mason. He had already confirmed it, first by calling other members of the News staff, then by calling Dean's very strange roommate, and finally by having his deputies do other checking. That was one of the great things about being a 24/7 operation—you had people available at all hours of the day and night to do your bidding. He had them checking out the *News* photographer all night long.

By the time Jenny Jeffries got to work, Wilson already knew the answers to the questions that he was going to ask. He knew that the *News* was missing a staff member, knew that the missing staff member was a photographer, and knew that the name of the photographer was Joe Dean.

The people of Teton County hadn't elected Wilson sheriff to sit on his butt and read newspapers, in his opinion—particularly when those newspapers didn't contain all of the news that was fit to print. Sometimes, you had to read between the lines. Sometimes, you even had to read between the reporters and the editors. Like now.

Wilson knew a little bit about the small-town newspaper game, having been a part-time sports reporter on the *Pinedale Round-up* for several years when he was a lot younger. He knew that editors send you out on stories that they want you to cover, but also keep you from going out to cover the ones that they don't. Editors, and the publishers who hired them, have their own political agenda—just like everyone else. Unlike everyone else, however, editors and publishers have better tools with which to pursue those agendas, to influence events far more than the average joe is able. What was it George Orwell said about equality? That some of us are more equal than others? He must have been referring to editors and publishers—and to most politicians—Instead of pigs. Maybe the world was more of an *Animal Farm* than he had supposed.

Jenny Jeffries had an agenda. What was it?

Without finding out what had happened to Joe-Dean-the-photographer-Joe-Dean, it would be hard to determine the editor's agenda. Dean was the key.

Wilson had been so sure that they would find a human body on the elk refuge this morning—or pieces of it. When they hadn't even found any bears he was mystified. Bears bury bodies for later consumption, he knew, but they had not seen any sign of that, and a fresh burial mound should have stood out like a sore thumb on the side of the bare butte, even if it were higher up. But, given a choice, would a bear carry a body up the steep side of a butte simply to bury it? Or would he be more likely to bury it down low? The answer was obvious.

That meant that they had missed the photographer's buried body—assuming it had not been completely eaten last night—when they scanned the butte. Makes sense. They were all using the magnification of binoculars to look up high. What they should have been doing was using their eyes to look down low. In effect, they had been too close to the forest to see the trees.

Wilson picked up the phone to dial Johnston. He had a proposition for him.

Chapter Twenty-Nine

THE FLOOR

Dan Johnston had pretty much decided that he was going to put off having his office floor waxed again, at least until next spring. His door was open. He saw the mayor coming back.

"Well, what is it this time, Mr. Mayor?" Dan asked, before Ashton could get the first word in. "Are we celebrating or complaining?"

"Where are the goddamn bears, Johnston?" The mayor appeared to be a bit irritated, as he quickly paced back and forth in front of Johnston's desk. There were big dark circles around each of his eyes, as though he hadn't been getting much sleep lately. "What did you do with the goddamn bears?"

"The bears are gone?" Johnston faked surprise. "I told Spellman to keep an eye on them." He looked through the open doorway. "SPELLMAN! Get your butt in here! Sorry about that, Mr. Mayor. Spellman must have forgotten to feed them last night." A young man instantly appeared at the entrance to the refuge manager's office, but hesitated, obviously expecting to get still another reaming.

"That'll be all, Spellman!" Johnston shouted, not even glancing at the young man. "Don't let this happen again!" Puzzled, and yet relieved, Spellman pivoted quickly on his heels, and hurried away, not daring to ask what that was all about.

"Think you're smart, don't you Johnson?" the mayor hastened. "Well, I'll show you what smart is when I contact your supervisors in Washington to tell them what kind of a job you've been doing."

"And just what kind of a job is that?" Johnston challenged. "First you storm in here wanting me to get rid of the bears, then you come back wanting me to help get the tourists closer to them, now you come in wanting to know what I've done with them. Just exactly what do you want, Mr. Mayor?"

"I want you to find the goddamn bears! How can people see them if they aren't there to be seen?"

"You mean, what's going to happen to business in Jackson if the tourists take their money and leave, or don't come in the first place?"

"That's *exactly* what I mean! It's our responsibility to protect the public! We can't do that with no bears on the elk refuge! You need to find those goddamn bears! Shoot them, if you have to, to get them back. But GET THEM BACK!" The mayor turned sharply and stormed out, the same way he had stormed in.

Johnston just shook his head. He didn't even bother to get up, go around his desk, and examine his freshly waxed hardwood floor.

His phone rang.

Chapter Thirty

THE PROPOJITION

"Johnston."

"Dan. Jack Wilson. Anything new on the possible location of the bears?"

"Well, I went to the library to do a little research on bear habits, and I've just been going over the topographic maps of this area, and I think they may have headed up Flat Creek Canyon. I suspect they're going to try to find a place to hibernate near the top of Sheep Mountain."

"Sleepin' Indian, eh? Hadn't thought about that."

"My guess is, they'll spend the winter up there, join the elk in migrating back to Yellowstone next spring, and we'll never see them again. I think our crisis may be over."

"What about the missin' photographer?"

"Who knows? Could have been eaten by one or more of the bears, could have been carried off, could have been stashed away on the butte. We probably won't see him again either. If the bears didn't polish him off, the scavengers will. Best we can hope for is to find some of his bones next spring."

"I wish I could leave it at that," said the sheriff. "But I have an obligation to find out now what happened to him."

"You think we ought to go looking for pieces of him up on Sleeping Indian?" Johnson asked, incredulous.

"I don't think we need to go quite that far," Wilson replied. "But I do think we should take another shot at findin' him on Millers Butte."

"What makes you think we missed him the first time?" Johnston said, somewhat surprised. "I thought we conducted a pretty thorough search."

"I'm not so sure we did," the sheriff said. "I think we may have had our sights set a bit too high, with too much magnification."

"You mean we shouldn't have been using binoculars?"

"That's exactly what I mean. We should have been lookin' with our eyes only, at close to ground level."

"Well, I suppose we could have missed something, under those circumstances," Johnston said. "But what do you want to do about it now?"

"I think we should go back out there and do another search—not like before. Just you and me this time, if you're up to it."

"Why just the two of us?"

"I don't want to raise too many eyebrows."

"Why do I get the feeling that there's something here that you're not telling me?" Johnston asked.

"Because there's something here that I'm not tellin' you," Wilson laughed. "I had a talk with Jenny Jeffries this mornin'.

She didn't seem to think that anyone else on her staff was missin' besides Cindy Mason."

"I thought you said Dave Hamilton had already confirmed the photographer's missing status."

"I did. He did."

"So why wouldn't the editor of a small-town paper know that one of her key people was missing?"

"That's the million-dollar question. Do you wanna be a millionaire?"

"What do you mean?"

"I mean you can help me answer that million-dollar question. If we can find some evidence that this Dean fellow was out there on the refuge last night we can probably conclude that he was with Mason. If they were both out there together, on some sort of cock-eyed newspaper assignment, Jenny Jeffries probably knew about it. If she knew they were goin' out there—and especially if she's the one that sent them—I think Charlie Barton over at the county prosecutor's office needs to consider filin' some charges."

"So what do you want to do, just drive around the refuge in your car or mine until we find something?"

"Actually, I think one of us needs to stay in the car, and the other one needs to get up in those low-set boulders on Millers Butte and look around."

"You realize, of course, that one or more of the bears may still be up there in those rocks?"

"That's why I'm volunteerin' right now to be the one who stays in the car," the wizened old sheriff hastened to add.

Chapter Thirty-One

THE MILLIONAIRE

Johnston and Wilson rolled onto the refuge in Wilson's Expedition at about three o'clock in the afternoon. The skies were overcast with puffy dark-grey clouds—threatening the first big snow of the season—but the sun was managing to sneak its rays through the cumulus cover every once and again. The smell of winter was in the air. As so often happened on the elk refuge, a stiff breeze was blowing, making it feel about twice as cold as any accurate thermometer would have indicated. On the normal refuge sleigh rides, especially in the months of January and February, most of the bundled-up elk watchers didn't realize just how cold they really were while on the flat and open Elk Refuge until their body temperature returned to normal a few days later.

The sheriff was driving. About a hundred years earlier, Johnston would have been regarded as "riding shotgun," except that his "shotgun" was a 30.06 rifle with split-point, 220-grain bullets that the manufacturer's advertising promised "would stop a bear." He sure hoped they were right. He'd never had an occasion to try it—and wasn't exactly praying for such an opportunity in the near future.

They planned to circle the entire base perimeter of the butte, starting at the southeast corner, going up and around, and coming back down the west side. As they got near the south end of the butte Wilson pulled off the road, edged as close as he could to the butte, then stopped to let Johnston out.

"Okay, let's do a radio check," Wilson commanded. "We need to be in constant contact so's I can warn you if I see somethin' comin' in plenty of time for you to get back in. You know, I was only kiddin' about me stayin' in the car. If you don't wanna do this, you just say so, and I'll do the walkin' while you drive."

"No," Johnston said, "I'll do it. I haven't been getting much exercise lately. Wrestling with a six- or eight-hundred-pound grizzly should burn off a few calories—if I live long enough." He pushed the transmit button on his walkie-talkie. "Bear Meat to Old Fogey," he said into the communicator's unseen mike.

"Ten-four, four-ten, thirty-ought-six, and any other weapons that we can bring to bear in this hunt," Wilson replied, smiling, into his own unit. "Okay. These things are set on voice-operated, so they should be on all the time, and we're usin' a frequency that nobody else normally does, so we shouldn't be interrupted. Plug in your remote mike in and pinch it to your collar. Snap the walkie-talkie on your belt, and see if it still works."

"Still good?" Johnston said at a normal voice volume, following Wilson's instructions.

"Loud and clear. Okay, keep your finger on that trigger, but for God's sake don't shoot me. You put a hole in this new shirt and Edna will have a fit. You and me both will get a good chewin' out."

Johnston began walking, making occasional forays up into the boulders of some ten or twenty yards. Wilson let the car idle along in low gear. If the Expedition began to get ahead of Johnston he would lock it in low axle to slow it even more. It didn't.

They made nervous chatter as Johnston walked and Wilson drove. Mainly, there were a lot of bear jokes and poor puns. Anything to cut the tension. Once, Wilson asked Johnston if he had any last words he would like him to pass along to his wife. "Yeah," Johnson had replied, mimicking the famous Arnold Schwarzenegger line. "Tell her I'll...be...back—and I hope she can stand the smell!"

"I'll come back myself with a broom, a bucket, and a gas mask to scoop you up in a couple of days. We'll make sure you occupy a special place right next to my old barn."

Johnston saw not a sign of the photographer on the east side of the butte, nor on the north. As he began to walk south along the west side he tried to think like a photographer. What am I here to take pictures of? A bear or bears. A bear sleeping? Nothing spectacular about that. A bear chasing elk? Right. Meat on the hoof. Okay, so where would the bear and elk be? Out there in the field. And where would I be? Not out there in the field. I may be dumb, but I'm not stupid. I would be...up a bit higher, to get a good angle. Up in the boulders. Not here, in the middle of the butte, because I'm going to have to run like hell after I take the pictures. Closer to the end of the butte. Like...there. Up in those boulders. That's where I'd be. I could take a couple of shots, get down pretty easy, run back around the butte, and hop back in the car before the bear even knew I was here. While he was still occupied chasing the elk.

Like Joe Dean, Johnston gave no thought at all to the possibility of encountering a *second* bear, one that had already been up in the boulders, watching his more-ambitious cousins chase food. Climbing up a bit into the boulders he soon found a bit of dried blood on some boulders, and then quite a bit more. In barely an instant, he knew exactly what had happened.

"Well, Jack, I think I know what became of our photographer friend," he reported. "There's enough blood up here to start your own slaughterhouse. If this is human blood it's probably Dean's. So far, I haven't found any body parts, but—wait a minute, what's that? There's something reflecting light down below me in a crack."

Johnson went over, stooped down on some angular rocks, and tugged on a leather strap. "It's a camera," he reported to the sheriff. Kinda banged up, but still in one piece. Aha! Lookee here what Santa brung me. We have one-each pair of night-vision goggles. Ex-pens-ive! Looks like they're fairly new—like they've been used just about once. How about that? Say, how much do I have to give the government out of a million dollars?"

"A lot more than the government deserves," Wilson replied. "I knew it! I knew that boy was up here last night. And a bear got him. The girl must have seen it happen, got scared, and lit out for home so fast that she didn't even see Bob Thomas as he was about to turn into the refuge. She plowed right into him. She was probably in so much shock that she didn't even know what happened."

"Sounds about right to me," Johnston agreed. "The only question I have is, what became of the body? It's not around here. It seems to me that the bear must have carried it off to eat it somewhere else, or else to bury it."

"I'm no bear expert," the sheriff repeated, "but if I were a bear that had just made me a kill, and there were three other fellows who were maybe gonna try to take it away from me, I don't think I would stick around here with it very long. And I surely wouldn't take it out there in the field to eat. I'd cut around the corner of the butte with the meat in my mouth and high-tail it for those trees up there on the side of the mountain. Okay, if you can't find anything else in the immediate vicinity, you'd better come back down here."

"Well," said Johnston, getting back in the car, "do you want to go up in the trees and check it out?"

"Not particularly," Wilson replied. "But it's a dirty job, and I guess somebody's gotta do it."

Chapter Thirty-Two

THE BLOOD

They parked the sheriff's Expedition alongside Elk Refuge Road, near the south end of Millers Butte. They both had high-powered rifles, and had changed frequencies on their radios to allow them to communicate not only with each other, but with the sheriff's office about a mile away if necessary. It was a only a couple of hundred yards to the tree line, although they had to climb up a fairly steep grassy slope to get to it, and they tried to take as short a route as possible, even though that type of climb would be tougher than doing switchbacks.

"You gettin' cold?" Wilson asked Johnston, who had by now spent a bit more time out in the wind-chilled air than he had.

"A bit, actually, but not enough to mention," Johnston replied. "Just enough to make me wish I'd worn a warmer and heavier coat. Like yours."

"Unless I miss my guess," Wilson said, "this shouldn't take too long. What we should probably do is walk this off by sections. Let's go over to the right about a hundred yards to start. You go in about twenty-five feet, and. I'll go in about fifty. Then we'll walk north for a couple or three-hundred yards and turn around. You go in about seventy-five feet. I'll go one-hundred. Then we'll make a sweep back. That should give us some idea, because we can look for broken branches and tramped down bushes at the same time. If he went through here we oughta know it by the time we do a coupla' sweeps."

By the time they had made just half of the first sweep they knew it. The huge grizzly came charging out of the trees at them almost before they realized he was there. They each got off a shot before the bear was on them, clawing at Wilson, who had instinctively tried to protect his head by raising his rifle with both hands. The bear snapped its huge canines around the barrel and wooden forearm of the gun, as Johnson put two more bullets into it, apparently hitting vital organs. The big bruin toppled onto Wilson, and they both went down to the ground. There was no more motion, or noise, from either of them.

"You okay down there?" Johnston yelled to Wilson, who was almost completely hidden under the bear.

"Yeah," Wilson responded after a moment. "But I don't think I'm gonna be able to get this booger off of me by myself. The damned thing must weigh a ton."

"Six or eight hundred, maybe. But it probably feels like a ton to you. Here, let's roll him downhill to get you out from under him." Johnston struggled to find a good grip on the bear. He finally managed to roll it off by grasping it around a shoulder and rocking it.

"That bear smells like a sonofabitch," Wilson said, as he got to his feet. He began brushing himself off. "Aw, look at this. Edna's gonna kill me. Look what that mother did to my coat and shirt!"

"Is that your blood or his?" Johnston asked, examining the torn black coat and brown shirt.

"Maybe a little bit of both," Wilson allowed. "Don't worry about it, though. I'll be just fine."

"Well, that's one down, three to go," Johnston said. "Do you still want to look around here some more for the photographer?"

"Actually," the sheriff said, in an obvious, growing amount of pain, "I think you should probably get me over to the hospital just about as soon as you can. It appears I may be leakin' a bit more than I thought."

And with that the old sheriff passed out.

Chapter Thirty-Three

THE HOSPITAL

Wilson woke up in a bed in a room close to the Emergency Ward at St. John's Hospital on East Broadway, only about three blocks from the end of Elk Refuge Road. His chest hurt, he had a few scrapes and bruises on his face, and a couple of fairly deep bite punctures on his right hand where it had been holding the forestock of the rifle. However, he realized, if he hadn't been able to use the rifle to block some of the bear's blows, and to give it something to bite down on, he could have been in a lot worse shape. As it was, the bear's long claws had raked some long furrows in his chest, deep enough to give him something to brag about for the next year or so.

"You're lucky," the attending emergency room physician told him. "Just a bit deeper on some of those wounds and you would have needed major repairs."

"I don't feel all that lucky," the sheriff replied, squeezing Edna's hand. She had been called to the hospital immediately, and was there at his bedside when he came out of it, as was Johnston.

"If we can avoid any substantial infection," the physician said, "you should be good as new in a couple of months. You're going to have a good bit of scarring, of course."

"I can live with that," Wilson said. "It's a lot better than the alternative. Thanks, doc." The physician nodded, and left the room.

"How'd you get me out?" Wilson asked Johnston.

"Well, first I used my radio to call the sheriff's office, described what happened, and told them to send some help. Then I turned you over on your back, tied your hands together with your belt, stuck my rifle through it, and pretty much dragged you down the hillside to the road, where the squad was just arriving. You might have to replace the heels of your boots when you get home."

"Thanks for the rescue. But it seems to me that you were keepin' your hands on your rifle just about as much as you were keepin' them on me." The sheriff made a weak effort to smile.

"Well, I was dragging enough clear evidence of what one of those grizzlies can do even with four slugs in it," Johnston conceded. "I wasn't about to turn all of my attention to saving your worthless hide and then have another bear attack me without being able to defend myself."

"Makes sense," Wilson admitted. He paused a second to remember the events. "You think we actually hit that sucker solid with four bullets?"

"Pretty sure. We each got a shot off as he was charging, and I hit him with two more slugs while he was dancing with you. I've read about grizzlies that took six or eight bullets and still kept coming. From the looks of you, we got him down just in time."

"Edna, when I get out of here we're gonna have to have Dan and his wife over for supper to show our appreciation. You can bake him one of your famous huckleberry pies."

"I'll certainly be glad to do that," Edna offered, beaming, but still showing great concern for her husband's condition.

"You'd probably better get some sleep now to regain your strength, Jack," Johnston cautioned. "If you say the word, I'll take a couple of your deputies back up there, retrieve your rifle, and drag the bear out. You can have Norris Brown stuff it for you as a souvenir, maybe pose it reared up on its back legs, holding your rifle in its jaws, with ripped-off pieces of your bloody shirt in its claws. While we're up there we might look around a little bit for Dean's body. It's pretty obvious that your guess about which way the bear took him was right on. That grizzly must have been eating him darned close to where we were when we surprised him."

"The word is said," Wilson replied. "Start with Dave Hamilton. Tell him to bring along a couple or two other guys. But whatever you do, be careful."

"You think I want to end up in here looking like that? Edna, Jane and I will be looking forward to some of that huckleberry pie! Take good care of this character. If we can't find the photographer's body we may need to get Jack back up there again as bear bait. He's the only one still alive who has had any close-up contact with them."

Chapter Thirty-Four

THE BUCKLE

Dave Hamilton had already received his marching orders from the sheriff by the time Johnston got around to contacting him. As second-in-command under Wilson he officially was the man in charge when the sheriff was incapacitated, but as a long-time friend of the sheriff Hamilton didn't have any plans to upset the department applecart while Wilson was away. So he welcomed Johnston into his office, breaking the news about his telephone call from the sheriff.

"Well, as far as I'm concerned you are quite welcome to run the show," Johnston conceded. "Officially, these bears are no longer my responsibility, having left the Elk Refuge. They're now on Bridger-Teton, so I guess their fate is now up to Jim Farson."

"Except they're still in Teton County, so that gives the sheriff's office a little bit of say," Hamilton asserted. "But I don't intend to conduct a major search-and-destroy mission here, just go back up to pick up Jack's rifle, haul out the bear, and see if we can find anything that looks like it may once have been a photographer."

"How are you figuring to get the bear out?" Johnston asked.

"Well, the traditional way would be to use a horse," Hamilton considered. "We've got plenty of those to choose from—including mine—in the Mounted Posse. We could use a four-wheeler with a tow rope, but having a motorized vehicle up there for any reason probably wouldn't go over too big with the Forest Service. So, it looks like we'd better use a horse. I'll take mine as far as the refuge road in a trailer, unload him, and walk him up the hillside. Should be an easy pull back down. We'll then load the bear into my pickup, and take it over to Norris."

"Sounds like a plan," Johnston agreed. "When do you want to do it?"

"The sooner the better, I'd say," Hamilton noted. "The longer we wait, the less likely we are to find either the bear or the photographer, not to mention the rifle. How about this afternoon?"

"Meet you there at two o'clock?" Johnston suggested.

"Two o'clock it is," Johnson replied.

It was just before two o'clock when Johnston, already waiting in his vehicle on Elk Refuge Road, saw Hamilton's pickup/horse trailer rig and one of the sheriff's Expeditions come over the little rise by the old Miller place. They pulled up behind his pickup and stopped, exiting their vehicles with high-powered rifles in-hand.

"Don't shoot," Johnston said, raising his arms. "I give up. I'll never do it again."

"Haha," Hamilton responded, walking to the back of the horse trailer. "Never heard that one before. All set to go?"

"Just waiting for you guys to start horsing around," Johnston replied. "Hope you fed this horse an extra ration of oats this morning. That bear's a big one."

"Old Dollar will pull him out," Hamilton assured him, patting the horse's rear a few times. "He's a strong horse. Aren't you, fella? Besides, looks to me like this is going to be downhill all the way."

"Might have a bit of a problem in those trees," Johnston noted. "There's a lot of underbrush to get hung up on."

"Well, let's go take a look at it," Hamilton said, beginning to lower the rear gate/ramp of the trailer and back out his horse. "Jack told me I could have all the steaks I could cut off this sucker for pulling him out." He glanced over at one of the other deputies, who was braced at arms-ready. "Charlie, are you going to shoot somebody or what? Look around. You can see for five hundred feet in every direction. Do you see any bears?"

"No, but that didn't make no difference to the photographer," Charlie observed. "So why should it make any to me? Besides, I told my wife I would be home for dinner. I didn't tell her I would *be* the dinner." They all laughed, but Charlie didn't lower his guard.

It took them only ten or fifteen minutes to get up the hillside, enter the trees, and find the grizzly and Jack's rifle.

"Jesus," Hamilton said, "no wonder Jack ended up in the hospital. That thing is huge. I wouldn't say I'd like to try crawling around with him on top of me. Dick, do you want to hold on to Jack's rifle? We'll let Charlie stand guard while we hook Dollar up to this thing." The horse, smelling the scent of the bear, was predictably skittish, and was reluctant to get too close to it, but Hamilton eventually got it to stand still and let Johnston hold its reins while he looped a makeshift rope harness under its shoulders and around its neck. "That oughta do it. Let's pull the bear out first, then come back up and see if we can find the photographer."

It was almost an afterthought. The strong cutting horse had no problem at all pulling the eight-hundred-pound grizzly out of the woods and down the hillside to Hamilton's truck. It was more of an effort for the four men to jack it into the bed of the pickup, although that would have been easier if Charlie had not insisted on keeping his rifle ready in one hand. With the bear loaded, Hamilton put Dollar back in the trailer and secured the door.

"Okay, fellows," Hamilton said. "Now the real work begins. Let's go find ourselves a photographer...or what's left of him."

They walked the woods for almost a half-hour before Dick spotted something shining in the afternoon sun. He reached down and picked up a leather belt, with a huge silver buckle on it.

"Look at this," he called to the others. "Somebody was obviously a big *Star Trek* fan." They examined the buckle, which had a molded image of the *U.S.S. Enterprise* flying through space on its front, and the notation "200th Anniversary, *U.S.S. Enterprise*, The Olde New England Mint, Copyright 1983, Paramount Pictures" on its rear. It even had a serial number: 5459.

"We should be able to find somebody who recognizes this," Hamilton speculated. "The person wearing it would stand out like a sore thumb. 'Beam me up, Scotty.'"

"You know, Captain Kirk never actually said that," Johnston corrected. "If you watch all of the episodes, you'll never hear it."

"Are you one of those 'Trekkies,' too?" Hamilton asked.

"Actually, we'd rather be called 'Trekkers,'" Johnston corrected.

"Well, Houston, we have a problem," Charlie interrupted, mixing his space movie metaphors. "This belt appears to have a lot of dried blood stains on it. Whoever was wearing it isn't going to be making any more trips into space – unless he's already there."

"Live long and prosper," Johnston said quietly.

In less than ten minutes, their additional searching produced the remainder of the photographer's clothes, and beside them most of the bones of his body. Between the bear and the scavengers that already had been attracted to the scene, there was little meat left on them. They put the clothes in one plastic bag, the bones in another, and walked slowly and silently out of the national forest.

Chapter Thirty-Five

THE STORY

Word of the discovery of the belt buckle and the bones reached Jenny Jeffries through the newspaper's reporter covering the sheriff's department beat. There had been a log entry about conducting a search just off Elk Refuge Road, and she had been sharp enough to pursue it. Under casual questioning, Dave Hamilton had revealed that they had been searching for a missing person, whom they suspected was the newspaper's AWOL photographer.

At this point none of the newspaper staff except for its editor even realized that the missing photographer was probably dead; they had just assumed that he was still out on one of his frequent offbeat assignments. It had not been unusual for Dean to be "missing" for days, then return with a bagful of film to be processed. It was one of the reasons the photographer had won so many awards—he was willing to go the extra mile and take the extra time to capture just the right images to tell a story.

So it was a shock to the newspaper's entire system when the beat reporter discovered the news about the belt buckle and the bones. Everyone who ever saw Joe Dean remembered the belt buckle. He always had it on him. He was a devoted *Star Trek* fan who had watched every one of the original episodes at least twenty times and could spout off entire scenes of dialog without error. There was no doubt that the buckle was his, along with the bones.

"I'll handle this," Jeffries told the reporter bluntly, as she arrived back at the office literally breathless with the news of the discovery. "Type out your notes and leave them on my desk. If I have any questions for you, I'll find you. Good job, Margie." Margie, of course, was both disheartened and upset at being told to hand over the biggest story yet of her fledgling career. She wouldn't even share a byline. But she quickly rationalized her loss by thinking that Jeffries, as the supervisor of a newly dead employee, probably wanted to give this story some special treatment. Margie reluctantly turned over her notes without any obvious protest, believing that she would at least learn how a real pro handles a story such as this.

It was a surprise not only to Margie but to the entire newspaper staff when Jeffries's three-paragraph story appeared the following day on page seven of the daily newspaper, nearly buried between two large ads, one promoting land-development restraints, the other selling high-end real estate:

Bones Found

Teton County sheriff's deputies Thursday found several bones in the trees next to Elk Refuge Road, along with a silver belt buckle.

The bones are believed to be human, a sheriff's department spokesman said, and may be those of Joseph R. Dean, 20, of Jackson. Dean, a local newspaper photographer, was apparently reported missing some days ago. Deputies have not ruled out the possibility that Dean may have been a victim of foul play.

The bones will soon be sent to Cheyenne for positive identification, deputies said.

"What happened to the bear?" Hamilton asked himself after reading the story. It was the same question that was on the mind of several other search insiders, including Jack Wilson and Dan Johnston.

Chapter Thirty-Six

THE DOWN TOWN

The normal Jackson economy has two peaks, alternating with two valleys. The peaks occur in summer and winter, the valleys in spring and fall. In the tourism-based economy, money flows when sightseers pass through town in the summer on their way to Grand Teton and Yellowstone National Parks and come in the winter to ski or snowboard at Snow King, the Jackson Hole Ski Resort at Teton Village, or at Grand Targhee, just "over the hill" near Driggs, Idaho. In March and April, and again in October and November, money is as tight as a new pair of boots.

There are many other activities available to area visitors in both summer and winter, of course—hiking the surrounding hillsides, horseback riding, mountain biking, mountaineering on the Tetons, scenic boat trips and whitewater rafting on the Snake, fly-fishing almost anywhere there's water, hunting, heli-skiing, snowshoeing, snowmobiling, and in recent years even dogsledding, thanks to Frank Teasley, the closest thing to a true "mountain man" that Jackson Hole has seen since the late 1800's. (Teasley spent his first five years in Jackson Hole camped out with his dogs in the forest.) But all of those activities are sharply seasonal. In most months the business health of the town is either way up or way down, far removed from the annual average.

At the moment, as the calendar approached late October, the Jackson Hole economy, and therefore the mood of the entire town, was down.

When the bears left the Elk Refuge the tourists followed. The "non-locals" had returned to Jackson in the economic "shoulder" month of October only because of the highly publicized Elk Refuge bruins. When the grizzlies disappeared overnight without leaving a trace very few of the sightseers had stayed behind, mainly to continue eyeing the arriving elk or to putter around Jackson's shops looking for pre-Christmas bargains, which were plentiful. With most Jackson merchants now willing to sell their wares at almost any price, the bargain-hunters were having a field day.

Sixty miles to the north of Jackson the south gate of Yellowstone had been closed to traffic weeks earlier. The pivoting pole barriers would remain chained and locked for the winter, except to snowmobilers going into the park on tours that originated mainly in Jackson, at Flagg Ranch, a private lodge/restaurant/service station enterprise situated just two miles south of the entrance, and at Togwotee Mountain Lodge, some forty miles southeast of the park. Closer to Jackson, Grand Teton National Park had also been closed, officially ending the region's summer park season.

With the cooler temperatures it was now possible for the area's mountain managers to turn on their snow-making equipment and begin building a heavy base for the lighter snow that was expected to begin falling from the sky at any time. In a normal winter Snow King—the first ski area in Wyoming (1939)—would receive 150 inches of snow in a season. Ten miles west, at Teton Village, the Jackson Hole Ski Resort would measure over 400 inches. But just across the mountain Grand Targhee would record over 500 inches of powder—some 43 feet. In the winter of 1996-97, Targhee's managers were jumping for joy with a record 659 inches of seasonal snow.

All eyes were on the skies, and the "Weather Channel's" local segment was the most-watched program in Jackson, especially among those business owners who were most-dependent on snow-related income. In the few days following the disappearance of the bears there had been a lot of teeth-grinding in the Jackson area, while the clouds were barren and the ground was dry. Lodging reservations were now down. Flight bookings into Jackson Hole were now down. Retail profits were almost non-existent. Even the obscenely high gasoline prices in Jackson were gradually starting to fall, as station-owners slowly came to the conclusion that it would be better to sell more gasoline at a reasonable rate of return than to sell less gasoline at up to thirty cents higher than anywhere else in the state and hope to sell out and skip off to Hawaii before the anti-collusion regulators wised up and cracked down on their strangely similar pump prices.

It did not snow. And then it did not snow. And then it did not snow some more. It was beginning to look like this was going to be a long, cold, snowless, winter in Jackson Hole.

Chapter Thirty-Seven

THE MAYOR

It was not quite as cold on this final day of October in Jackson as it had been in some recent years. Although there was not yet a blanket of snow in the valley the mountains had been masked with moderate accumulations of the "white stuff," and the skies above the entire area had been overcast for days.

There was some hope among the merchants of Jackson that skiable dumps of snow would be falling within weeks, allowing them to discontinue their profitless bargains while encouraging shoppers to begin buying for Christmas. But at the bare rear-end of October, with nothing else to attract customers and cold cash, most shopkeepers had resorted to stirring up more than the usual amount of hoopla for Halloween. Any store that could find any way at all to have a Halloween sale had had one. Several merchants had encouraged their hired help to add interest (and sales) to the occasion by allowing and even encouraging them to wear creative costumes the entire week leading up to Halloween. Earlier in the year, lacking much faith in the promotional leadership of the area's Chamber of Commerce, the downtown merchants had organized their own association. A couple of nights before Halloween the organization had sponsored a huge block party as its first big event.

More than the expected number of youngsters had decided to dress up for the downtown merchants party in all sorts of weird, scary, and cleverly conceived costumes—many of them, of course, oriented towards bears in general and grizzlies specifically. There were long bears, short bears, thin bears, fat bears, tall bears, bears that were barely recognizable, and several costumes that were nearly true-to-life. The merchants awarded prizes for the "best" costumes, the top prize being reserved for the "most-realistic" grizzly suit. That honor was taken by a freshman at Jackson Hole High School who had somehow sewn himself into an actual bearskin rug. For his amazing effort he had received one-hundred dollars in cash and a fifty-dollar gift certificate redeemable for merchandise at a longtime local electronics outfit, Audio Video Country. He had redeemed the entire certificate for cassette tapes.

Mayor Elvis Ashton was sitting at his desk in City Hall, sipping on a bottle of mineral water, when Dan Johnston entered the outer office, said a friendly hello to Ashton's pretty, young receptionist, told her who he was, and asked to be admitted to "His Royal Excellency's" office.

"Mr. Mayor, a Dan Johnston would like to see you," the young receptionist said into her desk intercom unit. "Shall I show him in?"

"Ask him to have a seat and wait a few minutes," Ashton commanded into his response unit, not realizing that the sound from his voice was carrying not only through his wired intercom station but also through his open door. "I'm right in the middle of reading some very important papers." Releasing the intercom button, Ashton contentedly flipped another page of the morning's *Jackson Hole Daily*.

Cutting off the dutiful receptionist before she could even begin to relay the mayor's wishes, Dan barged by her desk, saying, "Don't get up—I'll find my own way in." Initially inclined to present a protest, she merely tossed her shoulders, spun around in her well-padded desk chair, and resumed reading the popular romance novel that she had brought to work to occupy most of her time.

"Thank you for seeing me on such short notice," Johnston declared in the mayor's general direction, as he entered the office. "I know what an important elected official you are, and how very valuable your time is. How's old *Dilbert* doing today?" Embarrassed at being caught reading the comic strip on "taxpayers' time," Ashton hurried to hide the daily newspaper under some of the many other documents on his desk, but was unsuccessful.

"God damn it, Johnston, why can't you show a little respect for your elected officials?" Ashton shouted.

"I beg your pardon, Mr. Mayor," Johnston hastened to reply. "I believe that I was showing just as little respect for you as anyone else does. But that's not why I'm here." Johnston began to sit down in one of the two big leather chairs in front of the mayor's desk, thought better of it, and instead decided to pace back and forth in front of the Mayor's mahogany desk, perhaps scuffing the wooden floor. May as well play a little tit-for-tat, he thought.

"Alright," Ashton prompted, "just exactly why are you here? Have you found those goddamn bears yet?"

"Only one—the one that sent Jack Wilson to the hospital. But, as you already know, we had to shoot it," Johnston said, feigning regret. "I'm considering calling Yellowstone to see if they can send us a replacement."

"I'll take that as a no," Ashton smirked. "Never send a cub to do a...what the hell do they call a full-grown male grizzly, anyway?"

"Just about anything he wants to be called, I guess," Johnston parried. "But let's get down to business. I'm here to talk about tonight. Trick or Treat."

"Are you asking for a handout?" Ashton said, not amused.

"Trick or Treat. Beggar's Night. When little boys dress up like little ghouls and little girls dress up like fairies and other elected officials," Johnston explained. "They go around collecting candy."

"I believe I am familiar with the concept," Ashton said, pointedly. "So what about it?"

"From what I can tell, there are going to be a lot of kids dressed up like bears out on the streets tonight," Johnston said. "A lot of stores were pushing bear costumes all this week."

"So?"

"So, do you really think that is a good idea?" Johnston asked, in all seriousness.

"Good, bad, what makes the difference?" Ashton replied, defensively. "There's not much I can do about merchants selling bear costumes, even if I wanted to, which I don't. They may not be real, but they're certainly the closest thing we have to real bears around here right now, no thanks to you."

"But do you really think it's advisable to have them trotting around town at night in bear costumes? Aren't you worried about some little kid being mistaken for a real bear and getting shot?"

"Oh, I don't think there's much chance of that happening," Ash-ton opined. "To begin with, everybody in town knows the

Elk Refuge grizzlies are gone. And who would mistake a little boy in a fake bear suit for an elk-breathed grizzly weighing hundreds of pounds on Trick or Treat night?"

"Just about anyone that you terrified into overreacting with all of your news media comments before the tourists began to arrive."

"Oh, come on," Ashton added. "No one thought I was being too dramatic by pointing out the potential dangers of having bears on the Elk Refuge."

"No? Then why did all of the sporting goods stores tell the newspaper reporters that they had never seen such a demand for guns as on the morning after those stories appeared?"

"Blown out of proportion. Distorted what I actually said," the mayor explained. "They always get things wrong in the newspapers. Always. Well, I have to admit that they did accurately report my revised opinion of the bears the following week. Anyway, nobody's going to be shooting any little kids wearing chintzy bear costumes."

"Have you even seen some of those suits?" Johnston asked. "Put one of them on a fair-sized teenager—like the boy who won the block-party contest—and he could very easily be mistaken for a real bear. Particularly on a dark, cloud-covered night."

"So what do you want me to do about it?" Ashton asked, growing perturbed. "Outlaw bear costumes? Stop Beggar's Night? I would have just about as much success in trying to do one as doing the other."

"Can't you just get on the radio and the television and issue a general warning, advising kids to not wear bear suits for trick-or-treating and cautioning homeowners about being too quick to draw their Smith and Wessons?"

"Oh, that would really help the situation," the mayor discounted Johnston's advice. "All we need to do is increase public interest in guns. If they hadn't thought about buying guns for self-protection before now, that would certainly bring it to their attention. We have enough people shooting people as it is. No, I don't think I'm going to do that."

"Well, what are you going to do then, Mr. Mayor? Just sit there reading comic strips and wait for a tragedy to happen?"

"No. Actually, I was just about to ask you to leave my office," Ashton concluded the conversation. "Please close the door behind you. You never know what a bear will drag in through an open door."

Johnston glared at him in disgust for a long moment, spun around on the balls of his feet in an intentional effort to leave scratch marks on the mayor's floor, and left the office. He did not close the door on his way out. The mayor's young receptionist smiled politely at him as he went by then went back to her taxpayer-financed daydreams.

Chapter Thirty-Eight

THE BEAR SUIT

Bobby Allen had worked really hard on his grizzly costume. This was going to be his final year of trick-or-treating—he was getting too old for such a juvenile activity—and he wanted to go out with a bang. Even before the downtown merchants came up with the bear costume contest he had been working on the old bearskin rug for trick-or-treating. He was almost sure that he would win the top prize.

When the winner of the contest was announced, Bobby felt that all of his hard work had been worth the considerable effort. His costume was judged to be as close as anyone could come to looking like a real grizzly. He had even scared the bejesus out of his elderly grandmother when he first walked into the house from the garage where he had put it together, foam padding and all, using Velcro strips to keep it around him. She had run for the bedroom, yelling and screaming, slamming the door behind her, and if his dad—through his tears of laughter—hadn't gone to her rescue and convinced her that it was just a costume, Bobby didn't think he would ever see her again.

The only problem with the costume was that it was both hot and heavy. He had fashioned holes for his eyes in what would have been the bear's chest, and had come up with a way to strap its arms and hands to his so that he could carry a candy bag and knock on doors. But the bear suit was still so big and bulky that it was awkward to get around in it. On the other hand, his lumbering gait due to the unwieldy suit actually added to its realism. He had even found an old fur coat in the attic that he had managed to turn into a candy bag, so the overall effect was impressive.

Living on the east end of Jackson Bobby had started making his trick-or-treat rounds on north Redmond, walking south towards Cache Creek Drive, where he would hit all the houses as far as Rancher, go north on Rancher to Hansen, east on Hansen to Nelson, maybe try the apartments there, then keep going north on Nelson to East Broadway. On Broadway he would go west back to Redmond, passing by the Lame Duck Chinese restaurant. He definitely would swing in there. By that time, he figured, he would either have enough candy to last him a lifetime or would be so dead tired from carrying the bear rug around on his back that he wouldn't care if he never saw a piece of candy again.

Bobby made the circuit as planned, drawing both praise and laughs from the neighborhood residents and scaring the pants off his youngest competitors as he passed them along the way or joined them at the decorated doorways for a handout. As an additional but unexpected reward for his efforts he seemed to be getting almost twice as much candy per house as the other trick-or-treaters. Only a few of the residents in the neighborhood had been taken aback by the virtual reality of his costume, had not found it very funny at all, and had quickly retreated to the safety of their living room after giving him only a perfunctory piece of candy. Maybe it was the growl that did it, he figured; he decided to stop doing that.

Bobby had made his way along the entire planned route as far as the end of Hansen and was now hitting the houses on Nelson, the eastern-most street in northeast Jackson, immediately south of the entrance to the elk refuge. Several ranch style and two-story houses lined the street. Just to the east, a bare steep hillside rose to form part of the northern slope of Cache Creek Canyon. A bit more to the north, another bare hillside joined with the denser fir forest that made up the eastern border of the Elk Refuge. A bear management specialist may have viewed the whole tree-topped hillside as an "edge."

"Trick or treat!" Bobby growled, as the elderly man opened the door. Bobby was standing on the doorstep, with both hands raised in an imitation grizzly attack, his fur candy bag temporarily resting on the ground.

"Are you crazy, boy?" the old man asked, clearly frightened. "I almost grabbed for my shotgun to shoot you. Ever since the grizzlies came down to the refuge I've been keeping it loaded and ready to go."

"Sorry, sir," Bobby puffed through his small breathing and talking hole. "I didn't mean to scare you. Most people just look at me and laugh. Trick or treat!"

"Now, I gotta admit that's a pretty real looking bear outfit," the man said, reaching into a large pan of fruits and candies next to the door. "Best one tonight. Seems to me a lot of you kids are going around as bears."

"It's because of the elk refuge grizzlies," Bobby explained, accepting a piece of fruit and a box of candy in his bag. "Thank you!"

"Don't mention it. Happy Halloween." The old man partly closed the door, leaving it slightly agape to give him a better warning of the arrival of the next beggars. Bobby staggered down the walk. He had nearly reached the street when he was slammed in the chest by the charging bruin.

The lone grizzly had been sitting on the small ridge east of Nelson Drive, watching and listening to the activity below, as some parents drove slowly through the neighborhood with lights on, discharging and picking up their young trick-or-treaters and older youngsters paraded around singly, in pairs, and in groups. The bear had been drawn out of the trees to the edge of the ridge by the sweet smells of fruits and candy. At this stage of his normal food foraging activities the grizzly's diet would be rich in carbohydrates, the final foods needed to build his store of body fat to an acceptable level before finding a place to hibernate. It seemed like the night air was simply saturated with the assorted aromas of such food.

He had been reluctant to slip down the ridge and mingle with all of the noisy people and flashing lights until he spotted a rival that was already there. His ears instantly up, his nose twitching to smell and sort out all scents, the grizzly rose to his full seven feet and squinted to focus on the scene below him, analyzing both the potential threats and the food opportunities. With an almost dog-like woof the bear snorted and began his charge, ignoring any obstacles in his path as he sped down the hillside, seeking only to attack his apparently much smaller competitor and take possession of the disputable cache of carbohydrates. As the grizzly ran he rumbled, growled, and spat.

The old man was still watching Bobby Allen struggling back along the sidewalk in the amazingly realistic grizzly costume when he noticed the big black blob falling down the hillside—or was it something running? He had to hear only a few seconds of the growls being vented by the black blob to know exactly what was coming towards him—or, more specifically, towards the boy in the bear suit. An old hunter, he knew instinctively that the charging grizzly had perceived a rival, and was intent on doing something about it. He ran across the room to the hallway closet where he kept his over-and-under twelve-gauge shotgun, picked it up, opened and closed the breech to make certain that it was loaded, and ran back to the front door.

Just as the grizzly's head-on collision sent Bobby Allen tumbling backwards to the ground, the old man pulled one of his shotgun's two triggers. A close pattern of lead shot struck the bear in its upper chest and neck, only adding to its irritation, not doing any real damage to any of its vital organs. The further-maddened grizzly looked up to find the source of his unexpected pain, saw the old man at the doorway, and immediately lost interest in his downed and apparently vanquished opponent. He rose on his huge hind legs to get a better look at this new adversary, and began shuffling towards him, growling fiercely at the old man, stepping without concern over the unconscious Bobby Allen.

The old hunter instantly realized that his shotgun was not going to stop the huge bear. The first round of pellets had simply drawn the bear's attention. He had only one chance now—only a single shot—and it would have to be fired when the bear was right on him. He waited, as the massive grizzly ambled ever closer to him on the sidewalk, waving its arms in a threatening gesture and gnashing its fangs. When the grizzly was just at the doorway, less than three feet away from him, the old man shoved the barrel of his shotgun straight into bear's gaping mouth and pulled the other trigger. There was a solid click, as the firing pin struck the metal cap of the chambered shell, but no explosion. The weapon had misfired. There was no time to break and reload, even if more shells had been available. Using one of its massive paws, the giant grizzly simply brushed aside the barrel of the shotgun and kept right on coming.

Teton Deputy Sheriff John "Duke" Wayne lived on Nelson Drive, only a few doors down the street from the old man's residence. Still on-duty but taking a break he had been helping his wife pass out candy at their front door when he saw the grizzly run across the street to attack the boy in the bear suit who had been at their house just minutes earlier. When Wayne heard the shotgun blast and saw the flash flare briefly from its muzzle he grabbed for his temporarily removed service weapon and holster and began running, trying to buckle the belt around him and unsnap the retaining strap at the same time.

Nearing the old man's door, where the bear was clawing and biting him savagely, Wayne fired all eleven shots in his Glock 22.40 Smith and Wesson at the grizzly, aiming to miss the big shot-blocking bones of its shoulder and strike somewhere in the vicinity of its heart. He stood there astonished with an empty weapon and in fear of the bruin's response as it struggled to its hind legs, turned in place, and started towards him.

In less than five seconds—about a whole day, from Wayne's point of view—the big bear tumbled towards him, hit the ground, and rolled onto its side. The claws of its swinging right arm slashed deep grooves into the deputy's left boot. When he resumed breathing again, Wayne could suddenly hear the screams and cries of every kid in the neighborhood, and those of all of the mothers, too. But from the boy in the realistic bear suit, and from the brave old hunter in the doorway, there was nothing but silence.

Chapter Thirty-Nine

THE PANIC

It had begun even before the mayor entered his office. Word of the bear attack had spread throughout the community all night long. By the following morning it was being reported on all Jackson radio and television stations, in one of the two dailies, and by the breakfast grapevine in every open restaurant. Ashton's outer office was overflowing with outraged parents and non-parents alike. His receptionist was seated at her desk, writing out irate messages as fast as she could answer the phones. She had not yet had time even to open her newest romance novel.

"What the hell are you going to do about this, Ashton?" one of his staunchest supporters shouted at the mayor as he entered the office.

"We want all of those bears found and shot!" an unknown woman screamed. "Right now!"

"Who's responsible for this attack?" asked another man.

"Okay, okay, everybody just calm down," Ashton pleaded. "Give me a chance to talk to the appropriate authorities and see what they are going to do. I don't have any responsibility for the bears."

"The hell you don't!" shouted the staunch supporter. "We didn't elect you to sit on your ass in this office while those bears kill our kids. You find out how to put a stop to this, and stop it now!"

"Shoot the bears! Shoot the bears!" The chanting of one woman was picked up by all. "Shoot the bears!"

"Please! Everyone just go home or go to work and let me talk to the proper authorities about this," Ashton tried to interrupt. "Just give me a chance." Placing one hand on the shoulder of one of the seemingly less-agitated women he managed to begin ushering them all out of the outer office. The phones were still ringing, and his exasperated receptionist was still taking messages.

"Yes, thank you for calling, I'll be sure to give him your message," the receptionist was saying. "Yes, ma'am, I've already left word for him to call you right back." "No, sir, he isn't trying to avoid you." "Well, I can tell you that he will do everything he can to make sure this doesn't happen again, ma'am." "Yes, sir, he knows you are concerned about community safety, and he shares your concern." "He already has your first two messages, sir, and he's been trying to contact the proper authorities. But I'll tell him that you called again."

Ashton waved to the receptionist after clearing the office and locking the door. He went into his own office, glanced at the pile of pre-printed phone call messages—most of them with call-back requests and numbers—and plopped down into his plush chair. It was going to be a long, long day, and as yet he hadn't figured a way to get out of it.

"Johnston," said the refuge manager, as his office telephone rang again.

"Johnston, this is Mayor Ashton. What the hell's going on?" The mayor did not appear to be too happy. At least, Johnston thought, the mayor wasn't there personally in his office, pacing back and forth, destroying the fresh wax on his wooden floor.

"Exactly what I warned you was going to happen," Johnston responded. "I believe I told you, in terms plain enough for even a politician to understand, that it was not a good idea to have kids running around trick-or-treating at night in bear suits. I am only sorry that my prediction proved to be prophetic."

"Yes, alright, you told me that," Ashton admitted, and in so doing also admitted at least partial culpability. "I should have listened to your warning and given some kind of public notice. But I didn't, and now two people are dead, and I guess I'll just have to live with that. But the bigger question is, what now? Are you going to be able to stop this from happening again?"

"I don't have a whole lot of say about what grizzly bears are going to do," Johnston explained. "All I know is that two of them are now dead and the other two may still be around, somewhere up in the mountains east of the Elk Refuge. I'm not trying to shift responsibility onto anyone else, but strictly speaking they are no longer in my jurisdiction."

"Well, whose jurisdiction *are* they in?" Ashton asked, irritated by Johnston's apparent refusal to help get him off the hook.

"The bears are now under the jurisdiction of Jim Farson, at Bridger-Teton."

"Jesus! You federal people are all alike!" Ashton screamed. "A normal person has to go through every office in Washington to find someone who actually knows his job!"

"Since when did anyone ever accuse you of being normal, Mr. Mayor?" Johnston hung up the telephone, thinking two down, two to go.

Johnston knew that he was being procedurally correct in refer- ring the mayor to the supervisor of Bridger-Teton National Forest, but he did not feel morally right about simply turning his problem over to someone else. He had been personally involved in the initial decision of what to do about the bears on the Refuge. One of the grizzlies had killed the photographer on the Refuge. And he had been with Jack Wilson when the bear attacked him—just off the Refuge. He had a strong jurisdictional sense of wanting to be a part of the solution to the problem. He decided to call Jim Farson.

"Mr. Farson's office," said the woman who answered Johnston's telephone cal immediately.

"Good morning," Johnston said. "This is Dan Johnston. Is Jim there?"

"One moment, Mr. Johnston," she replied. "I think Mr. Farson has been expecting your call." The line fell silent for only a moment.

"Good morning, Dan," Farson greeted. "So now I suppose you're going to try to pass off your bear problems to me?"

"Well, I was sort of thinking about it," Johnston admitted. "You've got a lot more people to lose than I have. And it appears that some of those bears are still hungry."

"Looks that way. It was a damned shame about the boy and the old man."

"Well, I tried to warn the mayor about that possibility, tried to get him to issue some kind of public warning on the radio and television, but he didn't want to get people too excited about protecting themselves."

"Sounds like the old man certainly tried," Farson said. "It took a lot of guts to wait until that bear was close enough to stick the shotgun right into its mouth. If the gun hadn't misfired he probably would have killed it with that second shot."

"Maybe, maybe not," Johnston speculated. "But it sure surprised Duke Wayne when he put all eleven of his shots into the bear at close range and it just kept right on coming."

"I understand he's going to need a new pair of boots—and maybe some new underwear as well."

"I know just how he feels," Johnston said. "I nearly dirtied my drawers myself when that grizzly charged me and Jack Wilson just off the Refuge. Took four hits from our rifles to bring it down, and we were using heavy loads with hollow points."

"That's what I heard," Farson said. "Say, Dan, you do know that the bear that attacked you and Wilson was—technically—under Bridger-Teton jurisdiction?"

"Yeah," Johnston conceded. "It really should have been you up there getting mauled, not the sheriff. But seriously, that's exactly why I called."

"That's what I figured," Farson interrupted. "The two remaining bears seem to be in Bridger-Teton, so all of a sudden they've now become my headache."

"Win some, lose some," Johnston joked. "But since those bastards sort of started out as a Refuge problem—even though they got here by coming down through your forest—I'd still like to be in on the final solution."

"I understand," Farson agreed. "You got any ideas on what that final solution might be?"

"Well, no," Johnston admitted. "My first thought was to just let them find holes up on Sleeping Indian to hibernate in this winter, and watch them all go back to Yellowstone with the elk next spring where they belong. But it looks like they may be thinking about holing up more to the south, which will put them right next door to civilization. We could have more people problems if one of them decides to interrupt its hibernating to go out and find a midnight snack."

"Like maybe a skier on Snow King?" Farson speculated.

"Or even another homeowner back down in east Jackson."

"That would not be very acceptable," the supervisor cringed.

"Particularly to those who get eaten," Johnston agreed. "In any event, I think we the people need to get rid of those bears before those bears get rid of we the people."

"You're probably right," Farson concurred. "But—as you know—I'm going to have to go through the proper channels in Washington to see what they want me to do. If they say they want me to go in after them, are you up for a little hunting expedition?"

"You bet," Johnston gladly agreed. "I was going out today to see if I can buy a slightly bigger gun, maybe something along the lines of an anti-tank weapon."

"Let me know if you can get a better deal by buying two," Farson laughed. "Dan, I'll give you a call as soon as I get instructions from Washington. Gotta go."

"Take care, Jack." Johnston replaced the telephone handset, and issued a sigh of relief—or was it trepidation?

Chapter Forty

THE SNOW

Shortly after nine a.m. on November 1 it began to snow in the valley. All that morning many eyes had been watching the white-capped western mountains take on a foggy appearance, and most area residents realized that the variable white haze was actually falling snow. As the morning hours passed the base of the snow-fog cover crept farther and farther down the rocky mountains, until it settled softly on the valley floor.

It seemed as though the entire sky was trying to fall to the ground. Within an hour more than a foot of heavy, wet snow had covered the valley, but that was not even half as much as some of the overjoyed ski area managers were measuring at higher elevations. On the southeast edge of Jackson 17 inches of new snow was already resting atop Snow King Mountain. Ten miles northwest, above Teton Village, there was 23 inches of new snow at the top of Rendezvous Mountain. But on the Idaho side of the Tetons snow-depth gauges had registered 31 inches of the precious new powder at Grand Targhee since seven a.m.

The clouds above Jackson Hole were still downloading, and they did not appear to be running out of snow. The late-morning temperature in Jackson, instead of doing its normal rise, was falling slightly, and all of the bank thermometers were now flashing around 20 degrees. Instead of melting—the usual fate of the first significant snowfall of the season—this snow was piling up in and around Jackson, and the big plow trucks of the state, county, and town were everywhere. Teton Pass, the shortest distance between the two points of Jackson and the more-affordable bedroom communities of Driggs and Victor in Idaho, had been closed to all traffic since early in the morning and was supposed to remain that way through at least the next day, the pass being both impossible to keep cleared of snow and also posing a possible avalanche threat to motorists at Glory Bowl.

With the snow still coming down, and with all of the local forecasts calling for it to continue snowing for the remainder of the week, the managers of all three local ski areas decided to move up their planned end-of-November opening to the following Saturday.

Jackson's merchants were elated. After the disastrous summer and the disappearance of the Elk Refuge bears this was exactly what they needed to recoup some of their lost revenues. Opening the ski areas three weeks before Thanksgiving would both attract winter visitors early to the town and kick-start the Christmas shopping season, flooding the local economy with recirculating dollars. Within hours of the fall of the first few flakes in Jackson many merchants were revising their advertising plans and redoing their in-store displays. It was as though the grizzlies had been completely forgotten. There was not a single "bear-with-us" sale, not the first mention of grizzlies in the revised advertising of the business community. To all but a few administrators and law enforcement personnel the final two grizzlies were simply gone.

"Jim Farson," the middle-aged, no-nonsense Bridger-Teton supervisor spoke into his office telephone.

"This is Mayor Ashton," came the voice on the other end. Farson had met the mayor a couple of times at various civic functions, but did not really know him, and he did not really like him. He did, however, think that he knew why the mayor was calling, and he was right.

"I understand that you are now in charge of the killer bears," Ashton stated, with an obvious air of offense and mainly imagined superiority in his voice.

"Well, Mr. Mayor, I wouldn't exactly put it that way," Farson replied. "But the grizzlies that you seem to be referring to do appear to be temporarily residing in the Bridger-Teton National Forest."

"So you are in charge of the killer bears," Ashton repeated. "Let's not mince any words, Farson. My constituents demand to know exactly what you intend to do about those killers."

"Without guidance from Washington," Farson explained, "I can't do anything about them. I was in the middle of putting together a memorandum to send out when you called."

"You're just like that bastard Johnston!" Ashton interrupted. "A petty bureaucrat who is afraid to make any decisions on his own, for fear that he will be wrong. Are you going to wait for more kids to be killed before you go out there and shoot those sons of bitches?"

"I think you're just a little off-base here, Mr. Mayor," Farson said, trying to maintain his cool. "To begin with, grizzlies are still a protected species, and any shooting of one—whether by us or by anyone else—is subject to a rather full and detailed investigation. You just can't go out and shoot a grizzly because you feel like it. Secondly, we have certain procedures to follow, procedures that were set down in the interest of all parties concerned about the proper management of our 3.4 million acres, and we are not about to bypass them to appease some second-rate mayor. Finally, I have better things to do right now than to listen to an idiot."

"Are you calling me an idiot?" Ashton asked, both astounded and affronted by Farson's unexpected offensive rather than defensive stance.

"That depends, Mr. Mayor, on whether you are capable of understanding plain English," Farson said, "Good-bye. Have a nice day." Farson hung up the phone. At the other end of the line the mayor's cheeks were becoming as red as the whites of his now bloodshot eyes.

"This is Jenny Jeffries," said the young newspaper editor as she tried to hold the telephone handset to her ear while keeping several sheets of paper in both hands.

"Jenny," came the familiar voice. "This is Elvis Ashton. How the heck are you?"

"I'm fine, Mr. Mayor," she replied. "I was just going to call you to get some comments on the grizzly attack last night. I'm writing the main story."

"Good. Good," Ashton observed. "I will be most happy to comment. In fact, that's exactly why I'm calling you now."

"You knew that I was writing a story?" Jeffries asked, puzzled.

"Well, no," Ashton admitted. "I didn't really know that you were writing one of your excellent stories on the bear killings, although I did suspect that your paper would be running something tomorrow. I just wanted to make certain that everybody knows my position."

"Sounds like you have something good to say," Jeffries offered. "That is, something bad—if you know what I mean."

"I do, and I do," Ashton agreed. "I want the people to know that these killings weren't my responsibility, but the work of Dan Johnston and Jim Farson. I wanted to get on the radio and the television yesterday and warn everybody about wearing grizzly bear costumes to trick-or-treat in, but Johnston told me not to do that. He insisted that it would get some people unnecessarily stirred up about guns and cause undue concern about the bears."

"He really said that?" Jeffries asked, sensing the stuff of major headlines. "Johnston actually told you not to issue any public warning?"

"I would say that he went so far as to try and *order* me not to give anything to the news media that would allow members of the public to protect themselves," Ashton added. "I had to point out that he may run the Elk Refuge but I was elected by the voters of Jackson precisely to make difficult choices when necessary. Unfortunately, I decided to go along with his demand."

"Wow," Jeffries observed. "Another federal bureaucrat trying to interfere with our duly elected local officials—causing an innocent child and an elderly man to get killed."

"Exactly. If Johnston hadn't demanded that I keep all of this quiet, I am quite certain that the boy and the old man would still be alive today," Ashton insisted. "Johnston may even have been directly responsible for the deaths of your reporter and photographer, but as yet I have no confirming evidence of that."

"We are going to pin this guy's hide to the wall," Jeffries beamed, detecting not only news in the making but a possible escape route from her own complicity as well. "What about Farson? How does he fit into this?"

"Just another typical bureaucrat," Ashton pointed out. "Now that the bears are on Bridger-Teton and under his jurisdiction he's saying that he has to *protect* them, not shoot them, regardless of whether they continue killing people."

"He puts the safety of the grizzlies before the safety of the public?" Jeffries prompted, feeling an increasingly comfortable and somewhat stimulating warmth in the area of her groin.

"He's just as bad as Johnston," Ashton speculated. "Maybe even worse. At least Johnston initially wanted to get the bears off the Refuge, as you know. But then he soon saw all of the tourists coming in and thought the bears would be great publicity for the Elk Refuge. Do you know that he was even thinking about bringing in a couple of those glassed-in bear buggies like they have in Alaska so he could take people right out on to the Refuge? I had to talk him out of it. Can't you just see the slaughter that would have resulted if some small child had accidentally opened a door and tumbled out into the arms of a bear? Johnston thought the risk would be worth the extra income to the Refuge."

"This is just incredible!" Jeffries gasped. "Putting public safety behind the opportunity to add a few miserable dollars to the federal till. Why didn't you come to me before now with all of this great information?"

"Well," Ashton sighed, hoping to suggest his sincere regret that he had ultimately had to abandon his initial hesitance, "Johnston finally agreed to back off his idiotic plan when I pointed out all of the potential problems. And I didn't want to look like I was playing politics on any issue that would threaten people's lives. But now that the boy and the old man are dead I can no longer stay silent about it. I am just so terribly sorry that I didn't make all of this public in time to prevent that tragedy. I guess I'm just going to have to live with this deep sense of regret for the rest of my term—or, rather, for 'the rest of my life,' if you decide to quote me on that. I would now like to offer my sincere condolences to the families of all of Johnston's victims."

"Well, Mr. Mayor, this certainly has been a very informative telephone call," Jeffries said, smiling in anticipation of the story that she was now about to write. "Would you care to add anything else?"

"No," Ashton concluded, with an unseen, self-satisfied smirk on his face. "I think that should just about do it."

Chapter Forty-One

THE FRONT PAGE

"Johnston."

"Have you seen it?"

"Good morning to you too, Jim," Dan Johnston said into his office telephone.

"Have you seen it?" Jim Farson repeated.

"If you're asking me if I've seen the front page of the newspaper, yes, I have," Johnston finally relented.

"I don't know about you, Danny boy," Farson said, "but I'm certain that I ended up on the wrong end of the shaft in that story."

"Same here," Johnston agreed. "It appears that our local mayor is not above playing politics in a matter involving public safety and the death of grizzlies."

"Can you believe he actually said all of that?"

"Well, it appears to me that all he did was to take everything that he's said and done over the past couple of weeks and simply turn it all around," Johnston pointed out. "Whatever he did, he said he didn't do; and whatever he didn't do, he said he did."

"And Jeffries bought it all."

"And Jeffries bought it all," Johnston again agreed. "Hook, line, and sinker. But I don't think Ms. Stop the Presses was just putting on paper what the mayor was saying aloud."

"What do you mean by that?" Farson asked.

"What I mean is, Ms. Jeffries may have been using the mayor almost as much as he was using her."

"You wanna explain that?" Farson asked, suddenly confused.

"Remember the girl reporter who smacked into the sheriff's deputy as she was coming off the Elk Refuge?"

"The Mason girl? Yeah. I knew her," Farson said, his curiosity aroused. "I never did figure out exactly what that accident was all about—but I thought something was funny when it was reported that she was driving at a high rate of speed."

"Well," Johnston said, "the official story—what you read in the newspapers—Is that she started to go out on the Refuge, illegally, to do a story, then had second thoughts and was high-tailing it off the Refuge when she plowed into the deputy."

"But that's not what actually happened?" Farson prompted.

"Not quite," Johnston informed him. "Do you remember us finding the body of the photographer—or pieces of it, anyway—after Jack Wilson was attacked?"

"Yeah," Farson recalled. "But that appeared to be a separate incident, unrelated to the Mason accident."

"Not quite," Johnston said again. "The way Jack Wilson and I got it figured, both the reporter and the photographer had been assigned to do a photo story that night by Jenny Jeffries, their editor. We have no doubt that they were both out on the Refuge together on some dumb-ass assignment that Jeffries either approved or assigned them."

"Aha," Farson said, picking up the implications. "The inky plot thickens. The photographer got attacked by a bear, and Mason saw it and panicked, causing her to have the car accident. Ms. Jeffries apparently has denied all culpability?"

"Right. When questioned by Jack Wilson, she denied ever having a father or a mother. Immaculate preconception, I believe they call it. She didn't make the assignment, didn't know they were going, didn't even know the photographer was missing in action the next day. Jack had already confirmed that the photographer was MIA before he talked to Jeffries. So if *he* knew it *she* must have known it, too. Other than being guilty as hell Ms. Jeffries appears to be completely innocent."

"I see," Farson observed. "So, when our illustrious mayor approached her yesterday with all of those lies about you and me she was just champing at the bit to print them."

"Redirection. Putting the heat on us would help to take the heat off her."

"You think there might be something going on between the lady editor and the mayor?" Farson asked.

"You mean something like a little hanky-panky?"

"Something like a little dipping of the proverbial dipstick."

"Who knows?" Johnston admitted. "One of Jack's deputies did say that he thinks there was something going on between

Jeffries and Ashton. But it doesn't really make much difference. Her story makes the two of us look like a couple of bureaucratic assholes, who are more concerned about protecting the legislated rights of a few misguided grizzlies than about protecting the public. The mayor, of course, comes out smelling like a rose, as the sole defender of all local citizens and/or voters. And Ms. Jeffries gets to shift any awkward questioning away from her own personal involvement and towards our respective motives."

"Glad I haven't been involved in all of this up until now," Farson said. "I can still place the blame for everything on you. After all, if you would have just shot those bastards when you first had your chance, none of this ever would have happened."

"Thanks for your support," Johnston sighed. "I probably should be packing my bags right now for reassignment to Alaska or somewhere else just as removed from civilization. I can probably count my days remaining in this position on my fingers alone, and that's with one hand tied behind my back."

"So what're we going to do about this evil person?" asked Farson.

"Are you referring to Ms Jeffries or the mayor?" Johnston asked.

"Take your pick," Farson advised. "As far as I'm concerned, one is just about as devious as the other."

"Well," Johnston admitted, "I don't think there's all that much that we *can* do about either one. We could try to go to the other paper with the real story, but it would all come down to our word against the mayor's—and you know who's going to lose that one. Or we could write a joint letter to the editor, but that would accomplish just about as much, even if they didn't decide to cut out every other word that we wrote 'in the interest of space and readability.'"

"Looks like we're pretty much screwed here," Farson concluded. "About the only thing we can do is hope that nothing else happens before the two bears that are left go back up to Yellowstone."

"That and maybe get our respective accounts of these recent events back to Washington before they get their bowels in an uproar," Johnston suggested.

"Already too late for that," Farson informed him.

"What do you mean?"

"I've already heard from my bosses in Washington," Farson revealed. "Got a top priority message this morning."

"Your bosses apparently work a lot faster than mine," Johnston conceded. "What'd they say?"

"That these grizzlies are still an endangered species, that I am to avoid interfering with them as long as they don't create any more people problems, and that I am specifically ordered to forget about finding them and shooting them without proper cause and prior consent."

Johnston paused for consideration. "Wonder if grizzlies like salt on their skiers?"

"I sure as hell hope we don't have to find out," Farson said.

Chapter Forty-Two

THE SKIERS

In 1939, Snow King Resort was the first mountain in Wyoming to have a ski lift. Today it has three lifts and a tow rope. Located in the Bridger-Teton National Forest, the resort operates under a renewable permit from the U. S. Forest Service and now has more than 400 acres of leased terrain available for day skiing, snowboarding, and even tubing. The resort also offers night skiing every Tuesday through Saturday on some 110 acres.

Snow King's longest run—about nine-tenths of a mile—rises 1,571 vertical feet from the valley floor and is situated among the 300 acres of terrain that the ski area regularly grooms. In addition to this run, known as Exhibition (the steepest in the nation), many other trails twist through clumps of trees on the world-famous mountain. There are runs with such names as Bearcat, Belly Roll, Cougar, Bighorn, Bison, Elk, Snake River, Ravine, and Grizzly.

Grizzly Run is challenge-rated as "Most Difficult"—second only to the "Experts Only" label slapped on Bearcat, Upper Exhibition, Belly Roll, and the East and West "S" Chutes. Along with its western neighbor Elk, Grizzly is the broadest run on the upper mountain and is bordered on the east by Cut Off, from which it is divided at only one point by a small stand of trees. Skiers coming off Saddle Cornice at the top of the mountain can choose between Elk, Grizzly, and the eastern-most Cut Off before encountering easier terrain at mid-mountain. Just east of Cut Off is the end of the area that is regularly monitored by the ski patrol, the beginning of the forest that is densely populated with spruce, Douglas fir, lodgepole pine, and an occasional aspen. Bear management specialists might look at this treed ski area boundary and view it an "edge."

Late Tuesday afternoon, a handful of juniors and seniors at Jackson Hole High School decided to go skiing that night on Snow King. It had been snowing almost constantly for the previous week, the King had opened early (as had the Village and "the 'ghee"), and this was to be the first night under the lights.

All of the teenagers had bought season passes for Snow King, and all had been smiling all week with the early snow that was pointing to a long winter with better-than-normal skiing on the town mountain. Several of them had first argued for purchasing season passes at Jackson Hole, where the runs were longer and more-challenging and the snow was always deeper. In the end, however, it was the opportunity to do some quick night skiing overlooking the town that brought the group to a consensus in favor of buying their passes to Snow King. The girls, especially, had wanted to ski the mountain at night with the town's fluorescent, incandescent, sodium, and neon lights glittering down below them, softened and spread by the reflective blanket of snow. Even halfway up the mountain it seemed that they could see forever up the long valley, with the Teton Range straight north of them, the Elk Refuge to the northeast, and millions of sparkling stars overhead. It was a very romantic setting, filled with all sorts of interesting possibilities and opportunities.

Jason Washburn was looking forward to taking advantage of those possibilities and opportunities. Now a senior, he had spent the better part of his junior year cultivating a relationship with Mellady Music, who was one year behind him. They had attended several JHHS football games (most of which the Broncs lost), taken in a lot of movies at the three cinemas in Jackson, spent many Saturdays together on the slopes, and had naturally gone to the prom together. Next year he would be gone, at some out-of-state school that offered a broader curriculum than he could find anywhere in Wyoming, and so would she. Now, already into November, he was running out of time. Jason had been making and refining his plans all this school year to get Mellady out of her underwear. His latest tactic was based on night skiing on Snow King.

They all went home to change clothes and to pick up their equipment after school let out at three-ten. Although night skiing would run from four to eight they had decided to meet at Snow King Center, the mountain's ice-skating rink, at five. With the change from Daylight Savings Time back to Mountain Standard in October it would just be getting dark.

Jason, naturally, offered to pick Mellady up in his battered Bronco. She was to be ready and waiting when he arrived at her South Park home.

"All set, babe?" Jason asked, as he met her halfway, on the snow-cleared sidewalk.

"Just have to pull my boots and skis out of the garage," she smiled in response. "I made us a Thermos of hot chocolate to take along."

"How are we going to carry a Thermos on the hill?" he grumbled. If anyone was going to carry it, it wasn't going to be him.

"It's a new soft-side design that collapses and expands as you fill it with something hot," she explained. "I got it last Saturday at Gart's. You wear it under your coat, front or back, and it helps keep you warm. I'm wearing it up front, to help keep my chest warm."

Lucky Thermos, Jason thought. We'll have to see if it can warm up two people at the same time.

They went into the heated garage and chose Mellady's equipment out of about ten pairs of skis and almost as many pairs of boots. In addition to all of the alpine skis there were skis and boots for cross-country, three snowmobiles, several pairs of ice skates, three or four pairs of snowshoes, and assorted other winter sports equipment.

"Did you say your dad's name was Jack Dennis?" Jason joked. "This place is starting to look like a sporting goods store. I think these skis are multiplying. Look at those little ones."

"Those are my sister's, silly," Mellady observed. "We just seem to accumulate these things. Half of this stuff is probably worn out or doesn't fit anyone in our family any more, but we never seem to be able to get rid of it."

"You oughta take it to the ski swap," Jason suggested. "Or just give it away, take it to Orville's, haul it to the recycling center, or something. Hey, I've got an idea. Why don't you put everything you don't need on "Trash and Treasure"? You could probably sell it for enough to get more."

"Smart ass," she said. "The last thing I want to do is get on the radio and hawk junk like some kind of used car salesman. I can't believe that people actually do that. Next you'll be wanting me to run for public office."

"Sure! Why not?" Jason speculated, completely missing her point. "Run for county commissioner or something and I'll be your campaign manager. 'Vote for Mellady. Not Your Everyday Office Music.' "

She wasn't amused. She had been hearing such jokes about her name for the past sixteen years. "Are you ready to leave?" she asked, sounding a note of discord in the tone of her voice. He was, and they did.

All but two of them had assembled in the Snow King Center parking lot by the appointed hour of five, had unloaded their equipment, had located their laminated badges, and were only awaiting the others when one of the three cellular phones that they had brought with them began beeping. In a confused search that involved flying gloves and questions about whose phone was doing the beeping the call was finally answered. It was the missing couple, who had decided to go see the latest blockbuster at the Movieworks theater instead of coming with them.

"Just that much more uncut snow for the rest of us," one of them observed.

It was only a short walk to the bottom of the Cougar triple chair lift, which would take them as far up the mountain as they could go at night. Farther east, the Rafferty chair lift was also running, giving them most of the mountain to play on. To the west, the Summit lift that took skiers all the way from the bottom of the mountain, at 6,237 feet, to the top of Exhibition, at 7,808 feet, was already shut down for the day.

In twos they rode to the top of Cougar, hopped off, and skied down Cougar, Bighorn, Bison, Lower Elk, and Kelly's Alley. Some of them transversed Old Man's Flats and Old Lady's Flats, and came down Re-Turn Trail, to catch Rafferty for a ride back up the mountain. Although the snow was still falling, and the distant Tetons were all but invisible, the glowing, multi-colored lights, the bluish and greenish fluorescents, and the orange sodium lights of the town, along with those on the mountain itself, created a winter wonderland.

It was almost eight fifteen when Jason asked Mellady if she wanted to ride up Cougar once more, take one of the cat tracks over to Elk or Grizzly, and make a final run down Kelly.

"Are we allowed to do that?" Mellady questioned. "It's above the lights."

"No problem," Jason assured her. "We can still see well enough to ski. We'll have the upper runs all to ourselves."

"Well, okay, if you're sure we won't get in trouble," Mellady agreed, but still dubious.

"Great," Jason said, seeing his hopes and wet-dreams take shape. "We'll slip off our skis at the top of Cougar and walk over to Elk." They stood on the lift platform, looking backward over their shoulder, as the chair came up behind them and scooped them off their feet, while the lift attendant lowered the restraining bar. They began to climb.

Less than ten minutes later they were sliding down the lift exit chute. They began skiing eastward, along the edge of the trees, until a cat track joined the Slow Trail at a slight upward angle. As soon as the uphill skiing began to get difficult Jason stopped and said it was time to remove their skis and proceed on foot.

"I hope you know what you're doing," Mellady said, with continued uncertainty.

"Count on it," Jason replied, with a smile.

It was only a short transverse to the wide Elk run, but when they got there Jason said he would rather continue on over to Grizzly. Since the sideways walking was fairly easy, even in the still-accumulating snow, Mellady consented to accompany him.

When they got to Grizzly it was just a short distance more to Cut Off, through the small clump of trees, and Jason's urging soon convinced Mellady to join him on the King's eastern-most high-mountain run. Arriving at the middle of Cut Off Mellady quickly noticed Jason's hesitance to re-mount his skis.

"What's wrong?" she asked, seeing nothing that would keep them from putting on their skis and starting their final run.

"Mellady, isn't it beautiful up here?" Jason asked, edging closer to her.

"Really," she concurred, sensing something strange in his voice. "But what's the matter? Why aren't you getting into your skis?"

"What's the rush?" Jason asked. "There's still plenty of time to get down the mountain. Why don't we just enjoy this magic moment?"

"This isn't like you, Jason," Mellady asserted. "Something's going on here. Why are you coming up with all of these movie lines? Are you trying to seduce me?"

"Do you want to be seduced?" he asked.

"Well," she admitted, "yeah. Eventually. Probably. Some day. I don't know. Jeez, do we have to talk about this right now?"

"Can you think of a better time? Look at the stars, the lights, the snow. This is a regular winter wonderland. Doesn't it make you just want to take off all of your clothes and make love?"

"Are you nuts?" Mellady asked. "You can't do something like that here!"

"Why not? Who's going to complain? How many other people do you see around here?"

"What if some ski patrol guy came through here to check the mountain and saw us? We'd probably lose our passes—at least! Besides, it would be cold—and wet! Look at it snowing!"

"The snow will make it even better. And you could even keep your collapsible Thermos warmer on," he suggested.

"You're joking. And I'm seriously not going to do this."

"Look, we could go over there in those trees, just inside them, where the snow is probably not so deep, and it would probably be warmer. We could use our jackets and pants to lie on, and cover up with the rest of our clothes."

"You're really serious about this, aren't you?" she asked, trying to see through the entire scheme. She paused and thought a moment. "Have I been set up?"

"A little," he admitted. "I just wanted to make love to you in a beautiful setting. I thought this would be a perfect place. C'mon, Mellady, you know we're going to do it sooner or later."

"Well, I wasn't thinking about doing it tonight, up here on the middle of the mountain, in the woods, in a snowstorm," she assured him. She gave some more thought to the proposition. She had to admit that it did sound exciting. And he was right about them doing it sooner or later. She had even come close a couple of times to suggesting it herself. It might not be all that bad, actually, if certain rules were followed. "Do you...do you ...even have any protection with you? God, I can't believe I'm even considering this."

"Wouldn't leave home without it," Jason smiled, sensing her about to cave-in. "I haven't done this with anyone else, of course, but I brought two, just in case one breaks."

"I thought that was the whole idea," she said. "They aren't supposed to break. If we're seriously going to do this—and I'm not saying we are—you'd better put one on top of the other. Maybe the cold temperature makes them brittle."

"Anything you say, babe," Jason offered, smiling broadly.

"And don't call me 'babe' any more," she chastised him. "I never did like that."

"Wouldn't think of it," he said, starting for the edge of the trees. "Well, Mellady, my love, are you ready to make a little music?"

"I knew you were going to say that," she said, shaking her head. "I just knew it." She tried to walk in his footsteps as they went towards the woods.

"How's this?" Jason asked, as he looked around for a spot with less snow. They were about thirty feet inside the tree line. The mountain lights below them, as well as those of the town, were still visible, casting the first few yards or so of the forest in twilight. Although the skiers down the mountain were making gay noises as they enjoyed this first night of skiing on Snow King the snow-filled air was absorbing nearly all of the sound before it reached them. But in the branches above, the light wind was causing a whisper. Some of the falling snow was being blocked by the branches and fir needles. The trees must have been generating heat, because it felt a bit warmer.

"It looks like somebody's already been here," Mellady observed. "Look how mashed down the snow is. I don't think we should do this. We'd better just go back."

"Aw, c'mon, Mel," Jason pleaded. "We're here, and there's nobody around. This is probably where an elk or a moose was lying down."

"Well, what if the elk or the moose decides to come back? What are we supposed to do? Climb a tree naked? Or just put on our boots and take off down the mountain that way?"

"Aren't you being a little over-dramatic?" he asked. "Nothing's going to happen. Trust me."

"Where have I heard that one before?" she replied. "Okay, let's just get this over with." Having made the decision to "do it," she began removing her clothes. His jacket was already on the ground, and he placed hers alongside it. The bed continued to be made with his pants and hers.

"Do we really have to remove all of our clothes?" she asked. "It's too cold. And it's still snowing. We'll get wet."

"Not under our blanket of clothes. The friction alone will keep us warm and dry. Besides, I want to see you completely naked," he said. "Of course, you get to see me the same way. I think it would be kind of stupid to do it with some of your clothes on. Like fucking a sock."

"I wish you wouldn't use those words," she said. "You don't have to try to impress me with dirty language. I'm already doing this, although I'm not sure why. And another thing...."

"What?"

"Have you really ever fucked a sock?"

They shared the laugh, and removed their final articles of clothing, piece by piece.

"Well, that's about all I have," Mellady said, handing him her panties. "What you see is what you get. What do you think, lover boy?"

"I like what I see," Jason declared. "I can't believe we've never gone this far before."

"At least not in reality," she admitted, with a smirk. "Are you gonna save those shorts for a souvenir, or are you going to take them off and give them to me?"

"Sorry." He quickly slipped off the shorts and handed them over. "Don't lose them; they're the only pair I've got."

"Actually, I was thinking about taking them home with me, and saving them as a memento. It would be a fair trade for mine, which I assume you're going to keep. Is that a banana growing out of your groin, or are you just happy to see me?" She reached down and encircled it with her hand, and used it to pull him down to their makeshift bed. "Let's see if we can find some place to put this thing. What did you do with the condoms?"

He never had a chance to answer. Before he knew it the grizzly was upon them, flailing its massive arms and launching deadly assaults with its jaws and teeth. One of the grizzly's first swipes struck Mellady smoothly on her upper back and spun her headfirst across the snow. One of its first bites caught Jason around the neck, tearing flesh, muscle, and bone, completely severing the carotid artery. As he quickly bled to death, Jason didn't even feel the pain as first one arm and then the other was ripped from his body, and the stiletto-sharp claws disemboweled and nearly decapitated him. Some twenty feet away, as she lay in the cold, wet snow, Mellady regained consciousness, saw what was happening, and began climbing the nearest tree, stunned, scared, shaking, and completely naked.

It snowed on Snow King Mountain all night long, the kind of dry, fluffy snow that turns the malleable minds of young avid skiers and snowboarders into marshmallows. The wind blew gently through the trees, causing minor drifts at the base of each tree and on the leeward side of every rock. Lower down the mountain, a dense morning fog filled the colder valley air. And some thirty feet beyond the forest edge of Cut Off Run, Mellady Music sat alone near the top of a spruce tree, battered, bruised, and still stark-naked, watching the sleeping bear. For most of the night, she had witnessed the grizzly rip and tear apart Jason's body, eating it piece by piece. At first she had screamed, at a volume that was quickly lowered by the falling snow, and had tried to look away from the ghastly feast, to imagine that all of this was not really happening. And then she had vomited. She had soon lost her voice, and between the semi-screaming and the vomiting and the cold dry air, her throat was now raw. She was cold, and sticky, and itchy on her chest and legs, where she had scraped her skin while shimmying up the tree. But mostly it was her back that hurt, where the bear had slapped her with its paw, probably saving her life by knocking her out and tumbling her some twenty feet away from Jason. She thought she may have one or two broken ribs. She had a major headache. And she had to pee again. There was already an irregular icy trail below her in the branches where she had reluctantly but uncontrollably gone once before, but the unseen yellow holes in the snow on the ground had been concealed by the new white flakes that were still falling. Her stringy hair and icy skin were almost completely covered by snow, but she had intentionally let it build up on her, and she had tried to avoid knocking any of it off, knowing instinctively that it was only the cold but insulating blanket of snow covering her that would help her avoid freezing to death during the night.

She had survived the night.

Now, through reddened eyes, iced nearly closed with tears, Mellady Music looked around the bloody pink-and-white scene of the massacre as the sun started rising southeast of Snow King and the details half-hidden by darkness became clearer in the growing light. It was possible, she thought, that they would find some of Jason's body, eventually, but not very likely. For most of the night, in the dimmest light, she had watched the bear consume all the soft body parts. And in the silence of that night, spared only by the wind whispering through the trees, she had heard the repeated breaking and crunching of Jason's bones in the jaws of the bruin.

Chapter Forty-Three

THE NAKED AND THE DEAD

It had finally stopped snowing in the Jackson Hole valley early that morning, but the dark grey cumulus cloud front to the west confirmed the "Weather Channel" reports that more snow was expected later in the day. Crews had worked all night clearing the streets of Jackson and the state and county highways. Traffic was flowing on almost all major arteries except Teton Pass and through the Snake River Canyon, although it moved everywhere at a snail's pace.

There had been several "sun dogs" in the eastern sky that morning—more than anyone could remember seeing at one time—as the rising sun tried its best to shine through the clouds that still covered the mountains and valley. In the valley itself, due to the typical air inversion, it was colder than on the mountains, so a dense fog had drifted about most of the morning, until the warming air had finally burned it all away.

Marty Watson was sitting at his desk in second-period calculus, trying to make any sense at all of what his instructor was writing on the board, when Jackson Hole High School Principal Ben Capistrano entered the room, walked up to the class instructor, and whispered something to him. The instructor pointed towards Marty, and Capistrano began walking towards him.

"Will you please come with me?" Capistrano asked as he walked by Marty's desk. He fully expected Marty to comply with his request, so he continued to leave the room, without even looking back.

What the hell have I done now? Marty wondered. Shaking his head in mock disgust for the benefit of all around him, he arose and followed Capistrano out the door, into the hall.

"I understand you were with a group of juniors and seniors last night at Snow King," Capistrano said.

"Yeah," Marty admitted, not quite certain how that could be considered some sort of crime against humanity. "There were six or eight of us. We had a good time. The powder was awesome."

"I'm glad," Capistrano lied, disinterested. "Were Mellady Music and Jason Washburn with you?"

"Yeah, they were," Marty conceded, still not quite able to figure out what was going on. "Jason brought them in his Bronco. I made a couple of runs with them. What's the problem?"

"The problem, Mr. Watson," Capistrano said, "is that neither Mellady nor Jason came home last night. Both their parents have called the school wondering if anyone here has seen them. I understand the sheriff and police departments have also been advised of their disappearance. We are asking around, trying to help locate them. Do you know anything about this?"

"No, sir," Marty said, relieved that he didn't seem to be in any trouble. "I haven't seen them this morning, but come to think of it, I don't remember seeing them in the parking lot when we all left to go home."

"None of your other friends does either," Capistrano informed him. "As best anyone can determine, they never came down off the mountain. And Jason's Bronco is still in the Snow King parking lot. We have been trying to determine if they might have gotten a ride home with someone else."

"Why would they stay up there all night on the mountain?" Marty asked.

"That's what we have to find out," Capistrano said. "Okay, you can go back to class. Let me know if you think of anything that might help us find them."

"Sure thing," Marty promised. He went back to calculus, hoping that the interruption would have given him some magical insight into the chicken scratches on the board. It didn't.

"Dave?"

"Well, what do you have for me, Benny? Did any of the kids come up with anything about them?" Dave Hamilton spoke into the telephone handset.

"Complete blank," Capistrano said. "Apparently none of them saw them come down off the mountain. We're pretty certain that Mellady and Jason didn't catch a ride home with any of them."

"Very strange," the deputy sheriff observed. "We haven't tried to start the Bronco to see if it had a mechanical problem, because we may have to consider it the scene of a crime. We've got it taped off until we figure out what's going on."

"Has anyone searched the mountain?" Capistrano asked.

"We're getting ready to do that right now," Hamilton reported. "We were just waiting to see if your people got anything we could use from interviewing the other kids before we started out. We've scanned the runs with binoculars as best we could to see if anything showed up, but that was a complete waste of time. And we've had the ski patrol looking around and asking the early skiers to report anything they see. So far no one has found anything at all. Of course, it was snowing all night, so maybe something got covered up. But it looks like we're going to have to begin searching all of the wooded areas."

"Well, good luck," Capistrano offered. "Let me know if there's anything else that we can do here."

"I will, Benny," Hamilton said, already rising to leave his desk. "Thanks for your help."

They had assembled at the Snow King Center, as many sheriff's deputies, Jackson police officers, and Snow King ski patrollers as they could pull together on short notice. Some were sporting skis, others were carrying various wood and metal snowshoes, a few had nothing at all to support them on the fresh snow; they would be the searchers riding in the tracked vehicles that were used to groom the mountain.

"Okay," Dave Hamilton opened. "Let's get started. Can everyone gather round the map?" They all drew closer.

"There's a slim chance that these people are somewheres on these runs," Hamilton said, pointing to the various runs that had been opened for night skiing. "But it's more likely that they are in one of these wooded areas. What we are going to do is start over here on the east side of Summit and make a sweep of the trees from up here along Slow Trail all the way to the base of the mountain. We'll go all the way over to the patrolled area boundary. There are enough of us that we should be able to cover the whole area in one sweep, but we'll have to make a special effort to check out any lumps under the snow that might be bodies. We're going to take our time and do this right the first time. Any questions?"

"What if they went up above Slow Trail?" asked one of the ski patrollers.

"They could have done that, I suppose," Hamilton contemplated. "But right now we're just going to concentrate on the area that was lit up. Hopefully, we'll find them there. But if we have to go higher up the mountain we'll do that. Any other questions?" There were none.

The search began, with a string of men and women spread out over 600 feet from mid-mountain to the base, proceeding slowly and carefully through both the wooded areas and the broad open runs. They were finding nothing to suggest that Mellady and Jason had even been on the mountain. As they approached the eastern patrol area boundary there were grumblings and comments about being on a wild goose chase, and not a few observations about where a couple of high school youngsters who were well-known to be very close friends might have gone to shack up for the night.

The searchers reassembled at the lower end of Ravine Run, and Hamilton again addressed them.

"Does anyone have anything at all to report?" Hamilton questioned. "See anything at all that might have looked suspicious?" There were no responses, not even the discovery of a piece of clothing or an abandoned ski that could still be checked out.

"Okay," Hamilton sighed. "It looks like we're going to have to do the upper part of the mountain."

- BEAR EDGES -

"I can't believe they would have gone up there," one of the police officers said. "Most of the upper mountain is woods, except for Grizzly and Elk, and there's no reason they would have fought the snow to go uphill on skis. If anything, they might have thought about climbing up to the top of Grizzly or Elk to ski those runs."

"That's why we are going to reverse our search pattern this time," Hamilton replied. "We'll start in the trees at the eastern boundary and work our way across Cut Off, Grizzly, and Elk, before we get into all of those trees and cat tracks further west. Okay, let's form a line along the eastern boundary. We'll take the vehicles highest up, and those of you on skis can be in the middle, with the people on snowshoes taking the lower end, up to about this area of Cats where the trees start. Any questions?" Again there were none. The snowshoers began climbing, the skiers started off towards Rafferty to catch a ride up the mountain, and the groom vehicles headed back up Ravine, to Cats, where they would turn west onto Slow Trail and follow the edge of the trees up to the top of Cut Off.

It was beginning to snow again, the dry, powdery kind of snow that doesn't melt when it lands on mere lukewarm surfaces, that tends to cover all things animate and inanimate with a soft blanket of white flakes of amorphous unity. The second search had begun, with everyone at the eastern patrol border. Almost all of the searchers were now in the trees. Those in the groom vehicles had been forced temporarily to abandon them and go back into the trees on foot. Everyone was either walking or skiing west now, parallel to the base of the mountain.

Dave Hamilton was on the search line in the trees just east of Cut Off, where the East "S" Chute spills skiers into it. Only one

THE NAKED AND THE DEAD

other man, another deputy sheriff, was higher than he was. To Hamilton's right a Jackson police officer was next in line, and then another deputy lower down.

They had walked only a few feet when Hamilton thought he heard whimpering, almost similar to that of a pup or a kitten. The wind in the trees and the falling snow were dampening any sounds, so he couldn't be sure he had even heard anything. But then he heard it again.

"Listen!" Hamilton commanded of anyone who could hear him. "Stop walking and keep quiet a minute!" The other close-by searchers complied.

"I hear it too," said the patrolman next to him. "What the hell is that? And where is it coming from? I can't see a damned thing."

"Just listen," Hamilton ordered. "Try to pinpoint the source of the sound." The whimpering continued.

"Got it!" the patrolman shouted. "Over here! There's something up in one of the trees, but it's all covered with snow. It looks like...Jeezus! It's the girl! She's sitting up in this tree!"

"Hamilton to all searchers!" he shouted into his radio. "Hold in place. We have something here. We're checking it out." The searchers in the immediate area converged on the police patrolman, who was already beginning to climb the tree.

"Hold on, Mellady," the patrolman said, "I'm coming to help you. Hold on." She continued to whine as though she wasn't even aware of his presence. She didn't move an inch, except to shiver convulsively.

As the patrolman approached her through the branches, about twenty feet off the ground, he could see the bare skin and fine hairs on the downside of her torso, and could tell immediately that she was completely naked.

"What the hell?" he asked himself. He approached her cautiously, realizing that she must be in shock, and that any sudden move on his part might scare her and cause her to fall out of the tree. Before he attempted to touch her, or say anything else he got himself well braced to catch her if she bolted. It was a good decision.

"Mellady?" he asked, with as much tenderness as he could put into his voice. Who knows what this girl has been through, he thought. "Mellady? We're here to help you." She suddenly became aware of his presence—or of a presence, because her delirium did not allow her to recognize anything except possible danger. She started flailing her arms, causing an avalanche of snow to fall on the searchers below, and tried to kick the threat away with repeated thrusts. The patrolman grabbed her and held her.

"I'm going to need some help up here!" the patrolman shouted. "Someone climb up and help me with her! Get a blanket or something to cover her up! She doesn't have a stitch of clothes on her body!" She continued to fight him. "This girl is out of her mind."

A sheriff's deputy scrambled up the tree while another ran out of the trees to the groom vehicle to get blankets or whatever he could find to wrap around her. By the time he got back to the base of the tree the other two rescuers had her down to the ground. She was shaking violently, involuntarily, even with the patrolman's warm jacket wrapped around her. Her skin was as white as the snow she had shed. They quickly also wrapped her in the two blankets the deputy had found, and then rolled a canvas tarp around those.

"We've got to get her to the hospital as soon as possible," Hamilton said. "Joe, you and Frank go with the vehicle to get her down the mountain. I'll radio ahead for an ambulance to meet you at the bottom. We'll continue looking around for Jason. Get going!"

"Ju ... Ju ... Ju ... Jason," Mellady whispered, barely able to talk. Her eyes were almost completely iced shut. Her hair was tubed in ice. Her whole body was caked in ice, where the first snow that had fallen on her had melted on her skin, and was quickly covered with more. "Buu...buu...buu...buu...bear."

They were all listening to her weak effort to tell them what had happened. As soon as they heard that complete word, they all knew as much as they needed to know.

"Get your guns out!" Hamilton ordered. "Keep your eyes open! Don't shoot unless you know what you're shooting at! But don't let that bastard surprise you!" He pulled out his radio. "Hamilton to all searchers. We have found the girl. Repeat, we have found the girl. She's alive, but almost frozen. She was up in a tree, apparently trying to get away from a bear. I think the bear must have got the boy. Get your guns out and keep alert. If you don't have a gun, get close to someone who does. The boy's body is probably up here somewhere, and we're going to take a look around, but everybody do a search in the trees, working your way up the mountain towards us. We're bringing the girl down the mountain in the groomer." As soon as he got that message across Hamilton switched channels on his radio and called the sheriff's office to tell them what had happened, and to summon an ambulance.

With the girl gone, they began kicking through the snow, looking for her clothes and the boy's body. They could understand finding her in a tree—each of them would have tried to climb one himself if he had been attacked by a grizzly and had enough time. But her absolute nakedness had them all puzzled. Could a grizzly have torn off every stitch of her clothes and left no major marks? Not very likely. Had she become disoriented and thrown her clothes a piece at a time at the bear to deter it from coming up the tree after her? Again, not very likely. Grizzlies can't climb trees. And besides, they could not find a single piece of her clothing at the base of the tree. Had she spent the entire night in the tree, with nothing to protect her against the cold and the snow? Almost certainly. They were amazed that she was still alive. They expanded their search area, making a thirty-foot circular sweep.

"Oh, God," one of the deputies said, as his boots stirred the new-fallen snow away from a bloody mess below. "I think I've found him. There's blood all over this place, under the snow." They all converged on the deputy, and began brushing snow away from the bloodiest area with their boots.

"Look carefully for anything you can identify," Hamilton said. "Try not to step on any of his remains."

Using their boots, arms, and any branches that they could swing, they cleared the pinkish snow away from the apparent site of the attack as best they could. New snow was still falling, quickly changing the uncovered crimsons to white. They found a pile of clothes, and two sets of skis and boots, apparently those of both Mellady and Jason. They did not find Jason's body.

"Is this a skull?" one of them asked another, pointing down.

"Part of one," came the reply, as they stared in awe.

Chapter Forty-Four

THE ſPECIAL EDITION

The first night skiing of the year at Snow King had been on Tuesday. The naked girl and the dead boy's remains had been found on Wednesday. Both weekly newspapers in Jackson came out on Wednesday—too late to contain the news about the finding of Mellady and the discovery of Jason's remains. Jenny Jeffries decided that a special edition of the newspaper was warranted, to appear on Thursday morning.

Special editions, due to their cost, effort, and difficulty in preparation, are usually avoided by most newspaper editors and publishers. That's why they are special; they are reserved for only the worst tragedies, like the assassination of the President, or the most critical public warnings, like the unnecessary and somewhat disingenuous advice to duck when a once-in-a-million-millenia asteroid is discovered careening towards earth at forty-one zillion miles per hour and Bruce Willis is off somewhere beyond reach on vacation.

So it was no minor matter for Jeffries to assemble her staff and tell them to begin preparing copy and artwork for the special edition. The lead story, of course, would be the news itself about Jason Washburn and Mellady Music. Jeffries would write a front-page editorial pointing the finger of blame at Johnston and Farson again and demanding that federal officials augment their efforts in disposing of the two remaining grizzlies. Several sidebars and large photos would fill up the front page and jump inside. Any other local news that hadn't made it into the regular weekly pages also would be included. The remainder of the space would be filled with the normal display ads, classified ads, Associated Press stories, and the more-challenging material like a crossword puzzle, a daily horoscope, and some comics. Various staffers were given special assignments on top of their normal duties. They would be pressed for time, she told them, but that was the nature of the "special edition" beast.

While the others began to work on their own assignments Jeffries closed the door to her office, sat down at her desk, and began to think about what she wanted to say in the editorial. The most important thing, of course, would be to rake Johnston, Farson, and maybe even Wilson over the coals for allowing the situation to get out of hand. It was Johnston's manipulation that had allowed the bears to get off the refuge—after killing Joe and causing Cindy's death. It was Farson's misguided attempt to protect the grizzlies and not the public under the Endangered Species Act that had resulted in the death of the old man and the bear-suited boy. There seemed to be some confusion about the Music/Washburn incident—why they were even up there where they shouldn't have been, and why she was completely naked—but that, too, could be blamed on Farson, since Snow King was actually leased property in Bridger-Teton National Forest. If the bear hadn't been there it wouldn't have happened. She would have to portray Music and Washburn as innocent skiers—maybe dumb as hell for doing what they apparently did, but still completely innocent.

It was going to be tough to find a way to blame Wilson for any of this, since he really wasn't running the sheriff's office during his recovery and would have a certain public sympathy going for him after being mauled. But she was aching to get back at the bastard for privately insinuating that she—more than anyone else alive—had been responsible for the deaths of Cindy and Joe. That was true, of course, but there wasn't anything that she could do about it now, so why not just let it drop? So far, Wilson had apparently kept his conclusions to himself, but who could know when he might make them public? Could he have enough evidence to go to the county prosecutor and get charges filed against her? With what evidence? The evidence had to be circumstantial at best. Wilson couldn't have anything to link her directly to the assignment. And what charges could he file? Felonious Assignment? Reckless Reporting? Animal Photography in the First Degree? He had nothing. Well, he did still have Joe's camera—and was holding it for evidence—but what did that prove? Not a damned thing, unless....the film. Shit. What could be on the film? Bear shots, maybe. Elk. General refuge shots. Maybe nothing at all. Who knows what that idiot Dean got on film? But how could that incriminate her? It couldn't. Let them go ahead and process the film, if they even think about it. Nothing on it to concern her.

Cindy. She always had that damned tape recorder. Did Cindy have it running when they were getting the assignment? If so, there would be Jenny's own voice to incriminate her, telling them, yeah, okay, go out on the refuge against federal law and get yourself killed. Send the newspaper the bill. I'll make sure it gets paid. No problem. Big problem. That could be a very sticky wicket. But Wilson didn't say anything about finding Cindy's tape recorder in the burned car. And even if they had it there's no certainty that Cindy had recorded her voice. And even if she had recorded anything the fire had probably melted the tape and the recorder along with it. End of story.

Jeffries breathed a sigh of relief, having finally concluded that there was no way that she could be blamed for anything that had happened. So, if she personally couldn't be blamed, then someone else could be. That was a basic principle of editorial writing. She set her fingers on the keyboard, started a fresh file, and began writing her editorial.

Chapter Forty-Five

THE TAPE

Margie Larrimer tried to avoid going into her son's bedroom. It wasn't that she was afraid of what she might find, but that she simply wanted to give Tommy some space that he could call his own, a place where he could have room to think, and room to grow. Since her husband John's tragic death, their only child had been having some tough problems adjusting to the situation—as had she. It wasn't easy being a single mom.

Still, the room had to be cleaned, Tommy's clothes had to be gathered up for washing and ironing, and there was always a need for general straightening. Young boys weren't famous for maintaining spotless bedrooms. But then, neither were young girls.

Margie had spent almost a half-hour in Tommy's room, cleaning and straightening while he was at school, when she discovered the microcassette recorder. She was puzzled. What was a ten-year-old doing with a microcassette recorder? Where had he gotten it? When? How had he paid for it? It was a Panasonic model, with voice activation and two speeds. There was a tape in it.

She had some reluctance about playing the tape. To begin with, she felt that her son had a right to some privacy. By playing the tape in his absence, she would be invading that privacy—violating his implied trust. On the other hand, maybe she really needed to know his private thoughts—if they were even recorded—how he was adapting to being the only child of a single parent, so that she might be able to help him with any developing problems. If she didn't really know those innermost thoughts, how could she help him? Playing the tape without his knowledge would give her the advantage of having an insight that she would not otherwise be able to obtain. Ultimately, it would be good for both of them, would help bring them closer together. She decided to play the tape.

The cassette was not rewound, and she first had to figure out which way to move the slide switch to rewind it. Then she was confused by the single arrow on the volume control/voice sensitivity wheel. Did it increase the voice activation sensitivity or increase the volume when you spun the wheel to the right? Or vice-versa? As the tape ended its rewind, and she found which button to push to make it play, she spun the wheel left and right to adjust the volume.

What she heard made no sense. First there was a man talking—maybe a public official, whose voice was vaguely familiar—but he seemed to be discussing politics, or town administration. Why would Tommy have recorded that? And then there was the voice of a woman, probably one in her late teens or early twenties, recording notes like—a reporter? Then there was a confusing conversation involving several people, like they were in some sort of office. There were sounds of typing in the background. People talking on telephones. Newspaper terms like "copy," "head," "take," and "deadline." Definitely a newspaper office. And then she could make out a door shutting. Whoever was carrying the tape recorder had gone into an office and shut the door. There was more than one person in there. Two, the woman and a man, probably young. No, wait, here's another woman, about the same age as the first. Bears. Elk refuge. They're talking about the bears on the elk refuge, about going out to do a story on them. The one woman is giving them the assignment. The other woman is hesitant, and not quite sure that it's a good idea. The man—the man seems to be a photographer—says it will beat the competition. What does that mean? Who is the competition? The one woman agrees. Wow! Some language this woman is using to describe the competition. Did Tommy hear all of this? He must have. Now the woman is insisting that the other woman do the story. Important for her career. The photographer thinks it will get them a Pulitzer. Pulitzer Prize? I've heard of that.

Wait a minute. Margie stopped the tape recorder. This doesn't belong to Tommy. This tape recorder belongs to the woman reporter who was killed up the street as she was coming out of the elk refuge. It must have fallen out of her car when she had the accident. Tommy must have found it at the scene of the accident.

Margie put the tape recorder in a pocket, planning to ask Tommy about it when he got home from school, and continued cleaning, thinking off and on the rest of the afternoon about the contents of the tape. What else was on there? She wondered. She hadn't even played the tape halfway through. Maybe, she decided, it was better not to know.

"Tommy," Margie Larrimer asked her son that night at dinner, "where did you get that tape recorder?"

"Aw, Mom," he said, feeling reprimanded, "I didn't do anything wrong."

"I didn't say you did anything wrong," she said. "I was just wondering where you found the tape recorder. You did find it, didn't you?"

"Yeah," he admitted. "It was in the ditch up at the end of the street. I was just looking around where they had the car accident, and I found it."

"Did you listen to the tape?"

"Not at first," he said. "The batteries were completely run down. I had to get new ones. I think it belonged to the reporter girl and she was recording on it when she got in the accident. It probably fell out of her car. It just kept on recording until the batteries died."

"I see," Margie said. "So you've heard the whole tape?"

"Yeah, Mom, it's really neat! There's this bunch of reporters talking. And then there's some woman talking to herself about the bears on the refuge and how she shouldn't have done something. And then you even hear the crash! Awesome! And then there are ambulances and sirens, and people talking about the crash. It's great!"

"Tommy, this is something that the sheriff's department and police need to have," she pointed out, gently. "It's called evidence. You should have told me immediately about finding this."

"Am I going to go to jail?" he asked. "I'm really sorry."

"I know," she said, trying hard not to smile. "No, you aren't going to jail. The only thing you did wrong was not tell me about this. But that's not a federal crime—not yet, anyway. But we do need to take this up to the sheriff's office and give it to them right after dinner. You should be the one to do it because you're the one who found it. But I'll go with you."

"Aw, gee, Mom, can't we just give them the tape and let me keep the recorder?" he pleaded. "After all, I had to buy the batteries. If I didn't buy the batteries, we wouldn't have heard the tape."

"We'll see," she said. "Now finish your meatloaf."

Chapter Forty-Six

THE EVIDENCE

"Hello?" Jane Johnston answered their home phone.

"Jane, how are you? This is Jack Wilson."

"I recognized your voice, Jack," she replied. "I'm doing fine. How are you getting along with your bear wounds?"

"Oh, I get some chest pains every once in a while, but nothing real major," he admitted. "Just the skin healin' up. But thank you for askin'. Is Dan there?"

"Just came home a few minutes ago. Hold the phone and I'll go get him. Tell Edna I said hello."

"Will do," he promised, although Jane had already left to get her husband. He could hear her in the background telling him who it was. A few seconds later Dan was on the phone.

"How are you doing, Jack? I've been meaning to call to see if you ever got that bear over to Norris Brown's."

"Coupla days ago. I had to let Dave Hamilton carve off as many steaks as he could get in his freezer in return for haulin' it out."

"He said you were going to let him do that," Dan recalled. "I'm not sure the meat would still be good after the bear lay there for more than a day, but if Dave doesn't get sick from eating it I might ask him for a cut or two."

"You do that," Wilson advised. "I'm sure he'll be more 'n happy to share it with you."

"What's up?" Dan prompted. "Surely you didn't call just to talk about bear meat."

"Well, in a way I did," Wilson reported. "I thought you might be interested in hearin' a micracassette tape that just came in our possession. I was just listenin' to it with Dave. It has to do with bears and reporters and photographers and editors—even car crashes."

"Are you talking about what I think you're talking about?" Dan toyed.

"I guess that depends on what you think I'm talkin' about," the sheriff replied. "But I think we're on the same wavelength. Anyway, I thought you and Jane might want to drop by for some dessert, and listen to the tape. If you've already eaten, Edna made some of her famous huckleberry pie this afternoon."

"Well," Dan admitted, "I just got home, so I haven't eaten, but Jane's got dinner on the table. Can it wait for about an hour? Then I'm sure Jane would enjoy coming over and chomp on pie with Edna while you and I play the tape."

"Fine," Wilson assured him. "I'm not goin' anywhere in my condition. I'll have Edna put on a fresh pot of coffee to go with the pie. See you in about an hour or so."

"Count on it, Jack," Dan said. "Sounds to me like this is one performance I don't want to miss." He hung up the phone and went into the kitchen to tell Jane about their new dessert plans.

It was about forty-five minutes later when the Johnstons arrived at the Wilsons. As promised, Edna had made a fresh pot of coffee, and she had already sliced four pieces of huckleberry pie, which she served on her best bone china.

"Wow," Jane exclaimed as they entered the dining room. "What's the special occasion?"

"Special guests get special treatment," Edna smiled. "This is just some old stuff that's been lying around—for about a hundred and fifty years. It belonged to a distant aunt who was one of the first settlers in this area. It's a family heirloom. If you break it, I'll have to kill you."

"I'll bet," Jane laughed. "You have to be crazy to even put something like this on the table when Dan's around. At home, we call him Mr. Fumbles."

"I appreciate you, too," Dan contributed, mocking his offense. "At least they only call me that during the football season. But it could be worse. They could call me Dennis Miller."

"*Monday Night Football* sure ain't what it used to be," Wilson shook his head. "Next they'll be bringin' in a song-and-dance man to entertain us during the instant replays."

"I thought that's what they'd done already," Johnston rejoined.

"Good point," Wilson agreed. "Well, if we don't tear into Edna's huckleberry pie before long, I'm goin' to starve to death. Coffee?"

"Sure," Jane said. "Let me get it."

"Has to be better than that coffee you have at the office," Dan said almost simultaneously. "I wouldn't give that stuff to a horse!"

"Me neither," Wilson assured him. "The good stuff we save for the horses. What you had we only make for our rookie deputies. Well, let's dig in."

They continued their light-hearted banter through Edna's entire pie, with both Jack and Dan having two large pieces. Then, taking their second or third cup of coffee into the living room, they sat down to hear the tape.

"Where'd this come from?" Dan asked, before Jack started the tape rolling. "Or shouldn't you tell me?"

"No, I don't mind," Jack said. "A ten-year-old boy over on Nelson found it the mornin' after the Mason accident. Both the tape and the recorder it was in."

"I thought you sealed off that whole area for investigation," Dan said, puzzled.

"We did," Jack recalled. "But we apparently had our tape strung too close to the crash site. The boy found this in a ditch down the street a ways. The only thing Dave and I can figure is that when she was comin' 'round the corner, turnin' right, and smacked into Bob's car, she was holdin' the tape recorder in her hand. The door flew open on impact, and the tape recorder went flyin' way down the street. Somehow, it kept right on recordin'. I think it had something to do with what they call "voice activated." You'll hear the crash, and then the sound of sirens. It's amazin' how sensitive these things are. I'm thinkin' about gettin' myself one to record my thoughts for prosperity."

"Don't you mean 'posterity'?" Dan suggested.

215

"Not if I can sell my life story to the movies for a bunch of money," Jack laughed, having put one over on him. He was genuinely proud of himself. "It wouldn't be the first time those movie people made a mountain out of a molehill."

Wilson pressed the play button on the recorder, and they strained to make out all of the conversation on the small single speaker.

They listened to the tape for almost a half-hour, sometimes fascinated, sometimes angered, sometimes curious, even shocked to hear the sudden sound of the collision and realize that at this very moment in recorded history Cindy Mason was either dead or dying. After hearing the tape they had no doubt that Cindy and Joe had gone onto the elk refuge together—assigned by Jenny Jeffries to break a federal law. They had no doubt that Cindy had seen the bear carrying Joe's body, and had panicked, even as she continued recording her notes. And they had no doubt that she had not even seen Bob Thompson's vehicle approach the intersection of East Broadway and Elk Refuge Road; she was talking into the tape recorder right up to the very moment of the crash.

"Absolutely incredible," Dan said, as the tape ended.

"Isn't it?" Jack agreed. "I don't think I've ever had such a documented case of law-breakin' in my whole career. The entire sad story is right there, start to finish."

"What are you going to do with this?" Dan asked.

"Well, the next person who should hear it, I suppose," Jack said, "is Charlie Barton. After Jeffries told me she hadn't given these kids any such assignment, and after she told me she didn't know if Dean was missin', I think Charlie is going to want to see if he can't help her refresh her memory."

"You think she'll go to jail?" Dan asked.

"Oh, I doubt it," Jack sighed. "The newspaper'll probably pay some fancy lawyer big bucks to file all sorts of motions until the case either collapses or she dies of old age. That's the way they play the game today. It's not a matter of gettin' justice any more but how much justice you can afford to buy. The newspaper has deep pockets. No, she probably won't go to jail. But I'll tell you one thing, this woman is through in Jackson. Once this gets out she won't be able to get a job as a bone at the dog pound."

"Just for the possibility of winning some dumb-ass award," Dan pointed out. "Pardon my French, ladies."

Chapter Forty-Seven

THE MESSAGE

It was going to be a truly great day, Jenny Jeffries thought as she exited the shower. The special edition would already be hitting the streets, and she had no indication that anything similar was forthcoming from *The Guide*. This was going to be a complete sweep of the local news ratings for *The News*. Everyone in town would be reading her newspaper to get the story on the kids. Everyone in town would also be reading her front-page editorial blasting the federal government for allowing the bear situation to get out of hand.

If she had not already been occupying the leading editorial seat of the newspaper, Jeffries thought, she surely would be promoted. Even so, she felt she now had an outside chance at making assistant publisher.

Jenny finished her bathroom tasks, then dressed, putting on her smart green wool pants-suit and a silky white blouse. Although she absolutely hated the Jackson Hole standard "Pac" boots she slipped on hers anyway, neatly folding and tucking the legs of her pants inside the wool and felt lining of the boots. She decided to forego anything for breakfast, being anxious to get to the office to see the results of her efforts. Maybe she would pick up a donut or a croissant later.

It was still dark, and she had to scrape the frost from her windshield. She got in the car, started it easily, and flipped the heater and fan switches on full-blast, with the slowly warming air directed at the windshield on the defrost setting. That done, she grabbed the aluminum-handled scraper with the plastic blade and brush and began working on the windshield frost. This is a real pain in the ass, she thought again, for maybe the one-hundredth time since arriving in Jackson; I'm going to have to look around for something with a garage.

There were only a couple of staffers at the office when Jeffries arrived. One of them had already made a fresh pot of coffee, she noticed, and she went over to grab a cup. No sugar, a bit of cream. She stirred the styrofoam cup of coffee, then went into her office. A copy of the special edition was already on her desk. She unfolded it, top and bottom, and admired it. Good job, she congratulated herself. This should take care of those self-aggrandizing federal bastards. And the judges at the Wyoming Newspaper Association should really love the special color treatment. Maybe we could have gone a bit heavier on the sympathy angle. That always wins awards. Shows the newspaper's compassion, and its truc concern for the community.

Dick Martin, the paper's greasy but capable press foreman, entered her office.

"How's it look, Madam Editor?" Martin said, still wearing his traditional rimless hat made of folded newspaper.

"Very clean," she admitted. "Good work on the color. Good registration. No bleed, no smears. Excellent appearance."

Martin beamed. He was proud of his craftsmanship, and he looked forward to her rare bones of congratulations. "Thank you very much. We put a lot of extra effort into this one, because we figured you would be sending it out for judging."

"It shows," she acknowledged. "And you're right about the judging. We are definitely going to win some awards with this one." She continued reading what she had written in the front-page editorial. Martin left the office, relieved. The editorial was highlighted in a double-ruled box at the left of the page, and took up most of the space above and below the fold.

The Bad News Bearers

The tragic incident on Snow King Mountain that this Special Edition of the *Jackson Hole News* documents should be remembered forever by the local community as evidence of a complete and callous disregard for public safety by certain federal officials. It shows what is likely to happen when corrupt management practices are allowed to prevail in a situation where common sense would normally rule. Young Jason Washburn was killed not by any grizzly but by the uncaring managers of the National Elk Refuge and the Bridger-Teton National Forest, who have clearly shown that they are more interested in protecting the rights of a bunch of unrepentant bruins than those of unprotected members of the public.

This newspaper proposes the formation of a community organization aimed at holding those federal bureaucrats fully responsible for their actions, up to and including the filing of charges of murder.

In the past few weeks there have been repeated local deaths attributed directly to the policies put in place by the elk refuge and forest managers. We have mourned the loss of Cindy C. Mason, Joseph R. Dean, Robert D. Allen, Edward N. Oldfield, Jason L. Washburn—and who knows how many other locals and visitors whose mangled or half-eaten bodies have not yet even been discovered. It is very possible that there are many unreported missing persons in this state and elsewhere who have come to our beautiful Jackson Hole valley for a pleasant vacation only to find themselves attacked, torn, and clawed apart by members of a renegade band of bears that should have been shot immediately when discovered on the Elk Refuge. The true number of deaths attributable to these unprovoked attacks may never be known.

What is known is that....

"Ms. Jeffries?"

There were two sheriff's deputies standing at her open door.

"Yes?"

"We'd like you to come with us to the sheriff's office," the speaking deputy said. "We need to ask you some questions."

"Can't you ask them here?" she queried.

"We don't think you would like us to do that," the deputy replied.

"Well, I'm very busy," she lied. "Is this going to take very long?"

"I guess that depends on how you answer the questions," he said.

A strange conversation, she thought, as she grabbed her coat and slipped on the ugly Pacs. They must want to ask me about Ashton's accusations the other day. They probably wouldn't have seen today's paper yet. Wait'll they read this! She walked smartly ahead of the two deputies towards the front door.

"Nancy, I have to go out for a few minutes," she told one of the girls at the front desk. "Please take any messages for me and put them on my desk. Tell anyone who calls that I'll be back in about an hour."

If I were you I really wouldn't count on that, one of the deputies thought, not trying to conceal the slight smirk on his face.

Well, so much for my great day, Jeffries concluded when she walked into the room and saw who was gathered around the big table. There was Teton County Sheriff Jack Wilson, Deputy Dave Hamilton, Elk Refuge Manager Dan Johnston, County Prosecutor Charlie Barton, and a woman seated at a machine that she recognized as the kind used by court reporters.

"Good mornin', Ms. Jeffries," Wilson said as she entered. "We're all very glad you could join us. Please be seated over here next to me. I think you know everyone here, except maybe Miss Davis."

"Yes, I do," she said, glancing quickly and curiously at each of them, as she walked over to sit down. "What is this all about?"

"Well, we have a micracassette tape recordin' that we would like to play for you," Wilson said. "And then we would be interested in hearin' your comments on it. This is not a formal inquiry, you understand. But if you like, you sure can have your lawyer sit in. If you think you need to call him, we'll be happy to wait until he arrives."

"No, I don't think that will be necessary," Jeffries stated, rather brusquely. "I think I am quite capable of listening to a simple tape recording without an attorney being present. If I think I need to call him before I make any comments, I will."

"Suit yourself," Wilson said. "Miss Davies, you can do your typin' as you listen to the tape, so's we can get a transcript of it for Charlie and maybe Ms. Jeffries to use. Well, here goes. Let me see if I can remember where the play button is on this contraption." Wilson intentionally made a big deal about finding the play button, making sure Jeffries could observe the machine clearly, and maybe recognize it as Cindy's. He was interested in her reaction, and was watching her as much as he was fumbling with the recorder.

I've seen that tape recorder before, Jeffries noted, as Wilson blundered around trying to operate it. Didn't it belong to...Cindy? Oh shit. It was Cindy's Panasonic.

"I'm sorry to interrupt you, Sheriff Wilson," Jeffries hastily observed. "But I think I should have an attorney present for this questioning after all. Where is the nearest telephone?"

It took less than fifteen minutes for the newspaper's attorney to arrive. Wilson apprised him also of the informality of the session, and asked if he had any objections. The attorney said he had none immediately but would make any objections as the need arose. He advised Jeffries against making any comments or facial expressions that could be misinterpreted while listening to the tape or immediately afterwards without consulting him first. She agreed.

Wilson played the tape.

"We need to talk," the attorney said to the editor as soon as Wilson pressed the stop button. "Is there somewhere Ms. Jeffries and I could have a private conversation?" he asked the sheriff.

"Use the room right next door," Wilson offered. "Would you like to have some coffee brought in?"

"Thanks," the attorney said. "I think we may need it. We may be there for awhile." He turned to the stunned editor. "Ms. Jeffries, before we begin our private discussion, I should remind you that, officially, I am the legal representative of the newspaper, not your personal attorney. You may want to telephone an attorney before this matter goes any further to represent you personally."

Jenny Jeffries was truly stunned. She could barely hear what anyone was saying, and their words were very confusing. Her skin was as white as the snow that was falling outside.

"Ms. Jeffries?" the newspaper's attorney asked when she failed to respond. "Are you okay?"

Chapter Forty-Eight

THE NEXT STEP

Jenny Jeffries had listened to Cindy Mason's tape, had received legal advice from her personal attorney, and had returned to the conference room to tell Sheriff Wilson that she had no comments to make on the recording. On the advice of her attorney, Jeffries also declined to answer any of the Sheriff's questions regarding her part in the fatal assignment. At that point Prosecutor Barton had Wilson call in one of his deputies who had been standing by, to serve Jenny Jeffries with a previously prepared summons to appear in District Court to answer two charges of second-degree manslaughter.

"Well, that went just about as we expected," Wilson said to Dan Johnston after Jeffries and the lawyers had left his office. Charlie Barton was with them. "Charlie, what do you think?"

"I think Ms. Jeffries is going to be spending a lot of time in courtrooms over the next several months," Barton said. "She's a very ambitious, very self-centered young woman who seems to have a bit of difficulty telling right from wrong. It was her responsibility, as the newspaper editor, to "kill" that early morning expedition onto the Elk Refuge idea before it developed. Instead, she turned it into an official assignment—one that violated federal law and cost two people their lives."

"She doesn't seem to have a lot of remorse about it," Johnston observed.

"I noticed that too," Wilson said. "When Mason was talkin' about seein' the bear cross the road with Dean's body in its mouth, it didn't even faze her. Anybody with half a sense of guilt would have found that part a bit... untasteful. And she didn't even jump at the sound of the crash."

"Well," Barton added, "Ms. Jeffries is going to have a lot of time to reconsider her decision—for the rest of her life. Gotta go, Jack. I assume I'll be seeing you in court. Actually, I'll want to call you as a witness in regard to your telephone conversation with Ms. Jeffries on the morning after the Mason accident."

"Yeah, I thought you might want to do that, Charlie," Wilson replied. "Take it easy. I'll be seein' ya."

"Say hello to Edna for me. Take care, Dan," Barton said as he went down the hall.

"Well, Dan," Wilson said, turning his attention to the elk refuge manager. "What's up with the two remainin' bears?"

"They're now Jim Farson's problem," Dan reported. "I haven't talked to him since yesterday's discovery of the boy and the girl on Snow King, but the bears are probably still on Bridger-Teton. It appears to me that he will just have to go in and get them. Otherwise, we're going to see more bear-people problems."

"You gonna go with him?" Wilson asked.

"I was stupid enough to volunteer," Johnston confirmed. "As you know, I don't have any official authority to go grizzly hunting off the refuge, but I told Jim I would make myself available if he needed any more bodies."

"That's an interestin' way to put it," Wilson commented. "My personal feelin' is, those damned bears have been responsible for about enough bodies already. We really don't need any more.

If you go out huntin' with Farson, you be careful that you don't join the list. I can tell you from personal experience that gettin' a real close-up look at one of them grizzlies isn't a heck of a lot of fun."

"You coming back to work now, or are you going to take some more time off to heal your wounds?" Johnston inquired.

"I thought I might come in a day or two next week to see if I can take a full eight hours of bein' on my feet," Wilson said. "I've given my butt more than enough polish to last it for the rest of the year."

"Well, don't push it. Old fogeys like you don't heal as fast as normal people."

"Thanks for the thought. Say, Dan, in all seriousness, if you go out there, you be extra careful. I can't stop you from goin', but I can sure advise you to take care to come back."

Chapter Forty-Nine

THE RIFLE MAN

"Morning, Dan," Jim Farson answered the refuge manager's telephone call.

"Good afternoon," Johnston corrected.

"Yeah, I guess it is," Farson conceded. "Time sure flies when you're having fun."

"I couldn't bear the suspense any longer," Johnston replied. "Are we going to be doing a little hunting?"

"After that mess up on Snow King?" Farson asked. "I really don't see that we have any choice. I've called Washington and told them the latest, and while they still have some reluctance about killing any members of a protected species they agree that the two remaining grizzlies have got to go."

"Go as in trap and relocate, or go as in something more permanent?" Johnston asked.

"They left that up to me, of course," Farson explained. "But I think it's going to be hard enough to even find those two bears in the snow, let alone get traps up to them and lure them in. To me, the only answer seems to be going after them in snowmobiles with high-powered rifles. Which is just what we're going to do, unless you or someone else has a better idea."

"Sounds like that's about all that can be done at this point," Johnston agreed. "I think you should start looking for any sign up on Snow King, where the kids were attacked, then work your way northeast as far as Sleeping Indian. If those bears are ready to go into hibernation I think that's where they'll be headed."

"I agree," Farson said. "So what time will you be ready to leave?"

"You're going after them yet this afternoon?" Johnston asked, truly surprised.

"I just don't think we can afford to wait any longer," Farson replied. "There's no guarantee that either bear is ready to hibernate. I don't think we can give them any more opportunities to fatten up on people food."

"Well, give me a half-hour," Johnston advised, "and I'll be ready to go. You providing the snowmobiles, or do you want me to bring mine?"

"Bring yours, if you feel like it," Farson said. "We'll meet at the foot of Snow King. I already have some of my people getting ready to roll. With you, there will be five of us in the search party."

"Let's hope there really is safety in numbers," Johnston replied. "I don't want to end up like Jack Wilson. Oh, forgot to tell you. I went on the Internet and had them overnight me a new rifle."

"What'd you get?" Farson asked.

"A .458 Winchester Magnum Model 70 Classic Safari Express with three-shot magazine and twenty-four-inch barrel, scope, and a couple of boxes of Federal Trophy Bonded Sledgehammer Solid 500-grain bullets," Johnston replied.

"Jesus!" Farson exclaimed. "Whatever all of that really amounts to, it sure does *sound* impressive. If I was one of these grizzlies, I don't think I'd let you come within five hundred feet of me."

"Strangely enough," Johnston responded, "that's just about as close as I plan to get. See you in about a half-hour."

Chapter Fifty

THE HUNTERS

There were five of them, each on his own snowmobile, with a high-powered rifle either strapped to his shoulder or harnessed in a boot on the machine when they left the Snow King parking lot and headed up the mountain towards Cut Off Run. Each had a hand-held radio for communicating with the others. It was shortly after twelve-thirty. There was a light snow falling.

They stopped at the site of the attack on the high school skiers. The yellow warning tape with bold black letters isolated the area, which had been made nearly unidentifiable as the scene of an incident by the subsequent snow accumulations. They all dismounted from their snowmobiles, and began fanning out eastward in the trees to search for spoor—any sign of a track or a trail left by the bear as it left the kill area.

"Looks like I might have something here," one of the men radioed after about ten minutes of searching. "There seems to be some broken brush with half-filled holes in the snow that could be where a bear went through. It's kind of hard to see unless you look at it from a sideways angle, but it's there."

"Okay," Farson commanded. "Let's all get in a north-south line with Artie in the center and follow the trail eastward. Let him determine our speed. If the trail veers north or south and he loses it everybody keep an eye out for it coming towards them. Remember, keep looking ahead for a big brown bump in the snow that might be the bear curled up. I don't want any of us jumped by surprise—especially in the trees. If you see any other trails that might belong to the other bear, let us know. Okay, let's roll."

The search line formed up on Artie, and began moving slowly eastward. It was tough going. All of them had their headlights on in the afternoon half-light of the trees, and this helped some to identify the indentations in the snow. Still, several times Artie had to get off his machine and drop down to one knee for a closer look at the trail. At Cache Creek Canyon the bear headed east-southeast along the frozen stream, then soon switched back along the other hillside as it climbed up Gin Pole Draw towards Nowlin Peak. In a single-file line they followed.

At 9,861 feet, Nowlin Peak is almost a half-mile higher than the point on Snow King where the attack occurred. Nowlin itself is almost 1,000 feet lower than Jackson Peak, which is only one straight-line mile to the east. A grizzly could easily find itself a comfortable place to spend the winter on either peak. Once near the top of Jackson Peak, however, it would be a fairly easy eight-mile hike for a bear to relocate to Sheep Mountain (10,772 feet), where Johnston believed the two remaining bears would hole up for the winter.

Following the trail of the bear the snowmobilers zigzagged back and forth on the southeast side of Gin Pole Draw. Ironically, as the afternoon light faded the trail became more and more obvious in the headlights of the snowmobiles.

"You think we're going to find this sucker before it gets dark, Jim?" Johnston radioed. "I think he's gone around the north side of Nowlin, will cross South Twin Creek, and end up at Goodwin Lake. He's gradually working his way towards Sheep Mountain, taking the scenic route."

"You may be right, Dan," Farson replied. "Well, it's now about four-thirty. Let's follow him around Nowlin to see whether he goes up the South Twin towards Jackson Peak or goes north towards Curtis Canyon. We'll have a fairly mild ride down the mountain to the elk refuge from there, and it will at least give us some idea of where to start tomorrow. I don't want to do too much running around up here in the dark. Artie, can you hear me up there?"

"Gotcha, boss," Artie responded. "This is one of the best trail rides I've had in a long time. I'd forgotten how much fun one of these snowmobiles could be."

"Well, don't have too much fun," Farson advised. "This is supposed to be serious business. If you turn it into a vacation I may have to dock it from your pay."

"Boss, you wouldn't believe how much my back is hurting," Artie answered. "I think I'm even going to have to file for temporary disability when we get back. Ohhhhhh. Ohhhhhh."

"Knock it off, you crazy bastard," Farson warned. "We have guests. You don't want Mr. Johnston to think we run some kind of sanctuary for nut cases on Bridger-Teton, do you?"

"We don't?"

"Say, Artie, there's really no need for all of us to go this last quarter-mile," Farson radioed. "All we need to do is see whether the bear went north or east. Why don't you and the other fellows cut off here and make Dan and me a nice neat path northwest down the mountain to the elk refuge? When you get down there, you can double-up and go back to Snow King for the trailers. By the time you get back to the refuge we should be there. Dan, you think we can do this last quarter-mile alone?"

"I don't see why not," Dan replied. "If the bear left Snow King yesterday morning he should be well past that point by now. Good-bye, Artie."

"Good-bye, Dan. Good-bye, boss," Artie said, heading his snowmobile off to the left. "If you see any bears, don't tell them which way we went."

"Not me," Farson replied. "Have those trailers ready for us."

Artie led the four other Forest Service employees down the mountain, their headlights creating a serpentine pattern as they wound their way through the trees. Farson took over the lead, with Johnston close behind.

They followed the grizzly's trail around the north side of Nowlin at about the nine-thousand-feet contour level but it was unclear whether the bear was going north or east so they continued to follow its course, which wound around the west slope of Jackson Peak without much rising or falling. At the point where the grizzly might have turned east, to go to Goodwin Lake, it headed northwest, down the easy slope.

"You thinking what I'm thinking, Dan?" Farson radioed.

"I am if you're thinking that this bear's still hungry," Johnston replied. He smelled the scent of cattle, or horses, drifting southeast from Twin Creek Ranch. Looks like he went down there to get something to eat."

"That's the way I see it," Farson concurred. "Am I an idiot for sending the rest of our team home, or what?"

"Well, you can't do anything about it now," Johnston observed, "unless you want to try to raise them on the radio and have them meet us at the ranch. But it looks to me like we don't have much choice but to go after this bear on our own before he does any more major damage."

"I knew I picked the wrong profession," Farson moaned. "I could have been president, a used car salesman, or even a mayor."

"Same difference, Jim," Johnston claimed. "They all hand you a line that they know you want to hear, and you end up buying something that you wish you hadn't."

"Well, let's get at it," Farson sighed. "Better keep your trigger finger warm."

Chapter Fifty-One

THE BARN

Where Elk Refuge Road makes a ninety-degree turn to the left and heads straight north there is a ranch gate, one of those three-log symbols of the Old West with a hanging board bearing the name and the unique brand of a ranch that is more often seen today at the entrance to a multi-million-dollar estate or to a suburban middle-class housing subdivision.

When you drive through this log gate you approach a number of houses, barns, outbuildings, fences, and other assorted trappings of Twin Creek Ranch. There are cattle, horses, stacks of hay, and fields for pasture here. There are trucks and tractors and wagons and plows and other pieces of machinery necessary for conducting a full-time ranching business.

And at this particular point in time, there was also on the ranch one curious and halfway hungry grizzly bear.

It was now after five o'clock, and it was fairly dark on Twin Creek Ranch, although you could still see the faintest pink glow on the west face of the highest peaks of the Tetons. In a blink of an eye, that glow too would be gone, and the western, snow-covered mountains would loom like shadows at the edge of the sky.

All around Twin Creek Ranch there was an uneasiness among the livestock, as the vague scent of an unknown, unfamiliar but probable danger drifted about. There were perked ears and probing eyes, as potential victims sought to detect the stealthy approach of possible death in time to avoid it. Death himself was sitting on a hillside overlooking the quiet ranch, barely visible in the reach of several fluorescent pole lights, sizing up the situation and looking over the menu. He had decided to tackle a beefsteak tonight, so rare that it was still on the hoof.

The bear began his approach, a silent stalking behind bushes, trees, barns, and other buildings intended to conceal his bulky body until he was close enough to make a fast run and surprise his designated victim before it had a chance to escape. His ears were up, his eyes were focused on only one point, his stomach was rumbling with hunger and the gassy sounds of anticipation. He crept cautiously behind any available cover, setting each foot down softly and silently, being careful to avoid stepping on any stones, twigs, or other loose items that would warn and frighten away his prey.

Two-hundred feet. One-fifty. One-hundred. Seventy-five. Almost close enough to launch the attack. Sixty. Fifty. Aim for the neck, slam and break the backbone. Forty. Thirty.

Twenty feet away, to his right, a barn door opened, and ranch hand Jake Jorgensen stepped out, holding a heavy metal feed bucket in one hand, a four-pronged pitchfork in the other. Thwarted in his attempt to approach the steer in silence, and distracted by the man at the door, the bear growled his disappointment and stood fully erect on his hind legs.

"What the hell?" Jorgensen thought aloud, instantly seeing the bear and hearing its gurgling snarls. An occasional black bear hunter, Jorgensen knew without thinking that this was a grizzly, one that wasn't going to fake a charge and then just run off into the forest. The nearest weapon was a loaded .22 caliber rifle hanging inside the barn that was used for taking potshots at passing chiselers and coyotes. Not even close to having enough firepower to stop a determined grizzly.

"Hah! Hey outta here!" Jorgensen shouted in an effort to possibly shock the bear into abandoning his approach. "Gee-yah!" But the bear kept coming, making menacing threats, walking on its hind legs and waving its paws. Jorgensen threw the bucket at it, ineffectively striking it in the face, then seized the pitchfork in both hands and jabbed it hard towards the grizzly's chest. The fork penetrated a few inches, and seemed to catch the bear's attention.

Not waiting to withdraw the pitchfork and take another stab at slowing the grizzly, Jorgensen retreated to the barn, closing the door behind him and flipping the two-by-four inside latch closed. He ran for the ladder to the loft, diverting only long enough to reach for the loaded rifle on the wall. He began climbing.

Further maddened by the pain of the pitchfork, the grizzly snapped its jaws at the wooden handle and brushed it away with both paws. Now intent on going after the source of his problems, the bear pounded on the inch-board poplar barrier hiding his new interest, smashing the door as though it were sagebrush. Any pieces still stopping him from entering the barn he simply shattered by walking right through the door. He looked around for Jorgensen and saw him climbing the ladder.

Fully grown grizzlies can't climb trees, mainly because their paws are simply not shaped to grasp a tree's limbs. For the same reason they can't climb ladders. But small trees and thin ladders are obstacles only as long as it takes to push them over. The grizzly growled at Jorgensen's attempt to evade him by climbing, and began lunging at the ladder, which was nailed solidly to the four-by-eight supports for the loft. Its repeated shoving loosened the ladder, shook the supports, and allowed the flat boards to begin sagging.

In the loft, Jorgensen gave up on trying to stand on its disassembling floor, grabbed for one of the two-by-six joists that anchored the rafters for the roof, and flipped himself astraddle of it. He was now fairly safe—unless the grizzly decided to go after the barn's walls. He held the rifle to his shoulder, aimed, and fired repeatedly at the bear's chest, emptying the magazine.

Most of Jorgensen's shots smacked into the bear. None of them hit a vital organ. But the snapping sounds of the shots, and the pinching sensations that followed like so many stingers from hornets or wasps were enough to cause the grizzly to give up on trying to reach this prey that had eluded him. He returned to all four feet, snuffed his displeasure at being denied vindication for the meal interruption, and lumbered out of the barn.

In the loft, or what was left of it, Jorgensen breathed a sigh of relief, made a conscious effort to stop shaking, and noticed a sudden liquid chill all along the lower front of his jeans and left leg. But the bear was gone. It would be another half-hour before Jorgensen abandoned the relative safety of his shaky perch and found a safe way to get down to the barn floor.

Outside the barn the hurting grizzly took one look at the penned cattle that he had intended to attack and decided to go back up into the woods and lick his wounds. He hoped that lying on the cold snow for awhile would deaden his pain.

Chapter Fifty-Two

THE SHOT

They had followed the bear's trail for almost two miles downhill towards Twin Creek Ranch, which was still almost two miles away. The spoor was getting fresher; it was obvious that the grizzly had gone through this area only a few hours before. They decided to halt the snowmobiles in the darkness and attempt to see the bear on the mountainside in the increasingly bright moonlight. The snow had stopped falling an hour or so ago and the dusky clouds were starting to drift off to the east. The weather forecast had been right on the money—clearing skies and colder temperatures tonight. A few stars were now visible in the western sky.

"Think he may be down at the Ranch already, Dan?" Farson asked, turning the ignition key and letting his snowmobile idle to a stop.

"I wouldn't be surprised," Johnston replied, doing the same. "If we listen close, we should be able to hear anything unusual going on."

They stopped the engines of their snowmobiles and stood in silence, eyes in the general downhill direction of the ranch, trying to scan the surrounding blue-tinted slopes for any sign of movement that would suggest the presence of the bear. They paid particular attention to the edges, the junctures between the nearly treeless slopes and the spits of densely wooded forest. There was nothing out of the ordinary, no blurred images, no vague sounds of terrified animals running for their life—until they heard the gunshots.

The cracks were faint, but clearly those of a small-bore rifle. One, two, three, several—one right after another. Someone was trying to make sure he didn't miss what he was aiming at.

"You hear that?" Johnston inquired. "Gunshots. Someone down the mountain is either doing some early evening target practice, or he is pretty intent on taking something down."

"What kind of fool would be shooting at a grizzly with a pop-gun?" Farson responded. "That's small-bore gunfire—probably a .22."

"Maybe that's all he has to use," Johnston speculated. "I pity the poor bastard if that's the case, because he's just going to make the grizzly unhappy."

"We'd better get down there quick and help him," Farson said, jumping back on his snowmobile. "If he's in trouble, it's only going to get worse. Better try to get your gun in some kind of shooting position." He started his engine, and began to speed off, disregarding his own advice about preparing to shoot.

Moments later, Johnston had changed the location of his Winchester, moving the shoulder strap from a diagonal that crossed his back to a single-shoulder carry that he found to be too awkward to maintain. He went back to the cross-back carry; the gun wasn't as quickly accessed, but at least it wouldn't be bouncing around and possibly fall off. He started his own engine and zoomed off after Farson. Now, this is a real good idea, Johnston thought. Let's just charge right up on that bear with headlights blazing and engines whining. That'll keep him calm long enough to center him in our sights.

They sped down the mountain, mainly following the bear's trail, as fast as their concern for reasonably safe riding would allow. Johnston was the more conservative of the two, perhaps showing greater caution since his earlier encounter with the grizzly that had attacked him and Jack Wilson. Farson, on the other hand, was steadily pulling ahead of him, throwing caution to the wind. Farson's snowmobile was stirring up a considerable roostertail of snow behind it, adding to Johnston's reluctance to follow too close to Farson's red tail light.

They could now see the fluorescent lights of the ranch. It looked strangely normal, as though nothing at all out of the ordinary had happened, as though nothing at all out of the ordinary would ever happen there. In the growing darkness, with the Tetons in the background, and the ranch illuminated by its small fluorescents, the scene was very much like a picture postcard.

The downhill terrain was getting steeper as they approached the frozen North Twin Creek. Farson was going way too fast, Johnston thought, for these rocky conditions. Several times already he himself had found it necessary to swerve sharply to miss buried boulders that bumped into view only seconds before his snowmobile encountered them. Each near-miss had given him second thoughts about his speed, and each time he lost a little ground to Farson. By this time, Farson was probably two hundred yards ahead of him.

The sprayed white light from Farson's snowmobile suddenly shot up through the trees to its left side and then died out. He had hit, Johnston thought, either a buried boulder or something else—maybe a fallen tree—and had taken a tumble. Even in the dim moonlight that was reflected by the snow, Johnston had seen Farson flip off the snowmobile and land fifteen or twenty feet to its right, while the snowmobile remained tilted on its side, falling silent, the "dead man's grip" throttle design doing its intended job, instantly shutting down the engine.

However, there was something else. There was a shadowy blob as big as the snowmobile itself rising from in front of it. It was the bear. In his unfettered downhill rush to save the shooter at the ranch Farson had forgotten to pay attention to the terrain. He had run into the bear with the snowmobile. It could have been wounded, was climbing back uphill, and was resting when Farson's out-of-control snowmobile came careering along. It may never have been down at the ranch at all. Whoever was shooting the rifle could have seen it coming down the mountain and had scared it off with his several warning shots.

There was no more time to speculate. Being smacked by the heavy snowmobile didn't make the wounded bear very happy. It had struggled to its feet to find what had attacked it. The only animate object the grizzly could see in the general vicinity was Farson, and it was going over to discuss the rules of driver courtesy with him. Farson was already in considerable pain; he had broken something—probably a shoulder, and several ribs— and was rolling in the snow in agony, making noise, doing everything except the one right thing that might save him: play dead.

Johnston was too far away to help. There was no way he could cover the nearly 200 yards that now separated him from the scene of the accident before the bear got to Farson. He stopped the snowmobile, cut the engine, and unstrapped the high-powered Winchester. He had three shots, with one bullet in the chamber and two in the magazine. He would have time for only one. If he didn't stop the grizzly before it got near Farson he wouldn't be able to risk a second or a third shot. He also wouldn't be able to tell whether he was aiming at the bear or at Farson. He crouched down on the snow, in a three-point stance and braced his elbows on the soft seat of the snowmobile. He quickly clicked off the safety, and took aim on the center mass of the bear, trying to remember the standard shooting instructions. Hold the stock tight against your cheek. Grip the forestock firmly. Take a deep breath, then let part of it out. Squeeze the trigger—don't pull it.

Johnston was momentarily blinded by the yellow-orange flame that shot from the barrel of the Winchester, and was nearly deafened by the sudden sharp explosion. He couldn't tell whether he had hit the grizzly or not. Apparently not. As he slowly regained his night sight he could see the big form continue edging closer to the injured Farson. There was nothing else he could do now but watch.

When the grizzly got to Farson, Johnston watched it drop down upon him. In the dim light, he couldn't tell how badly Farson was being mauled. But the strange thing was, all Johnston could hear was silence. Had the shot in fact completely deafened him? He remounted the snowmobile, restarted it, and sped on down the mountain, afraid of what he would find, and fairly certain that he would be encountering a pretty mad bear. He did not realize that, while he was momentarily blinded and briefly deafened, he had sat the new Winchester in the snow, leaned up against the snowmobile. As he pulled away the rifle fell over and partially buried itself in the snow.

Chapter Fifty-Three

THE HELICOPTER

ello?"

"Jack Wilson, Harrison."

"How's it going, Jack? What can I do for you?"

"Well, we have a rescue mission. We need your help. Is your helicopter available?"

"Any time...during the day," the pilot said. "But I'm not too confident yet about flying it at night. What's the story?"

"We have a situation up above Twin Creek Ranch, in the forest. You know Jim Farson and Dan Johnston, the guys who run the Bridger-Teton and the Elk Refuge?"

"I think I've seen their names in the papers," he said. "But I haven't met either one of them."

"Well, Jim and Dan were up on the mountains east of the Refuge lookin' for the last two grizzlies that have been causin' us problems—you familiar with that situation?"

"A bit. The 'Elk Refuge' bears?"

"The same," Wilson said. "A coupla grizzlies. Anyway, Jim apparently bumped into one of them on the mountainside—like plowed right into the sucker—and got thrown off of his snowmobile. Johnston just radioed in and said Farson's in pretty bad shape."

"The bear got to him?"

"Well, you see, that's the thing," Wilson explained. "It looks like Farson may have broken a shoulder and some ribs when he was thrown from the snowmobile. But Johnston apparently shot and killed the bear before it could get to Farson. It dropped dead right on him. We have to get the bear off of Farson before we can even get him down the mountain and take him to the hospital. Apparently Jim is layin' up there in the snow with an eight-hundred-pound bear rug on him. Must be in a lot of misery. Believe me, I know the feelin'."

"Couldn't Johnston just use his snowmobile to pull it off?"

"He doesn't have any way to do it, no rope or nothing that he could use to tie around the bear," Wilson said. "Anyway, Johnston is afraid to try to roll the bear off with his snowmobile, for fear of causing Farson even worse injury. He thinks the bear needs to be lifted straight up."

"Well, there's not much I can do, Jack. I could probably lift the bear off with a rope hanging down from the helicopter, provided they're in a clearing. But it would be a bit foolhardy to try it at night, given my present level of competence. If I caused Johnston any further injury, or injured one of the rescue workers, or damaged something else, I could easily lose my flying license."

"I understand," Wilson said. "I understand completely. Don't worry about it. We'll see if we can't find somebody else's helicopter."

There was a pause, as both men considered the sheriff's fall-back plan, one of them already knowing that it was doomed to failure, the other one quickly coming to the same conclusion.

"Jack, you know as well as I do that there are no other helicopters around here for something like this. That's why I volunteer mine for these search-and-rescue missions."

"I know," Wilson said. He paused to achieve the desired effect. He had known Harrison for some time, and was pretty certain that he had, by now, figured him out. Something like this would be irresistible to him. After a few seconds he had the answer that he wanted and knew that he would get.

"Oh, what the hell," the pilot relented. "Meet me at the south end of the elk refuge road, Jack. I'll be there in about twenty minutes."

The old sheriff smiled.

At his isolated ranch southwest of Jackson, the middle-aged, scruffy looking pilot, wearing Pacs, tan trousers, a bomber-crew jacket, and an old fedora, hurried to the Bell JetRanger 206B that was parked in a field near the frame house, flipped various switches, checked various gauges, and began warming up the engine.

"Bears," he mumbled to himself. "I hate bears, Jack. Why'd it have to be bears?"

Chapter Fifty-Four

THE BEAR LIFT

Wilson, Johnston, and two of the Bridger-Teton snowmobile searchers remained in constant radio contact as they awaited the helicopter. There was not much Johnston could do for Farson except dig the snow away from him to make it easier for him to breathe and assure him that help was coming. The remaining searchers all hopped back on their snowmobiles and buzzed east on Elk Refuge Road, first to check out the story behind the gunshots at Twin Creek Ranch and then to come on up the mountain to assist in evacuating Farson. At the south end of the Refuge, Wilson stood beside his Expedition, watching for the single, forward-angled light of the helicopter.

Chucka-chucka-chucka-chucka-chucka-chucka.

Wilson could hear the chopper coming even before he saw it flying over the town, coming out of the southwest. The pilot made a single circle of the area, and sat the helicopter down gently right on the road. He waited at the controls for Wilson to walk with ducked head the short distance to the helicopter and slide open its single door.

"Thanks for doin' this, Harrison," Wilson said as he entered and slid the door closed. "Jim Farson is a good friend of mine. I hate to think about him bein' in so much pain."

"Don't mention it, Jack," the pilot replied. "I wanted to take up sailboating, anyway. Know anybody who wants to buy a fleet of planes and a helicopter?"

"If you think it would help, I'd be glad to put in a good word for you to the FAA. We can tell them your helicopter was stolen, and somebody else was drivin'. I'll fill out the missin' helicopter report myself. By the way, nice hat."

Harrison ignored the sheriff's implied criticism. "You know where these guys are?" he asked, as he increased the speed of the blades and their pitch, causing the helicopter to rise and bank.

"Close enough," Wilson said from his rear seat. "Just head out the Refuge Road until you get to Twin Creek Ranch, turn right, and look for the first grizzly. Johnston and some other guys are already up there in a clearing with their snowmobile lights aimed at Farson and the bear. We shouldn't have much trouble findin' them."

"Okay. We're going to need someone to drop that rope back there down to the guys on the ground and have them tie it to the grizzly. You think you're up to that, or do you want me to pick up somebody else?"

"I think I can handle that part," Wilson assured him. "After we get the bear off Farson you may have to find someplace else to land to load him into the helicopter. I understand they're in an area that's pretty steep. They'll have to put him on a stretcher and bring him to you."

"You already have EMTs on the scene?"

"Farson's men," Wilson said. "They were part of the team of snowmobilers out lookin' for the bear. They should be ready to load him into the stretcher as soon as you yank the bear off of him.”

“Well, then, this should be a piece of cake.”

“Where have I heard that one before?” the sheriff asked.

Following instructions, the pilot flew his helicopter straight up Elk Refuge Road, banked right at the ranch, and began climbing towards the converged light of several snowmobiles about a mile up the mountain. As he approached the scene he could clearly make out the grizzly up ahead of them.

“I thought you said the bear was dead,” he said to Wilson, with a look of confusion on his face.

“He is,” Wilson replied. “Johnston shot the bear and it tumbled onto Farson. That’s why we need your helicopter. To lift it off of him.”

“Well, then, that’s the fastest dead bear I’ve ever seen,” his flyer friend commented, motioning forward with a nod of his head. “Look at him barreling down the mountain.”

“Oh, shit,” Wilson said, spotting the bear. “It’s the last one, the one they hadn’t found yet. All of the commotion must have stirred him up. He’s goin’ after them.”

“They apparently don’t see him. Their eyes must be adjusted to the bright lights of the snowmobiles and looking at us. Somebody’s going to get really creamed when that freight train hits them.”

“Can you warn them with your radio?” Wilson asked.

“It’s not working. I’m getting a switch replaced that’s on-order. How about using your hand-held?”

"We seem to have a slight problem there," Wilson admitted. "Like a fool I left it on the seat of the car. Got any other ideas?"

"Well, I have one. But I doubt that you're gonna like it. Hold on." He gave the helicopter forward cyclic to lower its nose, and decreased the collective slightly.

In the white circle of snowmobile light below Johnston and the others had been watching the helicopter cruising toward them. All of a sudden it went into a sharp dive.

"What the hell?" Johnston exclaimed. "What do they think they're doing?"

"They'd better pull up," one of the others said, "or they're going to be mashed potatoes—and we're going be the gravy."

The helicopter whizzed over them, only a few feet off the ground, stirring up a perfect storm of snow. They all ducked instinctively, and followed it with their eyes.

"Jesus!" one of them shouted as he suddenly noticed the bear charging towards them. "It's the other grizzly! They're going after it with the helicopter!"

"Did someone forget to tell Harrison that you don't play games with grizzlies in a helicopter?" another yelled.

"Dan, you're the only one with a rifle now," the first man pointed out. "You'd better get ready to shoot." Johnston was already going for his gun, which was...where?" He suddenly remembered leaning it against the snowmobile, higher up on the mountain—behind the new bear. In his haste, he'd forgotten all about the rifle.

"Uh, we have a slight problem there, guys" Johnston explained. "It's still up there on the mountain. We might want to get these snowmobiles ready to roll."

"And leave Jim behind?" one of them hastened.

"We have no choice," Johnston conceded. "We'll have to come back and get him later."

They all watched as the helicopter slanted towards the bear.

"I don't friggin' believe this," one of them said. "Harrison's going to buzz that bear with the chopper."

In the helicopter Wilson now suspected what his friend was actually planning to do. "Are you really sure about this, Harrison? This doesn't seem like a real good idea to me."

"You got a better one, Jack, I'm willing to listen," Harrison invited. "But you'd better talk fast!" It was going to be tricky. He planned to bump the running bear with the nose of the helicopter while keeping the main rotor blades from smacking into the snow and tearing themselves apart. If he timed it just right the helicopter would intersect the path of the bear in a nearly flat clearing, giving him the maximum chance to control the helicopter. If his timing was even slightly off, well.... Maybe with a good scare the bear would just turn and run.

"Hold on, Jack!" Harrison yelled as the helicopter closed the distance to the bear. Just before they collided the grizzly followed its natural instincts and stood up to get a better view of an unfamiliar opponent.

"Rats!" Harrison shouted, as he saw the grizzly rise, knowing he was already committed to the collision. "I hate it when they do that!"

The helicopter hit the standing grizzly almost head-on. The bear's muzzle smacked into the plexiglas windshield only inches from Harrison's face. The half-bubble cracked, but didn't break inward, as fine fissures radiated outward from the point of impact. Harrison fought to control the tendency of the spinning main rotor to dip forward, quickly giving the blades extra aft cyclic. He succeeded—apparently. Since the windshield was heavily smeared with the bear's blood, it was really difficult to see through it.

Harrison moved his head around, trying to find a spot on the plexiglas that was not shattered or covered with blood, to determine what the helicopter was doing. Simultaneously, he used the collective to increase torque in an attempt to climb. The Bell JetRanger resisted. He added more torque, but the helicopter was still sluggish.

The 206B's right skid had slipped under the bear. Its left rear leg was lodged between the base runner and the horizontal step-brace right above it. The bear was struggling mightily to break free, flailing its arms at the cabin of the helicopter.

"This is not real good, Jack!" Harrison shouted to Wilson. "I was trying to knock him down—not pick him up!"

"You guys do this sort of thing a lot in the movies?" Wilson responded, a little levity hiding his real concern.

"Every damned day," the pilot replied. "Only we don't normally use real bears. We have stunt bears and computer images to play their parts. You may want to start saying your prayers about now."

"I said every one I knew before we even hit him," Wilson admitted. "Since then, I've been makin' up a bunch of new ones."

"Well, I've got to get us away from the ground. I need more room to maneuver. I can't get much lift. Helicopters aren't supposed to be able to fly around with bears hanging on them, particularly at this altitude."

"That was my own first impression," Wilson said. "But I've never done anything like this before."

"Well, it may not give you much comfort, but neither have I."

"Are you kidding me?" one of the ground observers asked, seeing the helicopter bear lift. "Did Harrison just do what I think he did?"

"You know, I always thought they just faked this kind of stuff in the movies," another added. "I never thought it was real. Looks like I'm going to have to go back and watch that *Star Wars* movie all over again."

The helicopter rose, slowly, encumbered by the weight of the bear and the normal loss of torque as it climbed in the thin mountain air. Harrison had to adjust the cyclic, to compensate for the tendency of the helicopter to tilt towards the right. As he fought to control the craft he couldn't help but notice the angry grizzly right outside his window, pounding and biting to get at him.

"This guy's gonna need a trip to the dentist when this is all over," he joked. "I can see three or four teeth that have cavities, and a lot of holes with no teeth at all. Some dentist's daughter is going to be getting a new Corvette for Christmas."

"Harrison, I hope you don't mind my askin'," Wilson deadpanned, "but what are you plannin' to do with this bear?"

"I'm working on it, Jack," Harrison replied. In truth, he didn't have any idea what he was going to do with the grizzly that was hanging on to the helicopter. He was really hoping that it would just fall off, and he was ready to immediately adjust the chopper's controls to compensate for the sudden loss of weight. They were now more than 200 feet off the snow-covered ground.

"He doesn't look like he cares much for flyin'," Wilson noted, looking out his own window at the struggling bear.

"I'm beginning to have second thoughts about it myself," Harrison added. He had an idea. "We need to find us a tree."

"Well, there are about a dozen gazillion of them down there," Wilson observed, nodding towards the ground. "It shouldn't be too hard to find one that you particularly like."

"I don't mean a live one, Jack," Harrison countered. "I mean a dead one."

"Them, too," Wilson pointed out. "What's your plan?"

"This bear needs a ladder so he can get off my helicopter."

Harrison aimed the helicopter to climb uphill, and pushed the stick forward, simultaneously making a manual increase in the throttle adjustment. They flew almost a half-mile horizontally, and several hundred feet vertically before he spotted the old dead tree that he was looking for in the helicopter's angled spotlight.

"Over there," Harrison nodded. "That's the one." It was more of a tall stump than a full-grown tree, with a lot of jagged limbs jutting out on all sides. At one point in recent years wind or lightning had knocked off almost its entire upper half. Only a chopped-off, ragged top remained.

"He isn't going to like this," Harrison said, "but at least it may get him down." He backed off the collective to descend as the helicopter hovered directly over the tree. Slowly, the 206B settled down, until it was only a foot or so above it. In the helicopter's forward-slanting searchlight the flying grizzly soon saw his chance for an exit, and decided to lunge for the top of the tree. As he did so, the bear's leg came untangled, and the suddenly lighter helicopter shot upward. The grizzly clawed for a grasp on the dead tree, but was unsuccessful. He crashed head over heels to the ground, breaking nearly every branch he came to, bouncing off the others. When he finally stopped falling he looked up at the helicopter and snarled, then started limping away, turning his head every few feet to make certain that he wasn't being followed.

"Sorry, pal. Wrong tree. But at least you're down," Harrison said, grimacing. "I bet that's going to leave a mark." He returned his attention to Wilson and the delayed rescue. "Okay, Jack. Now we go back down the mountain and lift that dead one off your friend."

"Fine with me," Wilson consented, breathing a sigh of relief. "I've had just about as much aviation as I can stand."

Harrison spun his head around quickly in a double-take. Nah, he thought. Jack Wilson has probably never even *heard* of Anne Heche. For sure, an old cowpoke like him has never watched *Six Days and Seven Nights*.

EPILOGUE

With a broken shoulder, a broken right arm, and two broken ribs, among other assorted cuts and bruises, Jim Farson was at his home in John Dodge taking some badly needed sick leave when Jack Wilson walked in.

"Ho, ho, ho," Wilson laughed. "Merry Christmas!" He extended a gaily wrapped gift towards Farson's bed.

"For me?" Farson asked, faking surprise. "You shouldn't have."

"I agree," said Wilson. "That's what I tried to tell the guys down at the office, but they insisted. Go ahead, open it up. Can you move that arm yet?"

"Even if I couldn't, I still would," Farson replied. "Just to see what's in this pretty little package." He unfolded and read the attached card: *"To Jim, From All of His Fellow Admirers. Bear With Us."*

"Gotta be something very serious, with a card like that," Farson mused, a strong hint of irony evident in his voice. "I'm wondering now if I should even open up this thing. It'll probably explode in my face."

"Go ahead," Wilson urged. "Make my day." He was beginning to like tossing movie lines into his conversation.

Farson carefully unwrapped the box, and cautiously removed the lid. Inside was a clear glass jar of...nuts—of a kind that he didn't recognize.

"Well," Farson said, momentarily taken aback while he attempted to figure out the significance of the gift. "You be sure to thank all of your people for these. Tell them I'll be thinking of them as I eat them." He paused—for as long as he could bear the torture. "Okay, Jack, I give up. What's the story here?"

"Why, whatever do you mean?" Wilson replied, stringing him along. This was more fun than working a big rainbow on a fly line.

"You know damned well what I mean!" Farson protested. "You guys give me a bunch of nuts that I can't even identify, and a card that says *'Bear With Us.'* There's gotta be a joke in here somewhere. I just can't seem to find it."

"Well, Jim, we all wanted to get you somethin' to commemorate your huntin' expedition," Wilson explained. "And we knew just how up close and personal you were to that bear...."

"So you got me a jar of bear nuts," Farson completed the explanation, shaking his head at having been had. "Very thoughtful of you. Right. Sure. Say good-night, Jack."

"Good-night, Jack!" Wilson complied, as he exited the bedroom, hooting wildly.

It was mid-March. The snow on the National Elk Refuge was beginning to melt. Some of the elk had already begun their long journey back up to Yellowstone—trailed closely, someone had noticed, by the fourth, early-rising grizzly. Dan Johnston sat in his office on East Broadway and looked north across the back lawn of the Refuge headquarters complex, over the wire fence, towards the several scattered herds of elk. His office door opened behind him. Johnston spun his chair around. Mayor Elvis Ashton walked in.

"Remembering it all, Johnston?" the mayor asked.

"There are a lot of things that happened last fall and winter that I'm never going to forget," Johnston observed. "And I suspect that I won't be the only one with such a good memory— especially when it comes time to elect a mayor again."

"Oh, c'mon, Johnston," the mayor pleaded. "We all make mistakes. You made some. I made some. We all made some. You have to get over them, get up, and go on with your life. It's how the West was won."

"Right," Johnston concluded, not at all appreciating Ashton's attempt at humor. "I'm sure you've already forgotten about all of the mistakes you made that contributed directly to the death of innocent people, and are now ready to step up to the plate and tackle even bigger issues."

"Exactly!" Ashton replied, not catching the drift of Johnston's mixed-metaphor insult. "That's exactly what I mean! I think we need to start planning right now for next fall."

"What do you mean?" Johnston asked, puzzled by the abrupt course change in the logic of the conversation.

"Well, it seems to me," Ashton speculated, "that we might want to see if Yellowstone can send us down more bears again with the elk when they migrate next fall—black bears this time, not grizzlies. I think that was our main problem, don't you? We just had the wrong kind of bears."

Johnston shook his head in amazement. He just never knew what the mayor was going to come up with. "Ashton," he said, "this office is Federal property. There's a little-known but very useful Federal law that gives Elk Refuge managers the authority to shoot anyone who comes onto Federal property spouting exceptionally dumb ideas. And that's far and away the dumbest idea that I've heard all week.

"SPELLMAN!"

The young Fish and Wildlife Service employee instantly materialized at Johnston's door.

"Sir?" Spellman beamed, anxious to please, and happy to be summoned away from his usual monotonous duties.

"Bring me my bear rifle," Johnston ordered. "I want to shoot the mayor."

"Yes, sir, right away," Spellman promised, quickly turning to leave, wondering what the hell that was all about. He was definitely going to fill out that transfer application tomorrow, he concluded. Maybe even later today. He'd had enough of this nonsense. Johnston was certifiably a few elk short of having a whole herd.

"Well, I can take a hint," Ashton sniffed, ultimately insulted. "Don't expect to see me in this office any more."

"Believe me, Mr. Mayor," Johnston assured him. "The pleasure will be all mine," Ashton spun sharply on his heels, and quickly left the office. Johnston got out of his chair, went around the corner of his desk, looked down at his freshly waxed wooden floor, and sighed.

"Damn!"

THE END

AFTERWORD

*B*ear Edges is a novel that goes well beyond believability. I mean, c'mon, who could actually imagine not just one, or two, but *four* grizzlies from Yellowstone migrating southward—all at the same time—to the National Elk Refuge? Well, apparently, I could, and did, in order to have enough bears and bodies to fulfill the needs of my plot.

In reality, however, it is absolutely true that Yellowstone's grizzly population is being forced to wander farther and farther southward in order to find food. Over the past few months there have been several reported area injury incidents involving bears. A resident of Tetonia, Idaho—about 40 miles northwest of Jackson, Wyoming—was unexpectedly confronted by a grizzly and mauled fairly seriously as he simply exited his home. (The grizzly had to be tracked down and shot by authorities.) Most recently, a jogger near Jackson Lake Lodge unknowingly came too close to a sow and her three yearlings while they were feeding on the carcass of a freshly killed elk, and ended up in the local hospital. The innocent grizzlies were allowed (justifiably) by park managers to proceed on their wilderness way, having done only what comes naturally.

Other stories abound involving recent sightings of both grizzlies and black bears in and around (and even south of) Jackson, which sits at the southern boundary of the National Elk Refuge. Each spring locals are warned in the news media by federal officials in Grand Teton National Park and Bridger-Teton

National Forest about the possibility of surprising cranky bears as they emerge from hibernation—with two or three cubs. Unexpected, injury-causing confrontations between bears and hikers (and even Park Rangers) are becoming more and more common in this area, often resulting in serious wounds to the weaker species. (That's us.)

Why are bears and other predatory animals such as wolves and mountain lions increasingly coming south from the Greater Yellowstone Ecosystem? The answer, of course, has to do with food supply. Obviously, those predators follow their migrating prey southward in the winter because it conserves vital stores of energy to chase and kill old, injured, weak, or newborn elk in herds where the impeding snow accumulations are measured in inches, not in feet as is typical in Yellowstone. Obvious, too, is the impact of global warming on Yellowstone. As higher ambient temperatures alter the growth patterns of vital food sources for the grizzly, such as whitebark pine nuts and all of those army cutworm moths, bears in those impacted areas are going to have to look elsewhere for food in order to survive. (Ironically, the same may be true for humans. It has just been reported that perhaps a third of the nation's honeybee population has mysteriously, inexplicably, and suddenly disappeared—without even leaving any bodies around for investigators to study and find out why. Honeybee cross-pollination of many fruits and vegetables is critical to our food supply, accounting for perhaps one-third of our total diet.)

Still, there is no doubt that Yellowstone's grizzly population is somewhat better off today than it was 30 years ago, when grizzlies were placed on the Endangered Species List. After three decades of close observation and study, bear population monitors have concluded that the number of grizzlies in the Great Yellowstone Ecosystem is no longer declining. The present grizzly population is estimated to be stabilized at 500 bears. As a consequence, even as this novel was being prepared for lulu publication, the grizzly was taken off the Endangered Species

List (May, 2007). Now, some are even wondering if Wyoming should establish a grizzly hunting season.

Stabilization of the area grizzly population in no way suggests that bear-human encounters in and around Jackson Hole will, somehow, come to an end. With the undeniable effects of global warming likely to continue altering the environment for decades, particularly near the poles and at higher and normally colder elevations, it is far more likely that the grizzly will be forced to abandon its former home and look elsewhere for the sustenance that it needs to survive. As it leaves sparsely populated regions such as Yellowstone it will necessarily have to intrude into those other areas that are far more populated by humans.

If you live in one of those areas that are being sought out by grizzlies, such as Tetonia, Idaho—or Jackson Hole, Wyoming— you might just want to keep one eye on those bear "edges."

Remember what happened to Sheriff Wilson, Jim Farson, Joe Dean the photographer Joe Dean, Cindy Mason, Jason Washburn, Bob Allen, Edward Oldfield....

As Yankees catcher Yogi Berra once said, "It ain't over 'til it's over."

And for the grizzlies around Jackson, it clearly ain't over.

About the Author

*Fred Whissel, a native of Sonora, Ohio, owned and operated a storefront business (Audio Video Country) in Jackson, Wyoming, with his wife for 20 years. He holds a B.S. in journalism (1968) from Ohio University, where he studied creative writing under Walter Tevis (*The Hustler*). He has won several state, national, and military awards as an editor, investigative reporter, editorial writer, and photographer for various U.S. Army Security Agency and civilian newspapers. Prior to moving his family to Jackson in 1984 he was public affairs manager at Ohio Power Company. His first* **lulu.com** *contribution,* Save Yourself! How You CAN Troubleshoot Your Own Audio/Video Problems, *was published in May, 2007, and is a self-illustrated book of how-to help and how-NOT-to humor that includes several of his experiences with such personages as Harrison Ford, Gerry Spence, Bo Derek, and Robert Ballard (The* Titanic?*).* Bear Edges *is a slightly revised reprint of his novel that was first published in 2003 by Canada's Trafford Publications. His next* **lulu.com** *work, also being published in June, is another self-illustrated book of "sort of" true stories about life in a very small town in Ohio in the 1950s. Other projects in the works include July publication of a book of drawings (to be entitled* Sports in Jackson Hole*), a collection of his photographs; a book of his favorite published editorials; a compilation of his short stories, and a compilation of his several screenplays. He is married to Barbara A. Whissel (who, at the time* Bear Edges *was first published, was the real-life cashier character in this novel at the real-life Jackson eatery, "Bubba's Bar-B-Que"). They are the proud parents of Jhon, Alicia, and Carl, who attended universities in Wyoming and Ohio. Whissel is presently listed as a work-disabled security screener at the Jackson Hole Airport.*